# "★★★★★!" Averag

★★★★★ "Fast paced, action-packed thriller, like Dan Brown without the padding."

"All the elements of a great read are here - stolen treasure, glamour, murder, revenge and a secret society that infiltrates the highest levels of government. The book is fast-paced; if you read 'The Da Vinci Code' but found it a bit flabby, then you'll love the tight narrative."
**DM, Amazon Review**

★★★★★ "Gripping read!"

"I read the whole book the day I bought it and thought it was brilliantly written. Was a gripping read and you just wanted to know what would happen next! It's a must-read!"
**KB, Amazon Review**

★★★★★ "Unputdownable!"

"An 'unputdownable' read, couldn't wait to find out what happened, at the same time didn't want it to end! Had to find a place with no distractions so I could finish it! If you like murder, intrigue, faction, and the glamour and beautiful locations of a Bond film, this is one for you!"
**JKT, Amazon Review**

★★★★★ "An exciting read!"
A well constructed thriller which has been exceedingly well researched. Keeps the reader's interest from start to finish with a great ending. So often this type of mystery can 'tail off', but Barnes keeps momentum throughout. The content is always informative and sometimes educational. Most enjoyable."
**KS, Amazon review**

*(Kindle version) at time of going to press

★ ★ ★ ★ ★ **"A very good read!"**

'Enesi' is a very, very good read, giving a fast paced twist on books like 'The Da Vinci code'. And, it really does give 'The Da Vinci code' a run for its money. I have read both and most definitely found this better. The concept is brilliant and I did find myself wanting to read on as you end up with incredibly powerful drama, intrigue, and breathtaking descriptive locations. I'm not going to spoil the story for you as I don't want to give anything away. It's just a treat from start to finish. I wish I could go back and read it again to experience the thrill I had when I started reading originally. In fact, I am!
**CP, Amazon Review**


"Very pacy, punchy and well plotted – a high concept thriller."
**Alison Finch, National Books Researcher**

# ENESI

# ENESI

## ROBERT BARNES

ferdinand books

First published as an eBook by ferdinand books in 2010

This US English paperback edition published 2011

ISBN 978-1456588250

1456588257

Printed in the United States of America

ferdinand books
28 High Street
Great Houghton
Northampton
NN4 7AF
United Kingdom

email: info@ferdinandbooks.com

On 1st November 2345 BC the earth tilted off its axis by a catastrophic 26.5 degrees. From an estimated population of 2 billion, only eight people survived the global disaster. The day is still remembered: the night before, Halloween, is marked worldwide.

In May 1987 a newly discovered grave near Mount Ararat was robbed. Turkish authorities later reported that a jeweled bodice from the grave had been sold on the black market in Istanbul for $75m.

# Prologue

THE TWO GRAVES held their breath in the burqa-dark night. Distant headlights revealed a tumble of broken rocks, stones and earth that pressed right to the edge of a pitted road. As the vehicle bounced its way through ruts and potholes, the beam's fingers scribbled along a steep embankment where the ground had fallen away. You could sense, rather than see, the mountains that surrounded the valley like black curtains of folded rock. That night, even the stars were shrouded in cloud.

Inside the battered white truck, Harutyun noticed a sign printed in both Turkish and English letters: 'Kazan', 'The Place of Eight'. He nudged his passenger awake. The two Armenians were unshaven, dressed in dark clothes and black woolen hats. When they had put them on, they knew there was no turning back from their purpose: they were committed to crossing the border, in spite of the danger, and carrying out their daring raid. Vartan yawned and ran a sleepy tongue round the inside of his dry mouth, rubbing one eye with the flat of his hand.

A small collection of houses appeared on the left. No streetlights, just the odd lamp here and there at the corner of an alley or above a doorway. Rough-plastered walls were spattered with dirt and windows, shuttered against the cold. A few thin lines of smoke threaded their way from chimneys poking haphazardly out of clay-tiled roofs. Vartan spotted an old car parked by a telegraph pole, its red paint faded to a dull pink.

The truck slowed. Across the road from the village were fields of rough grass humped with boulders. Turning to the right, the headlights picked out a pattern of low, shadowy stone shapes - possibly walls, animal pens, the remains of several structures including an ancient house, another building and two old markers, like gravestones.

Just before the headlights went out, the men could see that the grave markers were covered in lichen.

Worn door hinges and spent suspension creaked slightly as the Armenians got out. Harutyun reached back in and took a torch from under the dashboard. He shone it towards the stone slabs. Going over to the grave markers, he nearly tripped over a thick tussock of grass. Harutyun bent down, slipped the torch into his left hand and rubbed the stone with the ends of his fingers. The lichen fell away.

There were incisions cut into the stone. The torchlight showed a rainbow design carved on the left of each grave marker. Under the rainbow was the crest of a wave with a boat on top. Harutyun put his right index finger on the boat and traced the outline of the wave to clear out some dirt. To the right of this were eight stick characters: two larger figures, obviously male and female, accompanied by three smaller men and, behind them, three smaller women.

Below these images he could make out another picture showing the larger woman crouching down, head bowed and eyes closed, with the other seven walking away from her. Harutyun guessed this meant she was dead but the others remained alive. Still squatting, he hutched a step nearer to the second marker. This had carvings of the man as well as his wife, both with heads bowed, eyes now closed and the other three smaller men and women walking away. So then he was dead, too.

Harutyun whispered: "Incredible!"

"What?

"And it's been here all this time."

"What's so good?"

"Can't you see? What do these tell you?

"I have no idea."

"Well, for a start, you can see she died first."

"What? So this is where we're supposed to dig?"

"Never mind - we'll begin with her!"

"Let's get on with it. Before anyone comes!"

"Yes." Now, he thought, now we'll see what those foreigners, those tourists, have found! Whatever's in here belongs to us, not to the Americans, not the Turks, but to our people - no-one else! And we're going to be paid well for our trouble.

Vartan walked back to the truck. It was easier, now his eyes had adjusted to the dark. It was even possible to make out the rusty raised letters: 'TOYOTA' pressed into the metal tailgate, which he pulled down, trying not to make a sound. From the collection of tools lying there, wrapped in sacking, he picked out a spade and rested it against the truck. He found an axe and held it near the blade in his left hand. Finally, he grabbed a crowbar and slipped it under his arm. He gathered up the spade and turned back to the graves.

Harutyun put the torch down on the remains of a low stone wall to light up the bases of the marker stones. He took the crowbar and started to tap on the ground. Vartan began scraping the earth off with the spade in front of the woman's grave. First Harutyan's crowbar let off a steely 'ping!' as it struck something hard, then the spade made a loud, scraping screech that prompted Harutyun to signal with his hand for Vartan to stop. They listened for a moment. In the distance, a door slammed. The two men froze.

Without speaking or making any sign to each other, the Armenians attacked the area in front of the woman's grave marker as quietly as they could. As the grass and earth came away, whitish streaks emerged where they had scratched the stone underneath. After ten minutes they had uncovered the outline of a large slab of marble.

The men glanced up at each other. Vartan held out the spade and they swapped implements. He tried prising below the surface all round the stone with the crowbar while Harutyun dug a deeper trench along one side. As Vartan probed, his crowbar caught and he heaved on it. The marble slab moved. Harutyun stopped digging and came round to where Vartan stood. They both dug into a space just below the stone and pressed down. The slab moved away from them. A small triangular hole appeared at the end nearest the grave marker.

They should have thought about it, but neither was prepared for the hideous stench that escaped like leaking gas. Vartan grabbed for his nose, dropping the crowbar, but it was too late. The rotten air had already invaded his brain and he fainted, falling backwards onto the ground, legs collapsing like a puppet whose strings have been cut. Harutyun was more fortunate - he had stepped away instinctively and avoided the full concentration of noxious fumes - the rank, fetid odor of death. Still, it was enough to make him force the air from his lungs and hold his throat. He sank down on one knee and retched but nothing came out.

He cursed himself for being so stupid.

As the stillness slowly returned, he felt better, and Vartan hitched himself up onto one elbow. "Man, that was gross!" he declared, wiping his face with his hand.

"Sh!" warned Harutyun. "Let's get it over with."

They both stood up. Vartan sniffed around the gap but there was not much of a smell left. He picked up the crowbar and levered it against the edge. Harutyun put one hand up, anxious that they might be damaging whatever was underneath, but he was ignored. What looked like a flat stone lid slid further, widening the hole. Harutyun put his spade in the other end and pulled the handle back and down. The slab moved. They looked at each other and then into the hole. There was something gleaming with dull silver light.

"That's it!"

"Yeah."

"It's like a - a sarcophagus. See if we can move the lid a bit more."

They set to and heaved. The hole was now about two feet wide and ran the entire length of the grave - about eighteen feet. Harutyun knelt down and put his hand in.

"Hey, are the bones still there?"

"Yes, I can feel them."

"Oh, man, I don't know how you could do that!"

"It's what we came for. We can't let those Americans get it."

"But you shouldn't touch dead bones. It's bad luck."

"Too late to worry about that now."

He felt around and pulled something. It would not come, so he yanked it harder. Suddenly it was free and he fell back a little. He brought his arm out. In his hand was a chain of gold discs that sparkled with gems of different colors set between them. The men's eyes opened wider than either had thought possible.

"Quick, get the sack!" Harutyun waved his arm - Vartan ran mutely, mouth open, to the truck and brought back a large sack as Harutyun fetched the torch. He bent down and searched the grave, moving the torch from one end to the other. He reached in and pulled something else out, keeping his face away from the open

13

sarcophagus, still haunted by the distinctive fester of decay. He lay on his front and felt around with his hand, finding more and more objects - a jeweled bodice*, bracelets, rings, armbands. Vartan scooped each item into the sack - gold and jeweled pieces which flashed in the torchlight.

*According to 'Into the Forbidden Valley' (Jonathan Gray 2005), in May 1987 two graves thought to belong to Noah and his wife were robbed. The contents have never been found, but a jeweled bodice from the loot was later sold on the black market in Istanbul for $75m.

"I think that's everything. I can't feel anything else. Let's start on the other one."

Harutyun was just pulling himself up when there was a shot from the distance. He grabbed the torch and they both carried the sack, stooping as low as they could and running for the truck. Vartan leapt into the cab with the sack on his lap. Harutyun scrabbled round the front, slipped, got up, opened his door and slammed into the seat. He started the engine and found first gear. He left the lights off.

A bullet ricocheted from the front wing as the truck pitched forward and the driver's door banged shut. The wheels bumped over ridges and hollows in the ground, making the tailgate smack up against the body and down again. All the tools in the back jumped, then shook out onto the grass. More shots wanged into the side of the truck, a rash of silver on the white paint, as Harutyun swung the wheel to the left. They lurched onto the road and accelerated into the blackness.

# 1

THE NATIONAL MUSEUM OF IRAQ was built to look like the ancient gates of Babylon. But on the morning of 8th April 2003 its arched entrance and crenellated towers were almost invisible behind a cloud of flying debris. The Museum's sand-colored walls echoed to the sound of an unprecedented aerial bombardment that was ripping up the city of Baghdad: Donald Rumsfeld's 'shock and awe', designed to bludgeon Saddam Hussein's forces into quick submission.

Through the dust and noise, two palm trees in front of the Museum swayed with every blast of heavy ordnance. Dotted amongst the tank traps and concrete defenses, troops from the U.S. Army's Third Infantry Division, commanded by Lt. Col. Eric Schwartz, were trying to protect the Museum and its priceless collections, but there was gunfire coming from within the Museum preventing them from getting any nearer.

Schwartz, mindful of the eternal damage that his men could do, kept shouting: "Do not fire. Repeat, do not fire!"

A nearby office block burst into shooting spikes of smoke and powdered concrete, sparkling with the mica flash of a million shards of glass. The air sucked hard on a silent vacuum for three whole seconds before the sonic boom of the explosion rocked feet, hammered organs and snapped teeth.

Inside the Museum, Iraqi civilians and soldiers were looting its riches and shooting at the American troops from smashed windows. Priceless artifacts, statues, pillars, bowls, cylinder seals and other Mesopotamian treasures were in danger. Groups of Iraqis were helping themselves to exhibits - anything they could carry. The museum was being ransacked by a number of different gangs.

There was a great deal of shouting and arguing coming from galleries leading off the main hall. Here, two men stuffed supermarket carrier bags with gold arm bands; there, a group attacked an enormous alabaster vase until it snapped off, leaving its foot firmly fixed to the display plinth; down the stairs, more men were dragging a cast copper statue - the broken legs of a man.

Deep in the whitewashed basement, at the end of a barrel-vaulted corridor, three Iraqi men in well-pressed green army uniforms and metal-badged berets were trying to unlock a steel door. It was hard for them to see what they were doing in the dim glow of a single overhead lamp, and they couldn't agree on who was actually supposed to be holding on to the large key. Backs turned, panic confusing their movements, they were surprised by five men approaching from behind. The five were kitted out in black from combat boots to knitted balaclavas.

All three Iraqis were swiftly strangled to death by thin wires and the key fell to the ground. Chuck Kowalski, the leader of the five, pulled off his balaclava and crouched down, searching the stone floor with eyes and hands for the key. His short blond hair was almost shaved at the sides and stuck out like straw on top. He bore the high cheekbones and piercing blue gaze of the Slav, though any connection to the land of his ancestors had been forgotten a few generations back.

Larry Carson's round features appeared next as he rammed a balaclava in his right trouser pocket and pulled one of the bodies away from the door. His folks were from Tulsa, Oklahoma, and his

16

tousled brown hair matched a slightly vacant look that never left his face. The other three removed their headgear: Clinton, an African American from Louisiana; freckle-skinned Ned with his button nose from Middleburg, Virginia; and Tom, squashed like a boxer, from Fresno, California. Even down here, it was unbearably hot, and each man glistened with sweat. Larry, Ned and Tom wore large, empty military backpacks. Chuck found the key and stood up. Clinton prized a bunch of other keys from the hands of the man Larry had pulled aside, while Ned and Tom dragged the other two dead Iraqis a few meters back up the passage way.

Chuck opened the door.

The five advanced through a store room as dimly lit as the corridor outside. Rows of shelves held objects of different shapes and sizes, each wrapped in thick, cloudy polythene bags and labeled with Arabic script and Roman numerals. They came to another painted steel door. Chuck signaled to Clinton, who tried the first two keys on the bunch he'd retrieved. The third one fitted and they were in.

Chuck undid the button of his chest pocket and pulled out a folded piece of paper. He checked the bags in front of him, holding on to each label with his right hand and looking back at the list of numbers on the paper. They all began with the prefix '2345' - 2345/01, 2345/02, etc. As he worked his way along the shelf, he came to the end of the list. He folded the paper, put his arm out and pushed a line of objects to the right, marking the limit of what he was there to collect. Satisfied, he gave a 'thumbs up' to Larry, Ned and Tom who turned and faced the door while Clinton undid their backpacks for them. Chuck took two bags off the shelf and put them into Ned's backpack. He passed the rest to Clinton, who loaded the objects into the backpacks.

When the last three packages had been stowed and the flaps on the backpacks closed, Chuck tested the fastenings. Clinton put his balaclava back on and led the way out. The other men followed, pulling on their balaclavas as Chuck tapped them in turn to indicate that their backpacks were secure. He looked round the store room and ran after the others, stepping over the dead Iraqis and adjusting his headgear as he went.

# 2

SHE WAS A STRONG SWIMMER. She was also in great shape. Her long, tanned limbs pulled her gracefully in a professional front crawl through the topaz sea. The water was so clear, you could see the rocks and sand of the bottom, thirty feet below. You could also see the lime green bikini that kept her just this side of decent.

Vibrations in her ears told her that a boat was approaching - the thrumming whirr of a propeller that sounded almost tinny underwater. She stopped and looked up, treading water. The fine bones of her face were framed by long dark hair that spread out in the water below her shoulders. Cat's eyes the color of Columbian emeralds fixed on a launch that zoomed into view and circled behind her. She had not been expecting it for another twenty minutes or so.

The boat's twin turbo diesel engines burbled as it drifted nearer. She pulled at her small nose with elegant forefinger and thumb, blowing water out of her nostrils. Standing with one hand on the wheel, Gianni, a tall blond Italian in his early forties, wearing deck shoes, white shorts and navy blue linen shirt, hailed her: *"Contessa!"*

*"Alora?"*

*"Una telefonata. Urgente!"* She swam with an easy breast stroke to the stern of the boat and grabbed the top of the swim ladder. Placing her right foot on the lowest rung, she hauled herself out of the water and into the boat in one practiced movement. Gianni

passed her a green towel which she held to her face, wiping the salt water from her eyes. The sea beaded the skin of her flat stomach and ran down her legs to form a pool on the teak planking. She wore no jewelry, other than a man's steel watch and a gold ring round the second toe of her right foot.

As she sat on the nearest cushion, she asked, "*Chi è?*"

"Ariq Tafisi."

Ariq! She was alarmed but not surprised to hear from him. Gianni turned and pushed the two engine levers forward. The launch rose up and accelerated away from Vagia beach.

Sabina, Contessa di Volturara, leant her elbow on the gunwale and looked ahead to the rocky outcrop of Aghia Thekla. Her hair streamed out behind and she half-closed her eyes as the boat powered through the water. The only child of the fifteenth Conte di Volturara and his Armenian wife Arevik, at 29 Sabina was unattached - and burdened with a unique responsibility. A responsibility she had inherited on the death of her parents in November 2001 - almost two years ago.

It was not something she could forget, but the news of Ariq's phone call brought it rushing to the forefront of her mind. The unfairness of it all would never go away. Though her grandfather, Razmig Assadourian, who had started the whole thing, had been orphaned by the Turkish genocide of Armenia in 1915, he had managed to die peacefully in 1990 at the age of 76, while her mother and father had been killed in a car crash that was far from accidental.

The launch hit a random wave and bounced. Sabina looked up at the southern half of tiny Patmos - only twelve kilometers long and five wide - towards the Monastery of St John, squatting high on the tallest part of the island. Inside, she knew, parts of the building were almost delicate, with light gothic arches and whitewashed courtyards. But from here its massive gray stone walls and buttresses made it appear more fortress than holy place. The huge edifice certainly overshadowed the scattered little white box houses that nestled at its feet. Its physical presence, its brooding antiquity, its spiritual significance as the site of the Revelation of St John - all combined to dominate the entire island.

Late spring was the best time. She loved the air, heady with thyme, marjoram, sage and chamomile, and the wild flowers and warm sunshine. Sabina always tried to be here for Easter - it was celebrated with all the timeless pageantry that the Orthodox were so good at. She could smell the incense in the fusty church that hit you when you walked through the outer narthex even now, and picture the mothers pushing their babies' lips to the glass of the Byzantine icons. The only drawback was the water - the sea was always cooler here, and had not yet benefited from a long, hot summer to penetrate its chilly depths.

The launch swung to starboard. A steeply raked white hull could be seen behind the headland on the right. In so many ways, this 50 meter yacht - 'Viaggiatore' - was her home. The monastery might tower above the island, but her ship was not small and stood out wherever it went. Now, it filled the cove behind Aspri, the windows and portholes of the four decks reflecting the mid-afternoon sunlight. A pale green helicopter sat ready on its pad in front of the radar antennae.

As Sabina reached the sun deck, Gianni's wife Maria was waiting with a toweling robe. The Contessa rarely bothered with shoes on board during the day - part of her small rebellion against adulthood and responsibility. At one end of a large hardwood table surrounded by dining chairs were a phone and a tray holding a bottle of mineral water, a thick glass with ice and lemon and a small bowl of medjool dates. Condensation confirmed that the green bottle of water had just come out of the fridge. Sabina left the towel she had been holding on the back of a chair and turned with one arm out to Maria.

"*Grazie, Maria.*"

"*Contessa.*"

She held the robe so it was easy for Sabina to slip into. Maria was a comfortable shape, a warm character who liked to mother Sabina. She had dyed magenta hair, a plump face with a ready smile and sparkling brown eyes. Whatever the weather, when she was on duty Maria always presented herself in a white drill dress, buttoned at the front, which made her look rather like an old-fashioned matron - apart from the ample cleavage that was always on display. She fussed a bit, but Sabina was glad of her dependable nature. When Sabina had tied the belt of her robe, Maria handed her the phone, collected the towel and stepped away towards the open doorway of the main saloon.

"Ariq, Are you safe?"

"*Contessa*, it's the Museum."

"I know, we've seen it on satellite. What's happening?"

"Everything is gone. Everything is ruined."

"And - my Mother's gift?"

"Gone, gone too, *Contessa*! I am a dead man!"

Sabina was quiet for a moment, shocked by Ariq's answer to her last question. She looked up at the hard blue sky and bit her lip. This was the worst possible news. Bringing her head down again, she regained control. The man was frightened enough, and she had to reassure him. So much for not taking responsibility! "Ariq, calm down! You need to get out of there. Go home and wait. We'll send someone to look after you."

Gianni came up the steps from the boat garage and waited, looking out to sea.

"Thank you, thank you, yes, *Contessa*, I will be going now, I'll go home."

"Don't try to call me again - go home and wait for Gianni."

She closed the call and put the phone in the pocket of her robe. Full of troubled thoughts and racing emotions, she walked slowly over to the table. Sitting down facing astern, she opened the bottle - 'pfssh' as the cap unsealed - and poured a glass of water. She screwed the lid back on and settled the bottle deliberately on the white cloth lining the tray, embroidered with its green 'V' and coronet monogram. She took a sip of water and spoke to Gianni. At the sound of her voice he turned to face her. "I need you to go and rescue him I'm afraid. It's the least we can do. Are you ok with that?"

"Of course, *Contessa.*"

"Good. It won't be easy." She considered the problem some more. "Take the helicopter to Rhodes. Radio ahead to Andreas - tell him to prepare for a flight to Iraq. Think about how you're going to get in. Obviously you won't land anywhere near Baghdad - I'm sure you'll find a way! You'd better bring him back here until we've worked out what to do."

Gianni nodded and strode off towards the bridge, running a hand through his long wavy blond hair. Sabina stood up and took a date from the bowl. She moved towards the doorway and then turned back, overwhelmed by the possible consequences of what Ariq had told her. She stared at the deck for a moment, then looked across to the nearby hillside and put the date automatically into her mouth, biting off the stalk and placing it on the tray. For a long time she examined the rocky slope just across the water, paralyzed with anxiety. Small bushes of herbs and scrub dotted the gray stone like spots on a leopard.

Stepping into the owner's suite, she locked the door. She sat on the bed, rolling the date stone around in her mouth as thoughts tumbled in the lapidary of her mind. She realized she'd have to find out from Ariq whether her mother's 'gift' had been looted along with everything else, or stolen to order - which was what she feared most. If - no, once - it was discovered, even by accident, a chain of events beyond her control would inevitably follow.

Unless she could get to it first.

She stood up and went over to her dressing table, taking the date stone out of her mouth. She flipped it without looking into a metal bin underneath the table. It landed with a ding. She licked her fingers clean and wiped them on the toweling robe. Turning, the *Contessa* walked through to the study, where she aimed her attention at a sizeable picture above her desk. It was a 1964 Bridget Riley print - the original painting was kept at Sabina's castle in Tuscany - called 'Arrest 3'. Waves of black and blue-green hues, from strong to light, flowed in optical illusions to make one feel at sea, or in a landscape of folded hills stretching to misty distance.

She pulled open a drawer and pressed a button concealed by a green crocodile leather diary. The Bridget Riley moved down and revealed a large safe, about 60cm wide and 40 deep. She opened the small diary and looked on a page near the back. There were lines of dates and times - the last one: 10th April 2003 - 20.31. She checked a digital display on the safe door: '10:04:03:20:31'. She smiled.

Half an hour later, the helicopter lifted off.

# 3

THE RED BRAKE LIGHTS of a ministerial Jaguar flashed in the falling rain as it approached the private entrance to the Cathedral Close. Two automatic bollards barred the metallic gray car's progress beneath the carved stone archway. On either side and above, blackened stone walls had guarded the way in for over seven hundred years, though the cathedral was much older. To the left, a sign announced: "Rochester Cathedral. No Entry. Private. All vehicles report to security." Water dripped steadily from the arch onto the glistening tarmac below.

The car's driver, Neil, was a solid fellow, broad in frame and features, with florid, rough skin and deep creases crisscrossing his thick neck. He wore a gray double-breasted jacket and peaked cap. His fat hands and ginger haired fingers rested on the wheel as the windscreen wipers swept the glass. General Seymour Lyle - distinguished looking, with brown hair going white at the temples - sat up straight in a dark Savile Row suit on the parchment leather seat in the back. He stared directly ahead, though he wasn't focusing on anything in particular. He just had no intention of being distracted from his mission.

A security guard - Gerald King - stepped out of a doorway on the right, squinting to keep the rain out of his eyes. He had the bearing and uniform of a retired Naval Chief Petty Officer, with a five-medal ribbon above his left breast pocket and a remote control pad in one hand. Anxious to remain dry for as long as possible, Neil lowered the electric window at the last moment as Gerald bent to speak to him. "Good morning. How can I help you?"

"We have an appointment with Canon Barford."

"Straight through and park outside number 12." Gerald pressed a button on his remote control and the two bollards slid gracefully out of sight. The car's five spoke alloy wheels began to turn as the car moved off, flicking water out behind the wide-tracked tires.

Inside the Canon's Georgian grace-and-favor house, a shaft of light from a gap in the rain clouds streamed into the double-height hall through the fan-shaped window arched above the front door. Its rays landed on the limestone flags that were each cornered by black diamond-shaped tiles; they played along the banisters of the curved staircase that rose to a galleried landing; and their glow warmed the yellow-painted walls. A large oil of a highland scene, with cows drinking from a loch surrounded by reddish-brown hills and a duck egg sky, hung above a 'D' end mahogany table against one wall. The powerful scent of fresh lilies emanated from a glass vase on the table, next to a beaten metal bowl that contained car keys, a blunt pencil, old dog chew, boy's digital watch and sunglasses with one arm missing. Beyond the stairs was a single country Chippendale dining chair below a 17th century map of Kent, surrounded by framed family photos, some of which were reflected in the glass of a large mirror opposite.

Outside the white-painted door to the Drawing Room, Ralph ('Rafe') Barford and his wife, Amanda, were holding each other in a tight embrace. At just under six feet, he was five inches taller, allowing her to bury her head in his shoulder. A large tortoiseshell clip held her long straggly blonde hair casually at the back: his was dark brown, thick, boyish for a man of 44. Amanda had a letter in her right hand, the torn envelope in her left. She was crying.

Ralph was in his work clothes - dog collar and pale blue shirt. Amanda looked brighter in a dusty pink canvas smock, jeans and elastic-sided boots spotted with dried clay. There was even clay between the stones of her diamond and sapphire engagement ring.

Ralph spoke softly: "My darling, I'm so sorry."

"It's all right." She sniffed noisily. "It's been fine before and it'll be fine again."

"Yes, but I just keep hoping it'll go away."

"We both know it's something I have to live with."

"WE have to live with."

"Yes, I'm sorry. We. Oh, I just wish…"

"I know, I know." The doorbell rang. Amanda pulled away and Ralph let her go, gently.

"That'll be him. Do you want to make yourself scarce?" She noticed a damp patch on Ralph's shirt made by her tears.

"Oh, gosh! Look what I've done!"

"Don't worry. A noble stain!"

"You are so silly sometimes!" She stretched up to kiss him on the lips. "I'll let him in. Would you like coffee?"

"No, thank you darling - I don't want to encourage him. Oh, did you speak to Johnny?"

"Yes, he'll be back from Paris on Saturday. He's having a fantastic time. Will you be able to collect him from the station?"

"Sure - can't wait to see him."

"I'll be in the studio if you need me."

Ralph went towards his study at the rear of the house while Amanda moved to the front door, brushing her eyes. She had a quick look in the mirror to make sure her mascara hadn't smudged too badly and did a running repair with bit of lick and an old paper tissue from her jeans pocket.

The letter had given her a real jolt - she had not expected the cancer to return so soon, although it had been years since she had last tested positive. The old fears flooded in: fear of leaving Johnny without a mother, Ralph without a wife; the sense of waste, of a life half-lived. Deep below there was also the fear of her own death, but she knew from past experience that it was dangerous to focus on anything selfishly negative. The main emotion was anger - rage and frustration at this vile disease that had dared to invade her body and threatened to steal so much: an enemy that never quite left, hovering somewhere undetected after the 'all clear' - a malicious spider hiding under the bed, waiting for the moment of its choosing. That drove her to resist with all her force, and by the time she answered the door, she hoped no-one would have known that anything was troubling her.

The study was a darker room, facing north, lined on two sides with bookshelves. The other walls were taken up with a fireplace and large twelve-paned window that had shutters folded back into their boxes above a deep, low sill. The rain seemed to be falling more heavily now onto the lawn outside. Over the fireplace was a picture of an unidentifiable rocky cove - probably somewhere in Cornwall. The paint had been laid on thickly with a palette knife. In the centre of the mantelpiece was an unglazed porcelain sculpture that seemed to have been inspired by undersea creatures - one of Amanda's creations. Either side of the hearth were a galvanized bucket and a basket. The one was filled with large, shiny lumps of coal and a single blue rubber glove, the other sat packed with logs, an old Sunday newspaper and box of firelighters. In front of Ralph's wooden desk was a faded, scuffed leather tub chair that gave the impression it might be broken; behind it, a weird-looking modern office chair, like a saddle, that Ralph insisted was great for posture. Amanda thought it the ugliest thing she'd ever seen.

Ralph was putting a book away as Seymour Lyle came in. Lyle offered his hand.

"Seymour Lyle." He spoke with a deep, rather pompous inflexion that didn't sound quite genuine. He elongated certain vowels - his name came out as 'larl'.

"Ralph Barford."

Ralph took in the suit, the red and white Bengal-striped shirt and silk tie, the black Oxford shoes. Funny, he thought, how army officers make a uniform out of civilian clothes. He couldn't help noticing that Lyle's eyes scanned the room in a way that made him instantly distrust the man. He seemed mechanical, not even courteous enough to give Ralph the basic kind of attention that good manners require from a first encounter between two human beings. It reminded him of that appalling rudeness some men have, pretending to listen to you but eyeing up the attractive woman behind you and then moving on while you're in mid-flow with a kind of 'wah-wah sorry old boy, must circulate' excuse. Rather ungraciously for a man of his calling, he hoped the meeting wouldn't last long - and that it would be their last.

"Thank you for seeing me at such short notice. Bit of a panic going on in Whitehall."

Ralph waved Lyle to the tub chair. "Yes, you mentioned the looting of the Museum."

"Indeed." Lyle sat and settled back, testing the chair for a moment. He looked at Ralph. He wondered if the Canon was going to be any good to them. Obviously bright, but probably far too sentimental. Clearly a problem with the wife - why hadn't he been briefed about that? One son. Still, the man looked pretty fit. Played for his college, second row. What a waste! All these churchy types were the same. Bloody wet.

"It seems that some priceless artifacts have disappeared. We've come to you because you know Baghdad."

"I've not been there for a while." Ralph sat down on the 'saddle' behind his desk.

"No matter. You were the Church of England's representative there for eight years."

Ralph leaned forward, trying to hide a certain agitation. "You make me sound like an Ambassador. I looked after a Church."

"The point is, you know the city, you know the people. And you understand the significance of what's stored in the Museum."

"Oh, of course - its collections are amongst the most important in the world. I mean, the history of Mesopotamia goes back nearly five thousand years." Ralph got up and started looking at his bookshelves, trying to locate a particular volume. "Presumably you know it was established by a Brit - Gertrude Bell?"

Lyle was wondering whether he was referring to Mesopotamia or the Museum, when Ralph found the book, an illustrated guide to the Museum and its contents. "She started it in the twenties. Right from the word go, information on the exhibits was shown in English and Arabic Still is. There are twenty eight galleries and then of course extensive underground vaults." He opened the book at a page of photographs and put it on the desk. "It was closed in 1991 during the Gulf War and only opened again almost exactly three years ago - 28$^{th}$ April 2000 - Saddam's birthday." Ralph suddenly realized that Lyle had pressed all the right buttons, and he was just blurting out information - because it was a subject that fascinated and enthralled him. He attempted to collect himself and play it a bit cooler. "I don't suppose at this early stage you have any idea of what's missing?"

"No - not really. Probably the treasure of Nimrud. The Vase of Warka - and the Bassetki Statue." Ralph caught sight of enameled regimental cufflinks and a plain gold Omega watch as Lyle dragged a paisley handkerchief from his jacket sleeve and rubbed his nose with it in a languid, affected way. A rifleman, obviously, keeping it there rather than in his pocket like normal people, but he hadn't needed it - the gesture was pure affectation. Why was he playing the peacock?

"Goodness! They'd have needed a crane to have carried those off. The vase is three feet high and made of alabaster. The statue is copper - it must weigh a ton."

"Apparently it was dragged down the stairs and did quite a bit of damage - both to it and to the steps. But there is something else that has definitely disappeared and which we're far more concerned about." Ralph stared at him quizzically. Lyle put the handkerchief away with a flourish. "The Noah." The way he pronounced it, the word sounded like 'na-arr'.

So that's it. He's trying to score points. In spite of himself, Ralph was impressed with Lyle's knowledge - and profoundly disturbed by the news that he had so artfully delivered. "What? But no-one's supposed to know about that. It's never been shown, never been on display. Most people think it's just a rumor."

"But you and I know differently, don't we? You and I know what it is and why it's so important."

"Well, yes. I mean. It's one of the undisputed pieces of historical material associated with the Great Flood."*

* On 1st November[1] 2345 BC the earth tilted off its axis by a catastrophic 26.5 degrees[2]. The date corresponds to that calculated by some from biblical and other ancient data for the Great Flood. The estimated population at the time is 2-5 billion. (Please note that although the actual date for the Flood is more likely to be 3554 BC, (www.setterfield.org.), the 2345 BC date is assumed for this book.) (1 Jonathan Gray 'The Killing of Paradise Planet', Chapters 8 & 9) (2 Dr George F. Dodwell, director of the Adelaide Observatory, proved that in 2345 B.C. the earth was impacted heavily by an external force which changed the degree of its axis to an inclination of 26.5 degrees from which it

*returned to an equilibrium to the present inclination of 23.5 degrees during the interval of the succeeding 3,194 years to A.D. 1850. His research was confirmed by Dr. Rhodes W. Fairbridge of Columbia University in Science Magazine, May 15, 1970.)*

"Quite, but I haven't come here to discuss that. We - Her Majesty's Government - would like you to look into it, see what you can find."

"I wouldn't know where to start. How could I possibly help?"

"You know Ariq Tafisi, the Museum curator."

"Well, yes, I do, but he's in the middle of a war zone. I'm not a soldier. Or one of your agents."

"No, absolutely." Lyle studied Ralph again and thought how unsuitable he was for the task.

"Absolutely. But still, we'd like you to talk to him."

"How?"

"We have him. We - we extracted him- a few days ago. He's being looked after somewhere safe. I'd like you to go and see him."

"But why me?"

"He trusts you. He's asked to speak with you. I'll set it up."

# 4

THE FIVE MEN came out of the 'Arrivals' doorway of the American Airlines terminal building at JFK looking like tourists returning from vacation. Chuck Kowalski, the leader, sported a Hawaiian shirt. He was raising his eyebrows at Larry Carson, blank face all but hidden under a 'Tulsa Drillers' baseball cap. Like the others, Clinton strode purposefully, though he seemed quite chilled in his dark green chinos. Behind him came Ned in suede boots and blue jeans. Tom was last, still looking like a boxer in a gray marl tracksuit. Each carried an identical aluminum case of a size that qualified as hand luggage. They were laughing and joking with each other.

Chuck was teasing Tom: "Hey, Tom, you still ain't told us what you did with her!"

"None of your goddamn business!"

All laughed suggestively.

Larry joined in: "Come on, Tom. You looked kinda tired the next day!"

Clinton's eyes grew wide to show his opinion: "She was something, man!"

A cruder response followed immediately from Ned: "Yeah, see the body on her!"

Tom's eyebrows lowered: "That's enough guys. Now shut the fuck up!"

They came out of the terminal to where a line of yellow taxi cabs was waiting on the opposite side of the road. The men looked around. A Lincoln stretch limo moved in from the right, coming down the ramp of the lower road that served the airport's arriving passengers.

Clinton said: "Try all you like Tommy boy, but we'll get the truth outta you sooner or later!"

The car stopped right by them.

Chuck agreed: "Yeah! Say, here we are!"

The trunk popped up. Javier Mendoza got out. The limo's Hispanic driver wore a shiny black single breasted suit. He filled his clothes, and a slack face gave little indication of his considerable strength. He had dark eyes and dark wavy hair, oiled back.

Javier greeted the men: "All right boys? Let's get your bags in the trunk."

He pushed the trunk lid right up. The men noticed his creased, black leather driving gloves as they handed him their cases. By the way Javier moved them, they were heavier than they looked.

"Phew boys, whaddya got in here?"

The men exchanged looks. The truth was, the cases were partly lead-lined so that the contents were not recognizable on an X-ray. Chuck got into the limo, followed by the others.

Javier closed the trunk and got back in smoothly. He selected 'D' and the limo pulled away. As the airport building receded, Javier used his rear-view mirror to glance at the men. He offered them a drink.

"The boss thought you boys might like a drink to welcome you back. There's a beer in the fridge back there."

Larry, full of relief and joy, pulled open the small fridge door and cried: "Thank you, boss, whoever you are!"

They passed round cans of Coors and flipped them open.

Chuck raised his can and tapped it against the others. "Mission accomplished!"

Ned turned to Javier: "So, we finally get to meet this guy."

"Yeah, he's looking forward to congratulating you on a job well done."

Tom chipped in: "And paying us, I guess!"

"Oh yeah, he has the second half of your money ready and waiting. Now, just sit back and enjoy the ride boys. It'll be a while yet." He touched a button and the glass privacy screen separated him from the men.

Some hours later, having picked up the I-95 south of New Rochelle and passed through Stamford, the Lincoln turned onto Highway 7 at Norwalk and headed north. At the next junction Javier pointed the car east on Highway 1 - Westport Avenue. Not long after, the limo approached a low private gateway set into a long stone wall. The white-painted wooden gates swung back and the car entered a long driveway past immaculate lawns. Further back, polo ponies grazed in generous, undulating paddocks marked out with white fences. Javier just caught sight of the enormous red Dutch barn by a bank of trees to the left and then the car rattled over a cattle grid. Here, the gardens were planted with flower borders and hedges. The limo came to rest outside a large, brick-built Connecticut farmhouse. The trunk popped up.

Javier got out as the front door of the house opened. Senator Henry Billington III, tall, slightly stooped, appeared at the top of a short flight of stone steps. He wore a lemon yellow v-neck pullover and sky blue trousers. A rather tired looking Golden Retriever followed him out and flopped down by his white tasseled loafers. The skin on his right hand and head was mottled with sun damage and age spots. He kept his left hand in his pocket all the time. Billington walked towards the limo like a man in his early seventies, but there was alertness about his movements that spoke of his former athleticism.

"Everything go ok, Javier?"

"Everything's fine, Senator."

He squinted a little and bent slightly, peering at the back windows of the car, shielding his eyes with his hand but not really seeing anything. "The boys?"

"All done, sir."

The Senator turned his head, with its thinning white hair brushed straight back: "You know where to take 'em?"

"Yes, sir. I'll put the bags in your study."

He twisted round to go back towards the steps. Good. He was glad that problem had been dealt with - and that the raid had been a success. The idea of what was in the cases filled him with greater anticipation than he had ever known.

Like many of his Ivy League alumni, Henry Billington had decided at college that he was going to make money - a great deal of money. The only thing was whether to go into the law or banking. He had the brains, the ambition and the lack of conscience necessary for success along both paths. He could just as easily devote his talents to ensuring that wealthy villains walked free as to exploiting the personal debt of citizens in rich nations and the corrupt regimes of poor ones. In the end, he thought that his brain was less of a rapier and more of a broadsword - he was a trader, a plunderer rather than a man who lived by rhetoric.

But after a while, making money was almost too easy. He had served on the board of the World Bank and he had been admired for his charitable work. His name was proudly inscribed among the benefactors of such noble causes as the Henry Street Settlement in New York (he never missed the annual Art Show at the Park Avenue Armory), the Metropolitan Opera and Connecticut

36

Voices for Children, based nearby in Westport. But it was not enough.

Money, sex and power - those were the great drivers. He had the money, he could buy the sex, but… So he ran for office and had served in the US Senate for thirty years. And then? Then he had wanted even more. He had moved from national politics to something global. Yes sir, he couldn't wait to get those cases open.

He stopped and looked back at his driver. The dog raised one eyebrow. "Thank you Javier. Appreciate it, as usual!"

Javier went over to the back door of the limo on the opposite side to the house. He stretched his hands in his leather gloves a moment and then rubbed his fingers against the palms. The gloves creaked. He went to the door handle with his right hand and pressed the catch.

The door opened.

An arm lolled out.

He looked in.

The men were all dead.

# 5

IN THE OWNER'S SUITE, the Contessa was getting ready for dinner. 'Viaggiatore' had left Patmos and was heading south towards Kalymnos. It was dark outside and the bedroom was brightly lit. Sabina sat at the built-in dressing table brushing her hair. She wore a long ivory silk halter neck dress which complemented her tanned skin.

Tomorrow evening they would be arriving in the pretty harbor of Symi just after sunset. It was always magical - a wonder heralded by the smell of thyme and oregano as the sea breeze carried the scent of the island across the water. Then the first sight of the main harbor town, Yialos. As you stood on deck watching the tall rocky coastline riding by, suddenly a backdrop of white neoclassical buildings would appear at the end of a long bay, climbing from the water right up high, like seats in an ancient amphitheatre. One by one the lights would come on in the houses and restaurants and bars as night fell. Floating nearer, you would gradually recognize individual buildings, smell freshly caught fish being grilled over charcoal, and hear the chatter of people. Sabina's appetite was being whetted by the thought when the phone rang.

"*Pronto!*"

"*Contessa.*"

She recognized the voice immediately. "Alex. This is a surprise."

"A bigger surprise than you think. Have you checked your safe recently?"

"A week ago. Why."

"You might like to take a look. *Buona notte.*"

The phone clicked off. She looked at it with irritation. "*Ciao.*"

As she made for her study, the expression on her face changed from irritation to worry. She pressed the button that revealed the safe behind the Bridget Riley print. It slid down slowly - too slowly for her anxious mind. She checked the last entry in the diary - '10:04:03:20:31' and went over to the safe. The digital display read: '16:04:03:14:27' - yesterday afternoon. How could anyone have opened it? How could they have come on board? It could only have been Alex - Maria would never have allowed anyone else near the ship, and it would have been easy for him to land with the helicopter away. Sabina would feel much happier when Gianni was back, but he was still holed up outside Baghdad, unable to move and no nearer rescuing Ariq.

But Maria hadn't said anything. Had Alex threatened her? How had he made sure she remained silent? What had she, Sabina, been doing yesterday afternoon? Diving off Livadi Yeranou, perfect clear water, not a soul in sight. She remembered the blue plastic oil drum resting on the bottom, twelve meters down, along with an abandoned anchor - its frayed rope caught between two rocks - that someone must have been sorry to lose.

She pressed the digital keypad with the right combination. There were five flat jewelry boxes - red, purple, blue and black, embossed with logos of international fame - seven assorted ring boxes and some envelopes on the bottom shelf, which she took out and put on the desk. But the top shelf was empty. She felt inside - it was quite deep, big enough for two full-size cases, but there was nothing there. She put her arm in up to her elbow, but still nothing.

Her eyes widened in panic and a hand went to her mouth. She blew out through her fingers.

What was he playing at? What point was he trying to make? He knew perfectly well that it was safe with her - that no-one would ever find it. She'd kept her side of the bargain.

Again that pain which made her feel sick and faint at the same time. She sat in the chair behind the desk with her hands holding each side of her face.

She'd been in Los Angeles when the accident happened. Malibu, to be precise, the J Paul Getty Museum, her favorite building in all the world, a fabulous recreation of a Roman Villa, based on the Villa dei Papiri found under the volcanic ash of Herculaneum at the foot of Mount Vesuvius. She loved drifting through the main peristyle, with its long narrow pool, clipped box hedges, pillared colonnades, delicate bronzes and huge terracotta pots. It was so extraordinary to stand there, in the brightness of Malibu's Mediterranean light, and be able to feel what it must have been like in first-century Pompeii. Such a civilized, peaceful atmosphere, enhanced by the splash of water in the white marble fountains, and hot fragrance of basil and lavender on the breeze! And the interior garden, the atrium - it was paradise for Sabina.

Her parents were far from such a placid scene as their powerful midnight blue coupe hustled along the SR222 from Siena to Florence. Alex had suggested meeting them for an early supper in Castellina and they had been looking forward to it. The wood-fired oven pizzas there were the best, and sitting out on a September evening with a glass of prosecco and good company was hard to beat. After a day in Siena, shopping for clothes and visiting the marble works south of the city, they were ready for a relaxing evening.

Sabina's mother, Arevik, was pleased with what she had bought - especially the chic suit that would be perfect for the concert at Badia di Coltibuono later that month - but frustrated that the new malachite surround for her bath was still not finished.

Her father, Luca, Conte di Volturara, had been in a good mood because his bespoke shotgun had finally arrived and now sat in the trunk of the car, waiting to be given its first outing at the castle shoot on the weekend

But now Luca was not so happy. Just after Quercegrossa on the Via Chiantigiana, a log transporter had come up behind and sat menacingly on his rear fender. It had pushed him to go faster than he wanted, but the coupe had plenty of power and he pressed the accelerator until the automatic kickdown triggered, propelling the big car forward at a speed the transporter was unable to match. The road was pretty straight at that point for about two kilometers, and Luca wanted to put as much distance as he could between himself and the heavy truck.

He didn't see the transporter, out of sight behind him, slew across the narrow road and stop, blocking traffic driving north. He was obviously unaware of a tractor with its trailer full of newly harvested olives parked across the Via Stradale at Croce Fiorentina, south of Castellina, making it impossible for anyone to pass. By the time he saw the road works signs 'LAVORI IN CORSO' just before he would have slowed for the first sharp left hand bend on the top of the hill before Fonterutoli, he was traveling at 120 kph. Arevik screamed as the car braked and swerved violently to the right to avoid the 'STRADA CHIUSA' barrier that blocked their path. The road went down and to the left - the car flew straight on. Its front wheels smashed into the curb, flipping the coupe over lengthways. Inside, the screeching of rubber on tarmac stopped abruptly as the explosion of the air bags deafened Arevik and Luca. Their world turned upside down in a long, slow, silent half-somersault. The big car landed heavily on its roof, crushing the passengers' heads, and slid wildly for fifty meters, its momentum finally killed by the gauntlet of rough scrub and small trees between the road and the nearest cultivated field.

There was no sound, just the drip of fuel and hot tick-tick of contracting metal.

Two men in gray overalls ran round the corner towards the barrier when they heard the car hit the curb. One waved frantically at someone or something out of sight, while the other started dismantling the road signs and traffic cones. A white van reversed rapidly from the left up the road and parked the far side of the barrier. One of the gray overalls opened the back doors of the van and then helped the other one throw the cones, signs and red painted wooden bar into the back.

The doors were slammed shut and the two ran round to the front passenger side. As the second one got in, the van moved off. Three hundred meters later, it turned left onto the Strada Provinciale delle Badesse towards San Leonino and disappeared.

The log transporter reversed a little, stopped with a hiss of air brakes and then took to the road again, growling its engine with a dark belch of diesel blowing from the exhaust stack behind the cab. The pretty convertible and small saloon that had been held up behind it were relieved to be on their way.

The tractor driver brought his machine back to life with the twist of a key and found that he was, after all, able to continue on his journey to the olive press. No-one overtook him and he waved to the driver of the log transporter as they passed each other a hundred meters north of Fonterutoli, surrounded by the ripe Sangiovese grapes of the Mazzei vineyard.

Sabina did not discover what had caused the 'accident'. Her father knew the road backwards, and she knew he would never normally have driven so recklessly. She suspected Alex, but there was no evidence to show that it was not simply 'driver error'. Nothing wrong with the car, no trace of drugs or excessive alcohol in the passengers. There were no witnesses, and the police concluded that there had been no other vehicles on the road south of Castellina or north of Quercegrossa at the time. The dead couple were found forty minutes later by a farmer driving his little three-wheeled scooter-powered 'Api' truck. He was traveling slowly enough round the bend to catch sight of the upended vehicle in the undergrowth some distance from the roadside. It was he who hid the new shotgun under a pile of fruit boxes in the back of the truck, before alerting the police.

Alex's phone call that day had shattered the stillness of the Basilica in the Getty Museum. Sabina would never forget that defining moment: her parents both dead, the suspicion that they had been murdered, the cataclysmic sense of loss - and the first stirrings of fear for her own life.

She came back from the Tuscan hillside, back from the shattered haven of the Museum, back to the bright seaborne study, with its almost imperceptible vibration that told her 'Viaggiatore' was under way. Alex would be expecting her to call him back, but he would have to wait until morning.

Sabina no longer felt hungry.

# 6

A TRUNCATED GRASS ZIGGURAT surrounded by rigid canals appeared in the window next to Ralph Barford's seat. The water was black in places: in others it reflected the blue sky and puffy cumulonimbus with the perfection of a mirror. The helicopter swung round to reveal a quadrangular hole in the ground exactly opposite the ziggurat like an inverted pyramid. It, too, was covered in lush green grass. A sloping ramp spiraled round its four corners, down and down until it framed a small square pool of dark water at the bottom. Ralph was just thinking about how many people it would take to mow all that grass when a line of tall trees blocked the light. Ahead he could see an ancient avenue of limes that led to the West Front of an impressive building. Its white stone façade seemed to have more in common with the Loire Valley than the East Midlands.

Ralph had read somewhere that Boughton House, rather ambitiously known by some as 'The English Versailles', was one of the great treasure houses of Europe. Shut up for over 150 years until the early twentieth century, its fabulous contents had escaped the damage of sunlight that had faded so many fabrics in England's stately homes: more importantly, it had also escaped the architectural arrogance of the Victorians, and felt uncompromisingly seventeenth century. Now he could see the main front which looked even more French. In contrast to the formality of the masonry, the roofs - all two acres of them - were tiled in weathered Collyweston stone slates.

It was obvious from the surrounding English parkland, dotted with grazing sheep and gigantic trees, that one should really arrive by car. A helicopter gave you an interesting overview, but it spoiled the surprise of seeing the majestic building - palace really - set perfectly in its environment. As the helicopter landed on the lawn inside the stable courtyard, Ralph was embarrassed at its uncouthness, its noise and wind that disturbed the grass, the gravel and the peace.

The first thing that struck him as he entered the staircase hall was the peppery spice of wood smoke from an endless succession of log fires. He detected the musk of oak paneling; and the shut up dust of closed rooms clothed in tapestry, velvet, silk, wool. All gently fragmenting in the air that seemed to come from another time. It was like breathing in years that had once been and would never be again, and yet, strangely, had left behind some of their precious air for Ralph to filter through his lungs. He was just wondering about visiting the State Rooms upstairs when a man in a horizontally-striped blue and gold waistcoat appeared. "This way please, Canon."

The butler ushered Ralph into a room called the Little Hall - great portraits hung above an oak wainscot and a gallery ran along one wall. His eye was drawn, though, to the fireplace: not to the fire that flamed in the grate, nor to the huge carved stone over mantel with its five rows of shields bearing the Montagu griffins and lozenges that left visitors in no doubt as to the first duke's pedigree. No, his eye was drawn to the pathetic figure of Ariq Tafisi, huddling in the corner of one of the crimson damask sofas that faced each other in front of the fire. Dark-skinned, swarthy, disheveled, disorientated, his curly black chest hair sprouting out of a clean white shirt, he wore a jacket of indeterminate color, gray trousers and brand new training shoes. This Director of the National Museum of Iraq - a distinguished scholar - looked homeless, straight off the street. It would be hard to imagine a figure more out of place.

"Ariq!" Ralph went straight across to Ariq, motioning him to stay seated, but he insisted on getting up.

"Canon Barford! *As-Salaam Alayka*! At last."

"*Alayka As-Salaam*!"

The two men greeted each other, Ariq holding Ralph's right hand in both of his hairy paws. Ralph noticed each wrist - the copper bracelet on the left, the old steel Rolex on the right - before he met Ariq's stare. They searched each other's eyes for a while, until each was satisfied.

"Sit down, sit down." Ariq settled back on the sofa, nearest the fire. Perhaps he was feeling the cold, thought Ralph as he sat next to him, half turned so he could see Ariq's face. "Tell me how you are."

"I am very well, thank you, Ralph. And you, you are very well, too?"

"Yes, I'm fine thank you."

"And your wife, Amanda? And Johnny?"

"Amanda's not so good right now. It's come back."

"Oh, I am so sorry. The problem with the blood - the leukemia?"

"Not exactly, but - yes. It can be fixed but you never know. And it's horrible - the treatment. I don't know how she lives with it."

"She is a strong woman."

"She's the strongest woman I've ever met!" He closed his mouth for a moment and took a new breath. "Johnny is great. He's in Paris on an exchange. I'm picking him up this weekend. They went by train."

"Ah, the Eurostar. It is one of my dreams to go under your English Channel on the train."

"Ariq, you never told me! You are strange!" Ariq looked puzzled, hurt. "Oh, I don't mean that unkindly - just English humor, that's all. But enough about me. Tell me about you."

"Ah!" Ariq paused, lost for a few seconds in reflection. "Your people have brought me out of hell. I would want in so many ways still to be there, but there is nothing I can do to protect the Museum. So much has already been lost!"

"I know. We saw it on the news and General Lyle told me more." For no particular reason, Ralph looked round to the far end of the room and back. There was an awkward silence, then Ralph spoke with more urgency. "Ariq, I'm really pleased to see you and I'm glad you're safe, but you wanted to speak to me?"

"Yes, yes. In fact, I will only speak it to you. There is something you need to know about…"

"About the jewelry, the necklaces - everything from the graves?"

"Yes, the Noah. I cannot tell you here." He fumbled in his jacket pocket and brought out a crumpled piece of paper. He took Ralph's right hand and put the paper into his palm, closing Ralph's fingers over it so it was hidden. "Perhaps there is somewhere more private we can go?"

"I'll ask. We should be able to walk in the grounds." Ralph got up and went to the door, slipping the paper into his trouser pocket. Why was Ariq being so furtive? Surely they were safe here? "Hello? Hello?" He turned back into the Little Hall. "No-one there. I guess it must be ok. Let's see how far we get!"

As Ariq stood up, the butler walked in from a different doorway. "Canon Barford, I'm sorry but we're going to have to ask you to leave. The perimeter has been breached and we need to get

Mr Tafisi somewhere more secure. Another meeting will be arranged."

Ariq, standing between the two men, caught Ralph's eye. He reached out and held Ralph's right hand with his left and squeezed it for a moment before Ralph moved off with the butler. Sensing something solid in his hand, he kept his fist tightly closed. It felt like Ariq's watch.

Ariq was far from his usual self. Ralph had no idea what was going on, but there was clearly more to this than Lyle had told him. All he knew was that his friend was in trouble, and he would do everything he could to help.

# 7

THE WINDOWLESS ROOM at the back of Haretz Diamond LLC, 70 West 47<sup>th</sup> Street, New York was lit by fluorescent strip and a powerful desk lamp. Its walls had once been white, and were now decorated only by a Swiss railway clock, a trade calendar and a gray row of five-drawer filing cabinets. Reuben Adler was bent in concentration on a sapphire ring held in his crabbed left hand. He peered at it through a lens supported by a long brass shaft that was fixed by an adjustable bracket to a stand. The wispy white hairs of his head mingled with the equally sparse beard. A black yarmulke was attached to his skull by a large, flat metal hairgrip. In the light, magnified by the lens, the sapphire seemed deep enough to dive into.

Next to him on the fawn faux leather of the desk top was an open aluminum case like the ones brought in by the men who had raided the National Museum of Iraq. Several rolls and bags of black felt concealed objects of varying size and shape, resting on the gray sponge interior. What looked like a gold disc half-protruded from one package. Across from Reuben, Senator Billington's driver, Javier Mendoza, sat on a beige plastic chair staring intensely at the jeweler, a mist of perspiration on the olive skin of his face.

At that moment the door burst open and David Adler, Reuben's 42 year-old son, crashed in.

"*Av?*"

Reuben failed to react.

"Dad?"

Reuben looked up and twitched back a couple of inches.

"David? What?"

"Have you got the diamonds you were looking at - the emerald cuts?

"No, I put them back."

David looked round and saw a shallow wooden drawer on a filing cabinet in the corner behind Reuben. "So what's that over there?"

"Oh! Huh! I must a forgot."

David reached over and grabbed the drawer. Piled like so much road salt on its black velvet liner, hundreds of clear emerald-cut diamonds, weighing between one and two carats, twinkled like mini prisms as he turned under the fluorescent light.

"That's three times this week already!" Having made his point, David softened and looked enquiringly at his father. "So, anything?"

"This is a private appraisal, thank you!" snapped Javier, aiming an intimidating stare at David.

"Okay, okay! We're just always interested, that's all. I got a customer anyways." David walked out, balancing the tray of diamonds as he closed the door with one hand. Reuben took an eyeglass from the desk, caught sight of Javier's tie like a bluebottle fly in the lens for a moment and looked again at the ring.

"Well," he announced, sitting back but looking no less bent, "it's glass. It's very good, but it's glass."

Javier Mendoza stared at Reuben. "So, it's all fake? The necklace and the ring?"

Reuben handed the ring to Javier, whose open right hand hovered above the desk. "Yes, yes. My life yes! It's a very clever piece of work - a copy of something very old. Must have seen it in a museum somewhere - you don't get this sort of thing worn nowadays." Javier put the ring back in a small black felt bag in the aluminum case. He tidied up the other objects in their felt wrappings.

"So, tell me, how old do you think it is?"

"The design?" Reuben scratched his chin for a moment with his right hand. Javier could hear the bristles crackling against the dry skin. "Thousands of years. Ancient Near East. Babylonian. Or even Mesopotamian." Javier looked uncomfortable. Reuben's knowledge was deeper than he or Senator Billington had bargained for. He began to rub his fingers in his palms, the leather gloves creaking. "They've something like it in the Met, I think. Or was that the Brooklyn? I don't remember."

"But how old is this?"

"Oh, I guess it was made recently. Within the last ten years."

"Thank you. That's er - that's very helpful."

"So, do you still want to know what it's worth?"

"Not much I guess after what you said!"

"Hm. Not much. The materials are common, but the workmanship is fine. Very fine. Five thousand dollars. For everything."

"Five thousand. It could have been worse!"

"I'll give you an appraisal certificate - it will only take a few minutes."

"No, that's fine. I don't need it."

"You sure? It's no problem."

"No, no - you've told me all I need to know. It's not so hard to remember."

"So, okay, working on the time we have spent, the appraisal is $75.00."

"Okay. You take Visa?"

"Sure - we take almost anything!" Reuben laughed. Javier reached inside his jacket for his wallet. He pulled it out of the left inside pocket - a pale brown pigskin folded wallet with a single snap popper clasp. Rubbing the index finger and thumb of his gloved right hand as he examined the contents, he selected a credit card that was protected by a small plastic sleeve. He prized the card out of the sleeve and passed it to Reuben, who had moved the credit card machine from the side of the desk to in front of him.

Reuben stretched out his hand and closed his fingers over the card. "Thank you."

"Say, I have the cash. I just realized. It would be easier."

"As you wish."

Reuben passed back the card. Javier was careful to make sure that it went back into its sleeve before replacing it in his wallet. He took $75.00 in notes from the main section of the wallet and gave it to Reuben.

Reuben counted the money - three twenty dollar bills, a ten and a five. Javier closed the case and turned it so he could reset the combination lock that secured it.

"That all seems correct. Would you like a receipt?"

Javier stood up. "No, that won't be necessary."

"I'll see you out." Javier had already opened the door and moved into the corridor. Reuben got up stiffly and half-walked, half-shuffled round with his knuckles pressed to the desk and then shivered out of the room, past Javier. He pushed a switch on the wall, a buzzer sounded and Javier shoved open the door into the main shop, turning to the old man. Reuben held out his hand. Javier did not respond. Reuben looked a bit put out. "Goodbye then!"

"Goodbye. Thank you."

Javier strode through the shop. A young, dark-haired woman in a brown wool suit - skirt and jacket - gold chain necklace, rings on most of her fingers bearing enormous diamonds, red lipstick and square-heeled shoes pressed another switch and opened the door.

"Goodbye sir and thank for coming to see us today."

Javier grunted and moved through the door. Outside, an overweight man with prominent love handles on a cell phone, wearing yarmulke, beard and long side curls, stepped sideways to let him pass. As Javier turned right on West 47th Street towards The Rockefeller Center and Fifth Avenue, he caught the stink of sweat wafting from polyester-clad armpits and wrinkled his nose. From inside the shop, David Adler observed Javier with distaste.

# 8

JOHNNY BARFORD, a lanky blue-eyed seventeen year-old with blond hair gelled forward in a dramatic quiff, sat with his friend Laurent Poitevin at the Café Hugo in the Place des Vosges, Paris. They were largely sheltered from view by the red brick arcades that surrounded the square's lawns and central fountain. Johnny wore an orange T-shirt under a plain charity shop jacket. When he reached for his glass of bière pression on the square bamboo table, wreaths of friendship bracelets, a leather thong and steel bangle appeared from his jacket sleeve. Laurent, in gold-rimmed glasses, navy v-neck lambs wool jumper and striped shirt, seemed more studious and conformist, though he was a passionate anarchist - at least, his views were hard core left-wing, though his parents lived in the ultra-chic *banlieue* of Neuilly. Johnny might look a bit wild to the average Parisian - especially those whose tiny lapdogs poked their groomed little heads out of Faubourg St Honoré shoulder bags - but his outfit, complete with black drainpipe jeans and pointed boots, was the free time uniform of a harmless English public school boy.

Laurent sipped his small white china cup of black coffee and stared with concern at his friend. "*Mais, encore* - you're still shaking!"

Johnny looked at the beer in his right hand - it was trembling slightly. "It's not just me is it? I mean, those guys were really spooky!"

"*Non, c'est vrai.* They were very interested in you."

"Bloody hell! Who do they think I am?"

The two had enjoyed their time at the nearby Musée Picasso in the Marais district that afternoon. Laurent had wanted to take Johnny as he had not been there himself, though he had visited the Picasso Museum in Barcelona with his parents the previous summer. It was interesting for him to compare them. Laurent was enjoying the exchange - he liked Johnny and it was a great excuse to go to parts of his home city that he had never seen. The afternoon air was sharp with the scent of exhaust fumes and the promise of summer. As they strolled happily along the Rue des Quatre Fils, they discussed the genius of the man who put a simple bicycle saddle and handlebars together to create a sculpture that pulsated with all the menace of a charging bull's head, horns ready to gore anyone foolish enough to step too close.

Behind them, a black BMW 5-Series saloon squeezed out of a private courtyard onto the cobbled pavement. It slipped into the street and followed the boys as two high automatic wooden doors, one bearing a circular *'PRIERE DE NE PAS STATIONNER - SORTIE DE VEHICULES'* sign, sealed the courtyard from sight.

Johnny felt something indefinable, a sense of impending danger, and turned to see the car keeping pace with them. He went left at the next street, down Rue Vieille du Temple.

*"Qu'est-ce que c'est?"*

"That car - it's weird."

Laurent looked back and saw that the BMW had also turned left.

"It's just a car!"

"No, there's something not right."

Laurent raised his eyebrows but carried on at a leisurely pace. Johnny started walking faster, turning left again when he could down Rue Barbette. Laurent began to catch him up as the car entered the narrow one-way street at walking pace. The windows of the car were heavily tinted - too dark to see who was inside. It sped up slightly and drew alongside Johnny. The passenger window lowered and someone in scarlet bike leathers, a red helmet and aviator shades held up a camera. There was a flash and Johnny shouted: "What do you want? Why are you taking pictures?"

The window rose and the car came to a standstill. Johnny stared at the blank passenger window, trying to see inside. Pierre cautioned him.

"*Laisse-la*, Johnny!"

"No, I want to see what's going on!"

He stepped out in front of the car and peered at the windscreen. He raised his eyebrows and hunched his shoulders, opening his palms as if to say, "What are you playing at?" There was no movement from the car. Johnny glanced over to Laurent.

"*S'en vas!*"

"Stupid!"

Without warning, the BMW leapt forward and hit Johnny's shins, knocking him towards the hood, where he placed both hands to keep from falling. He shouted out in pain, then moved rapidly round to the driver's door. As he reached for the handle, the car jumped forward again - this time it accelerated, turning left onto Rue Elzévir. Johnny chased after it but he could not keep up. He stopped, shook his fist then rubbed his shins. Laurent caught up with him.

"*Complètement fou!*"

"Yeah, they're certifiable!"

"*Non - toi, mon ami!* Come on!"

Laurent led the way, going right then left for two hundred meters along Rue des Francs Bourgeois and into the Place des Vosges. Once inside, he strode past the central fountain towards a café in the south east corner of the square and sat Johnny down.

# 9

RALPH AND AMANDA'S BEDROOM was dated in a chintzy, swags and tails way that contrasted with the spare Georgian elegance of the ground floor. They sat up, resting against pillows and a worn buttoned headboard covered in a glazed cotton print. Pools of light came from under the pleated shades of white china lamps on tables either side of the bed.

Ralph wore a loose, plain navy T-shirt and striped boxers. Amanda was peering at the Royal Academy Members' magazine through a pair of pink plastic reading glasses she'd picked up in a supermarket. Her blonde hair was down, framing her pretty face and resting on the old white collarless evening shirt she had nicked from Ralph ages ago.

Ralph had bought a copy of Private Eye and was snorting his way through the cartoons when the phone rang. Amanda looked at him over her specs as he answered it.

"Ralph Barton."

"Seymour Lyle. I have bad news. The 'treasure' stolen from the Museum turns out not to be the real thing - a very convincing fake, apparently."

"Good grief! That means -"

"Yes, I know what it means - now we've got a serious mystery on our hands. And a major headache. And we've lost Mr Tafisi."

"Lost?"

"Dead. He was found about half an hour ago on the steps by the West Front. Cause of death as yet unknown but we've got a pathologist working on it. I'll keep you posted. I don't suppose you got anything out of him?"

Ralph thought about mentioning the phone number he'd found written on the scrap of paper, and the fact that Ariq had given him his precious watch - almost as if he knew he wasn't going to survive for long, but thought better of it.

"No - we didn't have time for much more than pleasantries. We were about to go for a long walk and a chat when I had to leave - intruders apparently."

"Hmm. Well, if you think of anything, let me know. For now, we're completely in the dark. I'll be in contact. Goodnight."

"Goodnight."

Amanda had put the magazine down and was listening carefully.

"Ariq's dead." Ralph exhaled hard through his lips.

"Oh, that poor man! I'm so sorry darling." She took her glasses off. "What are you going to do?"

"I don't know. Lyle's got nothing - no clues." She reached out and held his hand.

"There's something else, isn't there?"

"Yep. I'm sure you've guessed it. It's to do with that business in Baghdad."

"Well, I'd worked that one out! I don't trust him."

"No, nor do I. I don't know why, but I took an instant dislike to him."

"That's not like you."

"No. But Ariq gave me a phone number and for his sake I'm going to give it a try."

"Do be careful!"

"Of course! We know what the stakes are, but God's in control."

"It always worries me when you say that."

Ralph looked at her, his beautiful Amanda. They had met at Cambridge. He was studying Theology and Archaeology at St John's and she was reading Art History at Girton. It had been an instant thing - they both found out later that there was no question in either of their minds - or hearts. That spring and summer of 1979 had started at Heffers bookshop in Trinity Street and a walk past the daffodils along the backs, wound its days through picnics and punting on the Cam and was sealed at a May Ball. They had found out later that she had Non-Hodgkin's Lymphoma. It was a huge shock but there was no question of not being together. It was diagnosed early enough for treatment to be effective and had been in remission for years.

After Johnny arrived, it was clear that it would be too risky for her to have more children - difficult, because Ralph had always wanted a large family, but bearable: she was still alive, very much alive, and that was what mattered most. Going for ordination had also been difficult, because although Amanda was supportive, she did not share the same strength of belief. Still, the fact that she had stayed on at Cambridge to do a PhD - looking at Cezanne's progressions and regressions as an artist through his many paintings of Mont Sainte Victoire - had helped. Ralph had risen up the Church hierarchy with a speed that provoked jokes amongst his contemporaries and jealousy from older priests - the kind who studied *Crockford's obsessively and were incumbents more through intellect than genuine faith.

*Crockford's is a 'Who's Who' of Church of England priests, detailing qualifications, posts held, etc.

59

Their time in Iraq had been a vital key to his preferment, and a real risk, but Amanda was one of those rare English girls who just got on with it - she was never heard to complain, was the most unselfish person Ralph had ever met and seemed to radiate sunshine wherever she went. If she was ever upset, you could be sure it was something very serious indeed.

Now it was back. Soon there would be the hospital visits, the treatment of rituximab and chemo to contend with. And now he had another dilemma to resolve. The phone number - and what might follow from calling it. Or whether he should just leave things there, as they were, and forget about the business with Lyle. But Ariq would never have given it to him, or his watch, if it was not serious. And now he was dead - killed, probably.

Amanda brought him back from his reverie: "You won't forget to meet Johnny tomorrow, will you?"

"No - it's fine. Don't worry. I'm not going anywhere."

"Now, where have I heard that before?"

# 10

AN ALARM WAS SOUNDING at Haretz LLC as David pushed into his father's workroom.

"*Av* - what is it?"

Reuben sat behind his desk with a vacant expression in his hooded eyes. His head rocked slowly side to side and he looked paler than ever - as if he was about to be sick. He scratched his right palm with his fingers.

"Tell me?" David went round to where his father sat and watched him rubbing his hand. "What's wrong?"

Reuben spoke softly, pausing before he forced each phrase out with a breath. "I don't know." Breathe in. "My hand." Breathe in. "My - ." Breathe in. "I - feel so strange." He breathed in harder. "I pressed the alarm." He looked at David, pulling back his ears with tension, stretching the skin across his face. "I hope you don't mind."

"Of course not! What is it with your hand?"

"I don't know. Ever since - it's…"

"Ever since what?"

"He gave me that card."

"What card?"

"Credit card. Visa."

"Who - that creepy guy with the case?"

"Yeah, with the case." The light went out of Reuben's eyes. Saliva dribbled out of one corner of his mouth as his head lolled forward and his arms slipped off the desk. He would have gone right to the floor, but there was no room and his legs were trapped by the desk. His knees went sideways, arms hanging loosely, and his forehead landed on top of the desk.

"*Av? Av!*" David knew he was dead, but he brushed the old man's temple, moving his head round so he could see into the lifeless eyes. "Bastard!"

There would be revenge. He would find this man, this loathsome, repellent - what was that word his old English teacher used to use? Rebarbative! That was it. This rebarbative man. Track him down. Kill him. An eye for an eye, a life for a life.

# 11

TWENTY MINUTES' DRIVE from Avignon's small international airport at Caumont, south east of the city, the Contessa sat under a large square sunshade at a table covered with a starched white cloth. As a restaurant, Le Moutardier boasted one of the best locations in the country, if not the planet - its terrace was set on the broad ancient *place* opposite the 13$^{th}$ century *Palais des Papes* - home of the Papacy during exile from Rome in the Middle Ages. Sabina liked it because it reminded her of Patmos - the forbidding feudal façade of the *palais neuf* had remained unchanged since construction was completed in 1364. The food was also *gastronomique*.

Alex was obviously still playing games - they had agreed 12.30pm and it was now just after one o'clock. She had finished her Virgin Mary - must keep a clear head - and read through the menu so often she could probably recite it by heart. She had decided to begin with '*Daurade royale en croute de pavot*' - (gilt-head bream crusted with poppy seeds), followed by '*Exercice sur la Crème brûlée: Badiane* (Star Anise), *Vanille, Café, Pralinée, Menthe*'. Her favorite crème brûlée was lavender, but these five little pots sounded interesting, and the couple at the next table had chosen the fish, which looked sensational. She would order a bottle of Chablis Grand Cru - partly because she loved it, and partly because she knew it would rile Alex, who would most likely have suggested a white Châteauneuf-du-Pape.

Sabina went inside and found the '*Dames*'. She checked her outfit in the large mirror. There were times when a girl needed four inch heels, and this was definitely one of them. They gave her height and lengthened her legs - which were far from short to begin with. Skinny D&G jeans added to the effect, but it was the top half that was truly arresting. With her boyish hips, narrow waist and swimmer's chest, she had an enviable figure - the sort that made other girls come out with catty remarks about having difficulty bearing children, a sure sign of green-eyed envy. But now she had really pushed the boat out - or rather, her chest. La Perla was fine, but when you wanted to make a deep impression on a man there was no-one like Agent Provocateur. Her 'C' cup breasts were magnified and presented in a way that even she found alarming. Had she gone too far? On the drive from the plane, she'd worn a Hermès scarf around her neck, but now that she'd taken it off it looked as if she was wearing nothing under the black leather biker jacket - which was true, apart from the gravity-defying bra. At least she didn't look like an East European moll - but all those zips and studs! She had drawn the line at leather jeans - just too Eurotrashy.

"You're such a tart!" she said out loud, then panicked and checked the doors behind her in the mirror to see that no-one else was listening. She put on a sharp pair of Persol shades, checked her teeth in the mirror, put a thumb under the shoulder strap of her black Kelly bag and went out.

Aleksander Vittore Kovalenko was the product of a Russian father and Italian mother - both dead. In his late forties, he had watched others make obscene fortunes overnight as Boris Yeltsin handed out state commodities and Mikhail Gorbachov dismantled the former Soviet Union under the twin banners of *Perestroika* and *Glasnost*. Alex had done extremely well, too, but he kept it quiet. He was probably more ambitious than all of them, and saw that the way to survive and prosper was to maintain a low profile. Alex's profile was positively horizontal compared with those who competed to build the largest super yachts and own the most successful sports teams.

The paternal side of his family had strong connections with organized crime, and some tenuous links to the Romanovs. Determined to erase the former and strengthen the latter, he had sold all dubiously acquired assets, reinvesting in a portfolio of established blue chip companies, and grown a beard that made him look disturbingly like a nineteenth century Tsar. His liquidity had made it easy to become the châtelain of an exceptional Côtes du Rhone vineyard - Châteauneuf-du-Pape to be precise - that had belonged to relatives of Nicholas II. Alex had studied oenology and marketing at the University of Bordeaux - an MBA that had taken him to the wine-growing districts of Australia and South Africa, New Zealand and Italy, South America and California. The contacts he had made gave him an international network that was respectable beyond reproach. It also meant that he was on first name terms with some of the most powerful and influential families on Earth, like the Rothschilds. He recalled an evening in Tuscany, a dinner party hosted by the Head of a European Bank, when he, Alex, was talking with three men at the top of the Italian wine industry - the Marchesi di Frescobaldi, Barone Ricasoli and Marchesi di Barolo - about the forthcoming grape harvest. It was the moment he knew he had arrived.

Sabina, on the other hand, knew that Alex had not yet arrived - at least, not at Le Moutardier. She asked a waiter to clear the table of her empty glass and menu and decided to remain inside, watching for him. She was more than nervous. She had insisted on meeting somewhere public rather than her castle near Marcialla in Italy - she needed to be out in the open with him, where she presumed he would not dare to harm her. And this was local for him - his vineyard, Château Roüet-la-Dauphine, was just north of

Avignon. She did not know he was dangerous, but her intuition told her to be on high alert. There were so many things about him that did not add up. He had always been too friendly with her father - almost as if he saw himself as Luca's successor. And her father certainly talked of him in that way. Alex appeared kosher - he had an aristocratic English wife, though nobody had ever met her - but there was something almost too perfect about his background. Coming from a self-made family herself (on the Armenian side), she suspected that he was not all he seemed: that at some point he had reinvented himself. It takes one to know one, she mused.

Alex was irritated that Sabina had wrong-footed him by not being at the table he had booked when he appeared forty minutes late on purpose. He stood for a moment in a fine slate gray wool suit made by his Italian tailor and dark brown double monk shoes. He loved the flattering cut that was the trademark of the suit's Neapolitan craftsmen - that, and the clever way the trousers buttoned at the top of the fly. Comfortable in his skin, he looked at his watch on his right wrist a moment - he was left handed. Not for him the rapper flash of an oversized timepiece - he wore a simple Patek. It was ten past one when Sabina appeared and Alex's mouth dropped involuntarily for a second. He had never seen her like that.

Alex was married but behaved as if single. He had genuinely fallen for Elizabeth but discovered too late that, like her mother, she preferred riding to sex and had no idea how to dress with any degree of style. He would have divorced, but it was a match that brought significant social advantages. An estate in Leicestershire (Cottesmore country), a house in South Ken and a decent allowance had bought him sufficient freedom to make things bearable. Girls become their mothers, a friend had warned, and if he ever married again he would take much more note of his potential mother-in-law. Not that it was likely. He had been impressed by an Australian cattle baron, who told him never to make a permanent financial commitment to ships, planes or women. He put it more crudely than that: "I call it the rule of the three F's - if it floats, flies or fucks, boy, rent, don't buy!"

Alex thought this highly original, until the first two people he repeated it to told him they'd already heard it.

What was he going to do with Sabina? After the death of her parents, he had hoped that the Noah would pass to him for safe keeping. It was vital that the real article never saw the light of day. Now that Billington knew the 'treasure' of Baghdad was fake, it was only a matter of time until he - and others - would be on the trail that led to Sabina.

"*Ciao bella!*"

"Alex." She wasn't going to darling him, and kept her shades on as he pecked her on the cheek three times. *Oh, la vache!* He was becoming more French than the French. Still, she was pleased he had been struck by her appearance - in a positive way.

He pulled out a chair from the table she had already spent half an hour at. She sat, placing her bag by her feet. He faced her, his back to the Palace.

"So, you look very well. The Greek sun agrees with you?"

"Yes, thank you. You don't look so bad yourself." Ridiculous small talk, but she guessed this was how it would be to begin with.

"Nice place."

"Yes, I haven't been here for ages. It used to be very good."

A waiter brought two menus and the wine list.

"*Pour boire? Mademoiselle?*"

"*Un Bellini, s'il vous plait.*"

"*Et M'sieur ?*"

"*Vodka.*"

"*Glaçons et citron?*"

"*Glaçons et citron vert.*"

*"D'accord, très bien M'sieur. J'arrive."*

They both had the fish. Alex ordered cheese. He was unimpressed by Sabina's choice of crème brûlée. Unlike most Russians - and he saw himself as more Russian than Italian - he hated anything sweet. It was a sign of weakness - one of the things he had despised about Sabina's father, Luca di Volturara. He knew Luca had been more attracted to Castellina that evening by the home made Black Walnut ice cream you could buy from the local *gelateria* than the wood-fired oven pizzas. Not that it had made any difference.

"You know my visit was for your own protection."

Finally Alex had decided to broach the subject. "I take it you're referring to your trespassing on my ship and stealing my property?"

"It's technically yours but too important - and too vulnerable - to stay with you at the moment."

"What do you mean? It's been perfectly safe up till now."

"It wasn't difficult to take it."

Sabina didn't know how to respond. Before she could think of anything, he continued. "The people who stole your mother's gift from the Museum in Iraq have found out that it's fake. They're not happy - and nor am I. They will not stop until they have found the real thing. And that means it needs to be hidden somewhere very, very secure."

"For how long? I mean, the deal was - I'm its legal guardian. I know it's not the sort of thing that can ever really belong to any one human being, but it was my grandfather who found it and it belongs in my family."

"I understand how you feel, but these people, Sabina, are very dangerous and while they are hunting for it your life is in danger."

So that was it, she thought. Alex wins. She couldn't think of anything to say that would make any difference. And she supposed he was right. But she didn't like it. Not at all.

One small victory though: apart from looking her in the eye when she chose the wine, Sabina noted with satisfaction that Alex had addressed almost all his conversation for the past ninety minutes to her chest.

# 12

"HERE HE IS!" Ralph called to Amanda as he came through the front door, followed by Johnny, who was carrying a large black canvas holdall and a guitar case covered in stickers. Ralph closed the door behind him as Johnny put the bag down and shifted the guitar case off his shoulder. He placed it carefully against the wall.

"Hello you!" smiled Amanda, coming out of the kitchen wiping her hands on the pink hearts that covered her apron.

"Hi, Mum," said a rather embarrassed Johnny, realizing that a hug was not to be avoided. He loved his Mum, he loved both his parents, but he felt awkward and shy around them, especially when they came physically near him.

"Good trip?"

"Yeah."

"Well, not entirely," Ralph chipped in. "Johnny lost his iPod on the train."

"Oh, you didn't?"

"Yeah, I think so. I'm sure I had it when we left Paris."

"Oh, what a nuisance!"

"Yeah, well that money Uncle James gave me should do it."

"Even so, you should be more careful!"

"Relax, Mum, nobody died." Johnny immediately realized that this was ill-judged. He was also aware of an atmosphere that made him think maybe someone HAD died.

Ralph wondered if it was always going to be like this. He contented himself with the thought that adolescence didn't last for ever, and his son had a good heart. He didn't mean to be gauche, but he seemed to manage to upset both of them pretty easily these days.

"Sorry, um. What's for supper? I mean - I'll take my things upstairs."

"Don't worry darling - it's fine! Leave your bag in the hall - I'm sure it all needs washing anyway. Come into the kitchen and tell us all about it. Did you get to the Musée d'Orsay?"

Johnny followed his Mum into the kitchen. They both loved talking about art. He hadn't shown any interest in his father's passion for antiquity - it all seemed too dusty and boring to him. Ralph took his scarf off and hung it by the door. He chucked the car keys into the metal bowl on the hall table and stood for a moment. Johnny's guitar case started to slide down the wall and he jumped back to catch it, just in time. He put the case carefully back upright, testing to see if it was safe.

Amanda checked the lasagna in the lower oven of the Aga, turning her head away to avoid the sudden rush of heat. She pulled the terracotta dish out between oven-gloved hands and put it on the top. Johnny sat swinging on the back legs of a rush-seated chair.

"It's ready."

"Shall I lay the table?"

"All done!"

Johnny looked at the table and realized that it was all beautifully set up for his homecoming supper. "Yeah. Duh!"

Ralph walked in. "A little wine - or would you rather a beer?"

"Oh, beer please, Dad."

"John Smith's or Budweiser?"

"Bud'd be great."

"Here, I hope you're hungry!" Amanda passed Johnny a steaming plate of lasagna. "Help yourself to salad - and there's loads of garlic bread."

"I'm starving!"

"I'm not going to ask when you last ate!"

"I could always eat your lasagna, Mum!"

"Good. I'm glad it's still your favorite."

Ralph reappeared with an open Budweiser and a bottle of 1993 claret.

"Blimey darling - that's your best!" said Amanda as she saw the wine.

"I know. No reason why you and I can't enjoy it, even if the prodigal does prefer lager. It's time to celebrate!"

Johnny looked at his Mum and Dad. It was good to be back. The kitchen was warm, the food was great and he felt safe. He was knackered and the beer went straight to his head. There was definitely something wrong. Something they weren't telling him. God, why did people have to be so uptight? If something's happened, why don't they just get on with it and tell me? Why do we have to be so bloody English, pretending it's all fine when it so obviously isn't? It didn't occur to him that he himself was being just as 'bloody English' as they were: he hadn't mentioned the incident with the BMW, using the story about the iPod to explain why he was still a bit shaky. He felt protective towards his parents and didn't want to worry them.

Which was exactly why they didn't tell him about his Mum's illness.

# 13

THE PIECE OF PAPER that Ariq had thrust into his hand finally got to him. He could not rest until he had found out what it was that had mattered so much to his friend. Ralph closed the study door and took out his mobile. He wondered again whether he was doing the right thing, but above all else Ralph followed his conscience, and he had no real choice but to make the call. He spread the crumpled paper out on his desk and started to thumb in the numbers. It began with 0039, which he thought might be Italy, and the dialing tone confirmed that wherever it was, it was outside the UK.

"*Pronto!*"

'Oh bugger!' thought Ralph - who hardly ever swore - as he nearly dropped the phone. He was suddenly panicked by the fact that someone had answered. He was rather hoping there'd be no-one on the other end and he could forget about the whole thing. He could say that he had done his best. But now - a woman. A woman somewhere - he had no real idea where, no idea who. Was it safe? Was he being an idiot?

"*Pronto!*"

"Er, hallo? Um, who is this?"

"What? Who is speaking?"

"Um, it's Ralph Barford. I'm calling from England." He suddenly thought that was stupid, saying who he was and where he was - and giving her the upper hand.

"Why are you calling?"

"I was given this number by a friend."

"What friend?"

"Ariq Tafisi."

There was a long pause.

"Are you still there?"

"Yes, I am still here. How do you know Mr Tafisi?"

"I was in Baghdad, looking after a church. A few years ago. Um... I'm very interested in archaeology... We became good friends." Ralph now thought he sounded like a complete twit.

"So?"

"So, he gave me this number."

"Yes, you told me." Ralph was going to have to do better than this or the call would end.

"I think he knew he was in danger."

"When did you last see him?"

"Last Friday."

"Where?" Oh, what was he to say? Best to keep it vague.

"In England." There was another long pause.

"In England?"

"Yes." Now he thought she was beginning to sound a bit slow.

"And where are you in England?"

"Er, Rochester - but that's not where we met." Ralph knew now why he'd never be cut out for the secret service.

"And will you meet him again?"

"No."

"Why not?"

74

"Because he's dead." There was a much longer pause. Ralph waited this time.

"What did he tell you?"

"He wasn't able to tell me very much. Just about the looting of the Museum. He gave me his watch."

"He gave you his watch?" Ralph was beginning to feel better - at least, he wasn't the only one finding this difficult.

"Yes."

"What sort of watch?"

"It's the one he always wore."

"Describe it." Ralph fished the watch out of his top desk drawer and held it out.

"It's steel with a black crocodile strap - quite worn. The dial is silver. There's a magnifying bit on the right with the date and it says 'ROLEX Oysterdate'."

"Yes." Pause. "We should meet. I will send someone for you. What is your address?"

"12 Cathedral Close, Rochester."

"Good. Expect a man. He is quite tall, blond, Italian. His name is Gianni. Bring the watch."

The phone clicked off.

Ralph stared at the display screen, not quite believing that the call had ended. Or that it had happened at all. There was so much he wanted to ask. Who was this woman? What right had she to - what was he going to do?

He walked towards the fireplace, then sat heavily in the tub chair, which almost gave way, forcing him to hold onto the arms. He was in shock. Naively, he hadn't really expected anything to come of it. Now he was truly involved. How had he allowed himself to be drawn in to such strange circumstances? He supposed it had all started with going to Baghdad in the first place. And Lyle. And Ariq. Ralph had only been trying to do the right thing.

What should he say to Amanda? Perhaps, just that he had an appointment - something to do with Ariq? That someone wanted to see him and would be calling round? Fine. But what if she asked when? He had no idea when Gianni - or whatever his name was - was going to arrive. Better just say that he was expecting someone soon - they'd call to confirm - and hope for the best.

He twisted the wedding band on his left ring finger. It would be the first time he'd ever held anything back from her.

# 14

ALEX SAT AGAINST THE HOOD of his black Bentley Continental R, feet planted firmly on the gravel in front of the matrix radiator grill. Pulling on his beard, he gazed across the Gironde towards Blaye, beyond the Ile Nouvelle. As he breathed out, he glanced to the left, downriver past Pauillac, where an unwieldy oil tanker was maneuvering outside the refinery. It had always seemed strange to him that this large, ugly industrial site operated jut a few hundred meters from the vineyards of Château Lafite - and was in full view of the bedrooms at Cos d'Estournel. What must it have been like the night it was attacked by RAF Lancaster bombers in WW2? The kind of pyrotechnic display that would make the 14th July look like an afterthought.

But that was not really what was going through Alex's mind. He shifted his weight and placed his right hand on the red winged 'B' logo. He stared straight ahead in the bright spring sunshine, but his eyes were not focusing and he felt no warmth.

The meeting had gone well. A morning's presentation on ways in which Bordeaux's Cru Classé vineyards were exploiting the emerging Russian and Chinese markets was fascinating. Wealth was one thing, privilege another: as the owner of a prestigious wine-producing Château, he enjoyed being part of this exclusive club. He had really taken to the world of wine: with his family's background in organized crime, he had instantly understood the concept of 'turf'

- what a Londoner might refer to as his 'manor' - and the idea of *terroir* affecting the quality of wine was instinctive to him. He was hoping also to buy in the Haut Medoc, but prices were astronomic - up to two million Euros a hectare, the most valuable agricultural land in the world - and estates hardly ever came on to the market. What would you have to pay for the ground he was standing on - ninety hectares in production and over a hundred more in woods, meadows and formal gardens? Two hundred million Euros? More? But it wasn't just the money - these vineyards belonged to ancient families, French insurance companies or Japanese banks. For a private individual, there was almost no way in.

But it was an even more exclusive brotherhood he was plotting to join. Had he been part of it, he would still be inside the Château de Beychevelle behind him, rather than parked five hundred meters away, at the end of the track that led down to the river.

He had come a long way since his first deal, but one of the problems associated with climbing was that you became increasingly aware of new heights. It wasn't until you had ascended the mountain that had symbolized your life's ambition that you were able to see summits beyond - unsuspected peaks that enticed, tantalized and bewitched. When he started out, the wonder of having serious money of his own and the freedom to enjoy it outside Russia had been more than enough. Not that he had ever bought a Ferrari, a villa in Cap Martin or gambled at Monte Carlo - too obvious, too trite, too indiscreet.

Alex had always suspected that the world was ultimately controlled by very few people, and he wanted to be one of those people. He was not to be distracted by mere pleasure along the way - pleasure that sapped energy, pleasure that made you think you were a player but turned you into a spectator without realizing it. Succumbing to pleasure made you passive. Nor did he want to be dismissed as just another nouveau who had loaded his pockets with the spoils of a broken empire, a failed political system.

These people he so admired: he knew who they were now - at least, who some of them were. A few had been there that morning. Like him, they had enjoyed the private interior of the Château, with its eighteenth century paneling and Flemish tapestries, spectacular rugs and furniture, clocks and vases. Alex had watched two of them with special interest from behind an equestrian bronze of Louis XIV in the entrance hall before the presentation had begun. Like him, they had indulged in the nine course lunch, including some of the finest wines in the world. But unlike him, they had stayed on for another meeting of a very different type.

The great problem was that there was no road map. And you couldn't just muscle your way in to the Lucidi - a group whose families had been rising to the top and staying there for hundreds - in some cases more than a thousand - years. The easiest way to join was to become a successful international politician and wait for a tap on the shoulder at a G8 Summit or something. But that meant starting in local politics, and Alex was a very private person. He could never see himself on the hustings. Apart from one individual, Hari, his right hand man, he couldn't bear having people know about his life. If there had been close family, he would have distrusted them. He hated servants, the idea of people sharing your space, your moods. When traveling, he always drove himself.

He remembered with a new shudder the humiliation of his first visit to a grand private country house in England. Elizabeth's family were well-off and had a baronetcy, but he had been unprepared for their weekend as a newly engaged couple at friends of hers in Wiltshire. It was one of those stately piles that most of the population of the British Isles had never heard of - and of which the National Trust was completely unaware. Closed to the public, tucked away amongst thousands of acres of parkland and farmland, sequestered in one of those vast areas of countryside that are still like white spaces on the atlas, where mobile phones are useless, protected by three estate villages whose antecedents had been in service for generations, it was a magnificent Palladian mansion fronted by lawns, an enormous cedar and a lake. They were encouraged to leave the car at the foot of the front steps - it would be parked for them in the stable yard and their bags and guns brought in.

All was fine - splendid - until a member of the house staff led Alex and Elizabeth up to their rooms: separate, of course. He wasn't sure whether to tip then (he later found out that you did it afterwards, just before leaving - an envelope on the mantelpiece) and dismissed the old guy in a rather hasty embarrassment. He was dying for a pee, so made straight for the bathroom. As relief relaxed him, he was gripped by new tensions - what were his shaving kit, toothbrush, etc doing by the basin? He nearly wet his shoes trying to turn and see if he was right. In the bedroom, his case was there, but it was empty: all his clothes had been hung up in the mahogany wardrobe or neatly packed away in drawers. He was furious. The invasion of privacy was outrageous. Fortunately for him, Elizabeth entered at that moment and explained the system, preventing him from having made a total arse of himself at dinner.

So he was at a real disadvantage: he knew what he wanted, but he couldn't get there alone and he was essentially a loner. He had the credentials - several homes, over half a billion legitimately invested and a finely tuned network of people working for him inside the *Federalnaya Sluzhba Bezopasnosti* (FSB, formerly KGB) and other secret services, including the CIA and Mossad, where the relationship was suitably distant. But you had to be invited to join the Lucidi, the men who controlled the world.

And then the key had appeared, as if from nowhere. His father had had dealings with an Italian count - importing his first-class, cold-pressed virgin olive oil - and after his parents had died he had carried on as much of his father's lawful business as he could. The count - who only had a daughter - liked him, virtually adopted him as his son and, in time, took him completely into his confidence. And Hari, who worked for the count, had been the perfect accomplice.

But Alex had moved too swiftly. After years of stealthy preparation, he had misjudged the moment to strike, failing to get his hands on what he sought and creating unnecessary suspicion in the mind of the one who did inherit it. Now it was in his possession, but everyone was after it - at least, all those in the know, and his dream position had become a nightmare. As long as no-one knew that he had it, his life was in no more danger than usual: as soon as it was discovered, he was as good as dead. And yet, without letting the Lucidi know he had it, he was never going to be interesting enough for them to invite him to join them… The top card was in his hand, but just when he was about to play it, circumstances turned the ace into a death sentence.

He closed his eyes. After years in the West, and especially in the UK, he spoke English - he thought in English - most of the time. His Italian was perfect, and his French was almost fluent now. But when he was really passionate, he spoke Russian. Now, as frustration reached boiling point in his head, he exclaimed, "Так - что делать? Я не энаю! Я не энаю!"*

(*Tak! Chto d'elat? Ya n'e znayoo! Ya n'e snayoo! So - what to do? I don't know! I don't know!)

# 15

FIVE ALUMINUM CASES lay open on the inlaid yew wood dining table. The delicate color and fine patina of the wood were protected from the metal by thick, gray woolen blankets. Henry Billington III had asked his Philippino maid to move the twelve English Hepplewhite dining chairs that were normally set round the table and place them against the walls so that he could get close. His Golden Retriever, who went by the rather unoriginal name of 'Sandy', was not happy with this arrangement, and kept getting up and flopping down in a different part of the room to register his disapproval.

Billington stood, his legs touching the reeded edge of the table, staring at the black felt bags in front of him, his left hand in his pocket. After a moment, he looked up and out through the tall windows to where one of his stablehands was exercising a string of polo ponies. Without turning, he spoke to the other man in the room. He was angry and controlled his voice with difficulty.

"So what's going on here? We went to all that trouble. Five men dead here - more out there. A load of money and a load of effort. And it's a fake. Who would do a thing like that - go to so much trouble?"

"Well, actually, we think we know the answer to that now," said Seymour Lyle, who had come over on the early morning flight from Heathrow.

Billington swung round to face Lyle, who had misjudged the mood. The Senator did not suffer fools gladly, and Lyle was supposed to be working in his interests. "What? You know? And you didn't say? What kind of British cool is this?"

"No, no." Lyle responded with a half-smile, raising his hands in a mollifying gesture. "We didn't know beforehand. That's why I'm here. As soon as you told me what the valuer had said, we put extra pressure on Tafisi."

"He talked?"

"Yes."

"And?"

"And so we had to kill him, before anyone else could get to him."

Billington stepped back and sat on one of the dining chairs. It seemed that Lyle had kept him in the dark about more than one thing. "I thought you had that priest guy interview him? What's his name - Barford? Why'd'you get him involved in the first place?"

Lyle was now between Billington and a window through which light streamed. He moved to the right so Billington could see him more clearly - he didn't want to raise the man's blood pressure any higher, but he was enjoying the fact that he had the upper hand. This allowed him to be polite but also let Billington know who was in charge. As far as he was concerned, men like Billington had had their day. Lyle had had to wait long enough. "Tafisi said he wouldn't talk to anyone else. We saw no reason to get heavy at that stage. But when they met, we stopped it before it started. It was clear they were too close. My people are convinced Tafisi passed something to Barford."

"What did Barford say?"

"Nothing. Pretends that they weren't able to talk about anything that mattered."

"Which is true, right?"

"Yes, it's true. But I don't think he'll leave it there. We're watching him."

"Good. So, what did this Tafisi have to say?"

Lyle shifted a little further to the right so that he was framed by the astragal-glazed china cupboard behind him. It was filled with a 'Rothschild Bird Pattern' Herend dinner service. Billington liked to tell people it was a gift from a noble European family, but he actually bought it at auction from Christie's New York. "He told us that the Noah was robbed from the two graves near Ararat, which we already knew. The Turkish Authorities don't know where it went, but even they estimate the contents to be worth in the region of five hundred million dollars. He said that one man was behind the robbery, but used two teams."

"Two teams?"

"Yes. Apparently neither knew the other was there. The first team was surprised by the second one, who started shooting at them."

"Could've been disastrous!"

Lyle was pleased to see that Billington was less prickly. He was eating out of his hand - which just proved that Lyle was right - the man was past it. "Indeed, but this, er - mastermind - seemed to know what he was doing. He reasoned that one team might just make off with the whole lot. Anyway, the plan worked and both teams made the rendezvous back in Armenia. They were paid off, but having seen what they had looted, they weren't that happy with their reward. Three were shot dead, one escaped."

"So, what happened to the treasure?"

"Tafisi said that the man's family kept it securely locked away until he died."

"When did he pass?"

"What? Oh, um, 1990 - three years after the robbery."

"And then?"

"It seems his daughter took charge of it. She'd married an Italian - some count or other. He was terrified that someone would find out and try to take it from them. He knew it would be stolen to order by some gang boss or dictator and that they would be unlikely to survive."

"So?" Billington was urging him on, and Lyle was taking advantage, forcing the old man to ask questions, feeding him one morsel at a time.

"So the daughter decided to lay a false trail. She knew Tafisi from a big exhibition of Mesopotamian treasures he'd curated at the Metropolitan Museum in New York. She approached him with a proposal."

"Which was?"

"To make a gift of the Noah to the National Museum of Iraq in Baghdad."

"Baghdad? Why there?"

"Because that was where Tafisi worked. It was also a difficult place for Westerners to reach, and pretty secure from every other quarter. No-one wanted to get on the wrong side of Saddam Hussein - too many people were disappearing or dying in Iraq's jails. It was never to go on display, but the woman knew that even if someone found out about it, the chances of anyone risking trying to steal it were nil. In any case, by this time it was 1991 and the Museum had been closed because of the Gulf War - as Barford reminded me the other day."

"So that took the heat off her and her family."

"It certainly did."

"So, how come it's a fake?"

"Ah, yes. It seems the Countess wasn't quite so keen to give it up. Not even her husband knew at first, but she told him afterwards. She had a complete copy of the jewelry - the necklaces, rings, arm bands, chains, head dresses, bodice, tiaras, everything - made by a craftsman Tafisi knew."

"How could she trust Tafisi and this other guy?"

Lyle looked round and found a chair. He sat down, leaning forward with his forearms on his legs. Power had shifted, and he consolidated his gains by sitting in front of this man who had always commanded him. "In a way, she couldn't, but they were men who just needed to be comfortable - they weren't motivated by the idea of millions and they wouldn't have known what to do with the money. The Countess paid for the men's various family costs, new houses, education, holidays, cars, medical expenses, that sort of thing. She gave both of them presents from time to time and the arrangement seemed to be working."

"So they deposited the fake in the Museum?"

"Yes, and the Countess kept the real treasure on a boat."

"On a boat? You're kidding me!"

"Well, more of a ship really. I like the irony - the treasure of the ark spends the rest of its days at sea."

"Never mind that! Where is it now?"

"The ship?"

"No! Well, yes - if the Noah's still on board. Can't believe I just said that! Damn the woman!"

"We believe it is. The Countess and her husband died in a car accident about two years ago, not far from their castle in Italy. Ever since then, their daughter has lived on the ship and hardly ever returned to her childhood home. Too distressed, apparently."

"Any other kids?"

"No."

"Does she know it's there?"

"Yes. She spoke with Tafisi four days after our little raid."

"So. Now we target the ship."

"Now we target the ship."

"Where is it?"

"In the Aegean. Our info tells us it's currently moored just off the island of Symi - Dodecanese, close to the Turkish coast."

"You're tracking it?"

"Of course. Can you provide a team?"

"Sure. I'll get right on to it."

Lyle was ecstatic, though he was cool enough not to let it show. For the first time, it was he who had asked Billington to provide a team, and Billington had agreed. He had used the meeting to change the relationship for ever.

Billington was happy to be back in action. But he was aware of what Lyle had done. It was clear that once the Noah was found, it would have to be buried again. If Lyle had his way, it would be hidden in the vaults of the British Museum, and not the Metropolitan in New York, which was Billington's plan. He made a mental note to talk to Javier - tell him that if anything happened to him, he was to get rid of Lyle.

# 16

RALPH WAS IN TWO MINDS about the rendezvous. On the one hand, he liked the idea of being whisked away, jetted to some exotic part of the world to meet a mystery woman. On the other, he was beginning to worry about his position at the Cathedral and being involved in something so obviously dangerous. Ariq had been killed and he knew the raid in Baghdad must have been ordered by someone or some organization that was extremely powerful. Plus, Amanda was due to go to hospital any moment, and he couldn't not be there for her.

He had told her about the phone call later that day, while she was working in her studio - a converted outbuilding at the end of the garden. She was wearing old jeans torn at the knees, red baseball boots and a pink sweatshirt under a white apron - all spattered in clay and glaze. Her hair was pinned up and there was clay in it, as well as on her right cheek bone. She had been throwing a pot on the electric wheel when Ralph walked in, and her hands were covered in wet, red clay that was drying pink and pulling the skin on her arms as it shrank.

"So, when's he coming?"

"I don't know."

"Doesn't sound like you?"

"No. I don't know where we're going, either."

Amanda wiped her nose with the back of her hand. She got off the wheel and kissed his cheek.

"Are you sure this is sensible?"

Ralph moved close to kiss her, and then stepped back as he realized his clothes would be covered in dried clay. He brushed his gray clerical shirt. "Sensible? No - of course not. But I do believe I have to do it, for Ariq's sake if nothing else."

Amanda found an old towel and started wiping her hands. "Have you packed?"

Ralph noticed a tray of pots that were drying on a shelf by the kiln. "Hey, these are good. They're really thin. You trying that new technique?"

Amanda looked at him with a smile. "Don't change the subject. And yes, I am. It's going ok so far, but they could always explode in the kiln."

"Well, I've just packed an overnight bag. I shouldn't be away longer than that."

"As if you'd know!"

He picked up a ceramic kiln prop and started fiddling with it. Funny how they always felt heavier than one expected. "I can't be away right now."

Amanda could sense that he was struggling. She knew him well enough, and put her arms out to him. He stepped towards her and she held him close. This time he didn't mind about the clay. He just felt awful, as if he was betraying her, which he wasn't. He felt out of control, which he hated. Conflicting loyalties jarred and rubbed against each other, like a finger and thumb shaping a pot on the wheel - and he was the spinning clay in between. For a moment he thought he was going to give in to his emotions, and then he was suddenly all right again. He pulled back and Amanda let him go.

"It'll be fine. I'll just go and see why Ariq gave me this woman's number and I'll be back before you know it."

Amanda knew he was trying to sound strong - a sure sign that he wasn't - but she was wise enough to accept his words. Her darling Ralph - so clever, so daring in many ways, and yet such a little boy at times.

"Is Johnny ok?" Ralph asked.

Amanda, pleased to be talking about her son, looked thoughtful. "I'm not sure. There's something he's not telling us."

"I agree. It wasn't just the iPod."

"Perhaps he met some gorgeous girl in Paris."

"I think we'd have heard about that!"

"You're right! I'll keep an eye on him."

"I'm sure he'll tell you in time if there is anything. When's his exchange student arriving?"

"Laurent? Tomorrow evening I think. They're all going to the school first and Johnny'll bring him over afterwards for supper."

"I hope it'll be all right."

"It'll be fine. They're already good friends - J can't stop talking about him - and they'll be in school most of the time."

\*

GIANNI ARRIVED the following morning. Ralph was impressed by a rather wild looking figure - tanned, fit, in navy blazer, open-necked pale blue shirt, white jeans and boat shoes. Amanda thought he looked like a male model, and - even though he smelt of cigarette smoke, which she disapproved of - made him the strongest cup of coffee she could in the kitchen to impress him while Ralph fetched his things.

But the car was disappointing - Amanda could see that Ralph had been expecting something different, something glamorous. He liked his cars. If you asked him what sort of car someone had, he'd give you an answer that was precise, detailed and lengthy: if you asked Amanda, she'd probably be able to tell you what color it was, no more.

As they drove away, and she waved from the door, she began to wonder how her man would be. She worried that, with such an attractive employee, the employer might be more than a match for Ralph, and she was beginning to feel jealous already.

Ralph stretched in the stained velour passenger seat and settled down. He was glad he'd put on jeans and a casual shirt. At the last minute he'd swapped his sports jacket for a blazer: he had a feeling that he would be uncomfortable looking like a vicar - or a Geography teacher - in the presence of the person he was about to meet.

"So, Gianni, do we have a long way to go?"

"It's a little journey, but best if I do not speak."

'Oh,' thought Ralph. 'Well, this is going to be fun!'

He perked up significantly as Gianni turned the bland saloon - a hired Vauxhall Omega - onto Maidstone Road and followed signs for Rochester airfield. They parked by Hangar Two and Ralph waited while Gianni spoke with a woman at Reception. After twenty minutes of apparent confusion and heated discussion, a pilot came out and shook Gianni's hand. He waved to Ralph and the three walked over to a Bell 206 Jet Ranger helicopter.

It was the second time in a few days that Ralph had seen the English countryside from the air. He'd never been in a helicopter before Lyle had arranged for him to meet Ariq, and now, here he was again, taking to the skies. He loved it - but there was also a sense of foreboding, of the unknown.

He was beginning to wonder whether they were flying all the way to where this woman lived in the helicopter. He had been hoping for Italy - but that didn't seem right, especially as they appeared to be going in the wrong direction. About forty minutes later they started to descend to a landing pad by a lake. 'What now?'

thought Ralph. Perhaps they would travel by private jet, but there was no runway like there had been at Rochester.

Slightly mesmerized by what was going on - because it did not fit with his expectations of style and glamour - Ralph followed Gianni into a waiting taxi.

"The shopping centre?" asked the Asian driver, turning to Gianni. The man was about thirty, with sunglasses perched on top of greased-back long black hair, large brown eyes and an embroidered maroon shirt. The sleeves were partly rolled up, showing a watch and bracelet chain plated with cheap gold. He wore a similar chain around his neck.

"*Si*, yes," agreed Gianni.

The driver - Ranjit Patel - reset his meter with a prod of his chewed index finger and drove off, leaning forward to check the traffic both ways as he turned right, shifting his bottom on the wooden-beaded seat cover.

"So, mostly it's celebrities coming in here by chopper? - playing the MK Bowl, right?" Ranjit said, turning each statement into a question by his inflexion. "We've had Michael Jackson, yeah? U2, Madonna - all sorts. You famous, then?"

'MK Bowl!' thought Ralph. 'Oh no, don't tell me we're going into Milton Keynes!' He couldn't believe it. He had been dreaming of Portofino or the Amalfi coast.

"No - not us!" replied Ralph. Gianni gave him a quick stare - enough to let him know that conversation was not encouraged.

The taxi went over the A5 and on towards the centre of Milton Keynes. Ralph had never been there before - another first - and did not recognize the tall, futuristic bubble of the Xscape indoor ski slope, or the weighty dome of the cathedral, which seemed to have squashed the rest of the building into the ground.

Once they were on Saxon Gate they turned right down Silbury Boulevard along the half mile length of a tall shed punctuated by entrances and shop signs. The taxi stopped next to an open-air car park. Gianni and Ralph walked into the building through double glass doors, halting for a moment by the entrance to John Lewis, taking in the scene.

They were on one side of a large enclosed square. The roof was several stories above, giving a feeling of space and light. Crowds of people were moving like automata from shop to shop, and along two avenues that led off the far end of the square. Ralph and Gianni caught each other's eye: criss-crossing the scene like a pair of angry dodgems, Mr and Mrs Jabba-the-Hut patrolled the marble floor, each piloting a four-wheeled electric mobility scooter. Neither smiled but concentrated on steering one-handed while simultaneously refueling mid-flight - on a bucket of Dunkin' Donuts. As they dreamed of cashing in their high-yield benefit frauds for a life in the sun, they kept an eye on the walking sticks jammed like rifles in the forward-mounted on-board shopping baskets. Ralph was deeply disappointed at the choice of venue if, indeed, he was to meet the mystery woman here.

Gianni knew that this was the place, but he was having trouble locating the Contessa. He understood she was going to try and blend into the background as much as possible, but even he almost didn't recognize the girl in the blue baseball cap, gray hoodie and pink tracksuit bottoms with two white stripes along the leg. Had she been walking away from them, he might have made out a word in diamante just below the waistline, where the 'T' of a thin black thong poked out.

Sabina was worried that she had overdone it in the costume department - again - and confused Gianni - but she spotted him through her fake designer shades and raised her skinny latte. Privately, she was enjoying her sashay from Eurotrash to White Trash, but she had no idea what Gianni thought, nor did she particularly care. Ralph felt Gianni's hand on his back, propelling

93

him towards the coffee shop across the concourse. Sabina had a sports bag on the floor between her feet - she touched it with her ankles just to make sure it was still there without looking at it.

They took their coffees - an Espresso for Gianni and Cappuccino for Ralph - and joined Sabina at her table just outside the café. Ralph was completely unsure what to do, and nearly tipped his ribbed cardboard cup over as he sat down. He laughed suddenly with relief when Sabina greeted him in an accent that was half film star Italian, half pony club English. The voice he had heard on the phone.

"Canon Barford, thank you for coming."

She gave him her hand and they shook. He was aware of holding something priceless. It was as if she was merely visiting from another part of the universe. In that moment, he was captivated, though he would never have admitted it - to himself or anyone else. Sabina looked at him and he let go, abruptly realizing he had held on too long. She continued: "Do you have the watch?"

"Er, yes, it's here." Ralph took the watch out of his blazer pocket and handed it to her. He was put out by the fact that she hadn't introduced herself and hoped he'd done the right thing. Sabina checked the back of the Rolex.

"It is the one. My mother gave it him as a present." She passed it back and Ralph returned the watch to his pocket, out of sight. He recovered his confidence.

"So, if I've passed the test, what do we do now?"

"That depends," said Sabina enigmatically as she raised her cup to her lips.

"I mean, there are things I could tell you, but I don't know who you are and what you have to do with this. You're a friend of Ariq's, obviously, or you were. I don't know. I just think you should tell me a bit more."

"Ok. My name is the Contessa di Volturara and my family were, as you say, close friends with Mr Tafisi. He was very distressed by the looting of the Museum and he telephoned me for help. I sent Gianni to rescue him but it was impossible to get into Baghdad with the war. It seems that you or people you work with managed to get him out and you were able to talk with him before he died. I don't know whether you are a simple priest in the Church of England or an agent of the British Government. You must have some powerful connections."

Ralph was a bit annoyed by 'simple priest' but he let it go. He smiled at the idea of having some political influence. "Not really. The Government wanted me to talk with Ariq because I knew him and I knew Baghdad and they were worried about some of the things that had gone missing from the Museum."

"Exactly."

"So now we are going to have to trust each other if we're to get much further."

"Yes, we are. You can see from this," she waved at their surroundings with a dismissive gesture of her hand, and at her disguise with an even briefer movement, "that we have to be careful about being seen or overheard. I don't imagine anyone has thought of finding me here," she paused, "like this."

"Well, no. It wasn't what I was expecting either! The thing is, the Government went to great lengths to make sure that Ariq was safe and that our meeting was secret, so there must be something serious at stake. Especially as he was killed."

"Killed?"

"I believe so. I think he must have known it might happen - otherwise why would he have given me your number and his watch?"

"It doesn't take a great mind to understand that he wanted us to work together. He trusted both of us, and I think we must trust each other. Do you agree?"

Ralph looked at her. Somehow she had just asked him the same question he had asked her a minute ago, and got away with it. She was far from what she seemed. Even behind the mask of her underclass outfit, he could see that she was formidably attractive. She spoke and moved in ways that revealed an aristocratic background - title or no title. She was obviously used to getting her own way, and had to be wealthy to have set all this up - you don't simply send a helicopter for someone. Must've cost a fortune, just that. And how did she get here? Where had she come from? What choice did he have? "I agree. My wife's a bit nervous about all this-" Sabina cut him off:

"As you are."

"Oh yes, I don't mind - I mean, life was dangerous in Baghdad, and I'm happy about risking everything for God, but this is different."

"Perhaps not as different as you think. There is something…" She stopped herself mid-sentence. "Do your friends in the Government know that you have contacted me?"

"I don't think so. I don't think there's any connection. They didn't see Ariq give me your number or the watch as far as I know. I think they'd have said something otherwise."

"Unless they're being very clever."

"And they're not really my friends."

"Good. That should make it easier." To Ralph's surprise, she stood up, her sports bag in her left hand. She held out her other hand. He took it, standing as he did so, still feeling awkward in her company. "It was good to meet with you Mr Barford. I will be in touch."

"Yes, you have my number?"

"Of course. *Arrivederchi.*"

"Er, goodbye!"

Sabina nodded to Gianni and walked away. Ralph stared after her, relieved that he could return to Amanda having kept his promise just to check things out and come straight back. And he'd be in time to see Johnny and meet Laurent. But he wondered about what the woman thought, about how much she knew. Did she have any idea the Baghdad Noah was a fake? She was obviously aware something important was going on, but she'd told him almost nothing. His relief was short-lived. The more he thought about it, the more disturbed he was. Disturbed by the feeling that doors leading to jeopardy had opened, not closed. And a new door, a door he had not known existed, had slid ajar too easily on its hinges, exposing him to feelings that unsettled the core of his being.

Sabina couldn't wait to get out of those awful clothes and into the stuff she'd brought in the bag. On the other hand, she quite enjoyed the fact that no-one really noticed her - it had been a success. What a strange man! Well, not strange so much as unusual. In her world, she had never met anyone without guile, and yet Ralph Barford - he was not naïve, more innocent. Out of his depth, but not stupid. She didn't imagine they'd meet again. He couldn't possibly know what was at stake.

Now, a taxi to Newport Pagnell, just a few miles away. Her father had left an Aston Martin DB5 in the garage at the London house in Lancaster Mews, and she had had it recommissioned by Works Service at the factory. The drive back to town would be fun!

And she was looking forward to getting back to 'Viaggiatore'. She felt safer there, somehow.

# 17

HARYUTUN HAD CHANGED MORE than might be expected in the sixteen years since that night in the Ararat Mountains: thinner, a deep line engraved on each cheek, his dark hair prematurely badgered with white, eyes noticeably paler.

But the greatest difference was not seen close up: from a distance he was slightly crooked, as if he'd eaten something that didn't agree with him. He had never forgiven his boss, Razmig Assadourian, Sabina's Armenian grandfather. The man hadn't told him and Vartan that they were just part of the gang, that another team had been sent and they could have killed each other. And having seen the treasure he'd dragged out of that stinking grave, off those rotten bones, he was disgusted with the pathetic amount of money Razmig had paid him afterwards. All four of them had gone back to see the man, to get more out of him, but Assadourian was waiting and had had them shot before they reached his house. Only Harutyun was left alive, and it was all he could do to run and hide and escape being found.

The anger that festered deep in his bones had brought arthritis to the knees that had once bent over those ancient graves. He walked stiffly now as he crossed the cobbled courtyard between the *chai* where he had been watching Jean and Henri racking the wine - topping up the first year barrels - and Alex's office at Château Roüet-la-Dauphine.

It had taken him five years to track down Arevik Assadourian, Sabina's mother, whom he discovered had become the Contessa di Volturara on her marriage. Moving to Italy, he had changed his name, told everyone to call him Hari and bided his time. He worked first picking grapes for the Chianti harvest, then at a restaurant in Florence, picking up Italian and turning himself into a native. Getting a job working for Arevik's husband the Conte di Volturara had been simple, and since she had never met him, there was no possibility of him being recognized. Old age had cheated him of the satisfaction of ending Razmig's life, who died in his sleep three years after the robbery, so Harutyun had determined that he would avenge himself on the man's daughter.

As he knocked on Alex's office door, he again thanked his lucky stars that he had met this man, a business partner of the Conte. Some feral attraction had drawn the two men to each other and Harutyun had been easy to recruit to help carry out Alex's plans. He had never let Alex know that his motive was vengeance, or that he had any connection with the family, but he had been more than happy to be paid for his part in the murder of Sabina's parents. The roadblocks created by the log transporter and tractor had been the product of his devious mind. Less agile than he used to be, but still skilled at the wheel, Harutyun had driven the white van while other associates of his had set up and dismantled the barrier. It had been a perfect crime and he didn't imagine that the truth would ever come to light.

So now, here he was in southern France, employed by Alex as a trusted manager. He was uneducated but intelligent, a quick learner who had become skilled at overseeing the practical running of a vineyard, though Alex left the actual making of each vintage to experts. And, of course, he was useful to Alex in other ways.

It was Harutyun's involvement in the raid on the ship that had made him realize that matters had turned to his advantage beyond his craziest fantasies. Entrusted with carrying the two Louis Vuitton boxes from Sabina's safe on 'Viaggiatore', Harutyun had not been able to resist a quick look inside. Returning to the Château, Alex had left him for a moment in the small basement strong room while he made a phone call. Harutyun didn't hear the actual conversation, but he did open one of the boxes and it was all he could do to conceal his elation as he recognized part of the treasure he had extracted from the grave.

"*Entrez!*" called Alex. "Ah, Hari - how's the racking going?" He was sitting on the arm of an Empire chair behind the desk - an ebony bureau-plat with ormolu mounts. The room was full of hard surfaces, and Alex's voice echoed off the white stone walls, reflecting light from three French windows opening onto the courtyard. He waved Harutyun to a painted, cane-seated chair, which scraped on the small hexagonal terracotta tiles that covered the floor. Harutyun was glad to sit down. As he answered Alex's question, he glanced behind his boss's head at the familiar map of the vineyard, each field marked with the type of grapes planted - Grenache Noir, Syrah, Mourvedre, Cinsault, Clairette, Picpoul Blanc - there were thirteen varieties approved for Châteauneuf-du-Pape - and the age of the vines.

"Good. Jean and Henri - they're good workers."

"Excellent." Alex seemed distracted and Harutyun knew him well enough to realize that there was something on his mind; something that had nothing to do with wine. It was always a sign of restlessness, when he sat on the arm of a chair. He had clearly been staring out of the window rather than working at his desk.

His agents in the UK kept a close eye on Seymour Lyle. Alex suspected that he might be useful to him - to helping advance his ambition to join the Lucidi. The General wasn't at the Château de Beychevelle for the most recent meeting, but he'd seen him there in the past. At first Alex was dismissive of the man's visit to some obscure Canon in Rochester, but he should have known better. Lyle never wasted energy on anything or anyone unless he thought it could assist him. They missed the visit to Boughton House and the business with Tafisi, but after intercepting Lyle's call to Barford he'd ordered them to keep a closer eye. Just as insurance, he'd given Johnny Barford a fright, but it didn't seem to have had any effect. Perhaps the boy hadn't mentioned it. He wouldn't be the first teenager who'd withheld something from his parents.

But no-one was more surprised than Alex by the report on the Canon's helicopter flight to Milton Keynes.

"You wanted something?"

"You know that boy in Paris?"

"The one we hassled?"

"Yes. Johnny Barford. Well, it looks as if his father really could cause me problems and I'm not sure they got the message."

"He was shaken by it."

"Oh, I know you did your part."

"And Natalia got a good picture of him, which really upset the kid."

"Yes, but I think it's time to have another go. He's got that French boy, Laurent, staying with him in Rochester at the moment. Follow them, pick your moment and make sure he gets this." Alex took an envelope from his desk and passed it to Harutyun. "I want you to give him the note inside, and make sure you're wearing gloves so it can't be traced. Then burn the envelope."

Harutyun took the envelope, nodding to show that he understood and was in agreement.

"When?"

"Next train to Paris. Stay in the flat tonight. Take Natalia. At least, she'll take you - on her bike."

Harutyun immediately thought of his knees and her Ducati 748, which was more of a racer than a touring bike - not a good mix.

"It's a long way on the back of that thing."

"Ok, take the Eurostar. She can come out of the tunnel at Folkestone and meet you at Ashford station, which is on the way."

Harutyun was relieved. "Yes. Good."

# 18

IT WAS A BRIGHT, EARLY MORNING in New York, and the jeweled window displays along the north side of West 47<sup>th</sup> Street flashed rainbows as the sun's rays hit the Diamond District from the east. Most of the stores had not yet opened, and gems of emeralds, rubies, sapphires and diamonds were being set out behind bullet proof glass. Here, a hand withdrew from an 11 carat Asscher-cut yellow diamond ring; there, red-painted nails closed a black velvet door that separated a fiery necklace of Burmese rubies from the retailer's interior.

Standing opposite in the blue-shadowed entrance of Haretz Diamond LLC, David Adler was smoking a cigarette with Binyamin Neumann, his head of security. Mayor Bloomberg's new ban on smoking in restaurants had just come into effect, but the Adlers had long insisted on a no-smoking policy for their establishment.

David exhaled and the smoke rose across the street, defining the limits of the sun's reach as it struck a beam of light shafting theatrically from the top edge of the building behind him. Binyamin kept his filter clamped between his lips, the smoke curling upwards. It was a trick David had never mastered - smoke tended to go in his nose and sting his eyes, ash fell on his trousers - and he had long since given up trying. He decided it didn't look that cool anyway.

Binyamin liked to pose as a bystander on a cell phone outside the store. From this vantage point, he could photograph people who entered and left, while keeping in touch with the staff inside. David flicked the filter of his cigarette and looked at Binyamin. Even at this early hour - and coiled in smoke - David detected the odor of stale perspiration and kept a slight distance from him.

"Javier Mendoza - you're sure that's his name?"

Binyamin leant his heavy bulk against the stone ledge that ran under the shop window, flat feet slabbed on the sidewalk. David almost expected the building to shake.

"Yep - tough to track down but I always get my man. We had him on CCTV as well as the cell pictures. He's got an interesting record." He spoke without looking at David, playing with his phone, addressing his words to a passing yellow cab. The sun had started to scald the water from a pre-dawn shower and the tarmac was steaming.

David brightened. "Done this kind of thing before?"

"Yep. My clinical toxicologist buddies tell me it was probably thallium, which can be absorbed by the skin. They used to use it in rat poison, but it's been banned since 1965. Saying that, it's not hard to pick up on eBay." He took a pull on his cigarette and squinted. Each new word came out accompanied by a little cloud. "There would have been something else to speed things up, as thallium takes a much longer time to take effect than the few hours between his visit and your Dad dying. They're working on it - should have an answer for you in a few days. The real beauty is that it can't be traced - death appears natural."

"And this man's up in Westport you say?"

"Yep. We have the address."

"Thanks Binyamin. Let me know."

"I will."

David closed his eyes a moment and prayed quietly. He would get his father's murderer if it was the last thing he did. He flipped his eyelids open and half-smiled at the cliché. But he was deadly serious. The heat of the cigarette burned his fingers and he dropped it, crushing the filter, paper and tobacco into the stone of the sidewalk with the toe of his rubber-soled work shoe.

# 19

IT WAS NOT SO INTERESTING taking Laurent round Rochester. The city was quaint, but hardly Paris, and although there was plenty of potential sightseeing with the naval dockyards at Chatham, the Dickens connections, the cathedral, the castle - it just seemed dull, ordinary, normal. Perhaps that was how Laurent had felt about their time in Paris. Johnny's Dad had pointed out that King's Rochester, where he was at school, had been founded in 604 AD, but that really didn't help. It wasn't ancient history they were after. Good job London was close by. They were going to do the National and Tate Modern with his Mum on Saturday. She'd promised them a decent lunch and a look at a major department store to show Laurent that the country was not a completely lost cause.

Johnny had Upper Sixth study periods all afternoon, so he and Laurent decided just to mooch round the shops. They were joined by Johnny's friend Andrew and his exchange student *Gilles*, who was from the same lycée in Paris. Laurent found England - what little he had seen of it on this first visit - quite backward: the people seemed to have no idea of what to wear and Rochester was a monument to petit-bourgeois tastes, or so he liked to pronounce. His arrogance appeared rude to Johnny, who started feeling defensive about his city. Wishing to avoid any kind of friction, the four of them diplomatically sought common ground and went into a shop to look at games for Andrew's laptop.

*

AMANDA POURED THE WATER - just off the boil - onto the ground coffee in the glass and chrome cafetière. She put the kettle down by the side of the Aga and closed the lid on the faster hotplate above the oil burner. Ralph stood, staring out of the window at the lawn, fiddling with a garlic press. He'd forgotten now why he'd picked it up.

"Do you think she'll call?"

"I've no idea. I hope not. Well - no, I hope not." He turned to look at her. He hadn't worn his clerical dress since returning from the trip with Gianni, and Amanda detected a subtle change in him - less English? A hint of rebellion? She couldn't put her finger on exactly what, but he was not the same.

"You don't seem sure?" Amanda stirred the coffee, put the top on, chucked the spoon in the sink and rested her back against the cooker, hands on the towel rail.

"Don't look like that!"

"Like what?"

"You know."

"I'm sorry darling but you look so serious!"

"Yeah. I'm sorry. It's just not knowing. And the whole thing was so weird." He put the garlic press in a drawer, took two mugs off the shelf in front of him, bumped the drawer shut with his right hip and brought them to the table.

"Well, it's not every day you take a helicopter to Milton Keynes."

"Oh, don't remind me! That place! If ever you needed God's help to love your fellow human..."

"What, worse than India?" teased Amanda. She plunged the cafetière and carried it to the table as Ralph fetched a four liter plastic milk bottle from the red retro fridge in the corner.

"Completely different. At least on the sub-continent you feel they're not responsible for their misfortune." He was distracted for a moment by the sight of an unwrapped piece of stilton next to the butter. "But what do I know? It's dangerous to judge." He closed the fridge door with a thunk and the lever clicked shut. Amanda sat down on a rush-seated kitchen chair.

"Easy, though."

"Too easy. You'd have hated it."

"So we're not going there for my surprise birthday then?" said Amanda, eyebrows raised, as she poured coffee into the mugs.

"Correct." Ralph sat down with the milk.

He had just had a first slurp of coffee and exhaled in satisfaction at the taste when the doorbell rang.

"I'll get it," said Amanda, standing up. 'No peace,' thought Ralph.

The bell rang again. "Coming!" shouted Amanda. 'Good grief,' thought Ralph, 'what's the emergency?'

The door opened and shuddered as Johnny banged into it, knocking Amanda back. "Sorry Mum!" he shouted. "You all right?"

"I'm fine. What about you? Where's your key?" She still had her hand on the Yale lock and stared at him in surprise.

"Dunno. Couldn't find it. Just needed to get inside. Hey, Laurent, *allez, allez,* mate, come in, quick, close the door."

The two boys stood panting on the doormat. Amanda shut the door. "We're in the kitchen." She led the way. "It's the boys. Something. I've no idea."

Ralph faced Johnny and Laurent as they came in. "What's up?"

Johnny pulled at the blond quiff that seemed to be standing prouder than ever. "Oh, Dad, it was the same guy!"

"It was a woman!" interjected Laurent.

"Yeah, well, I think you're right."

"What woman? Sit down. Have a coffee. Tell us from the beginning."

Amanda fetched two more mugs. "I think it'll just stretch. Black for you Laurent?"

"Yes, please *Madame* Barford."

Ralph gazed expectantly at Johnny, who hugged his mug like a security blanket. "In your own time."

"Yeah, well. I didn't tell you. In Paris."

"I knew there was something."

"Sh, Ralph, don't interrupt, he'll tell us. What happened in Paris, darling?"

"This car. We were just walking along and this car - a black BMW, I think it was a 535i - started creeping along next to us. It was weird. I went down the next street, see if it was following us, and it was. Then it went past and this guy or woman in red bike leathers took a photo."

"It was her," added Laurent. "*Désolé*, but the woman on the motorbike just now, it was the same. She had the camera."

"Yeah, maybe you're right, but you couldn't tell because whoever it was was wearing a helmet and shades in the car. Anyway, then it stopped and I went round the front and tried to find out what they were up to."

"Eh? Why were they so interested in you?" asked Ralph.

"I really don't know. They drove at my legs and I jumped out of the way."

"Darling!"

"It's ok Mum, it didn't hurt."

"It was quite bad. I ran with your son to a café and we stayed out of the way for a while."

"But why didn't you say?"

"I didn't want to worry you."

"You are silly! What did you think we'd do?"

"I dunno. I just - I felt stupid."

"Come here!"

"No, it's all right Mum, I'm fine now. I need to tell you about just now. We were by the pedestrian bit…"

"We being?" asked Ralph.

"Me, Laurent, Andrew and *Gilles* - Andrew's exchange. Andrew and *Gilles* went off to get something to eat. All of a sudden, this bike comes out of nowhere from behind and stops right next to where I'm walking. There's a guy on the back who taps me on the arm, really hard. I went to rub it and he gave me this envelope. Then they just took off. Laurent's right, she was driving. It was the same red leathers and helmet. But the guy on the back was older. I couldn't really see his face - it was the way he moved."

"It's true, *M'sieur*. Just as Johnny has said. I saw."

Ralph blew out air and scratched the back of his neck. Amanda caught his eye and twisted her head a little as if asking him something. He knew what it was - don't be too hard on him. It hadn't occurred to Ralph.

"And are you ok? In one piece?"

"Yeah, think so. Bit shaky, that's all."

"I'm not surprised. I'm just glad you're both all right. I must apologize, Laurent. This sort of thing doesn't normally happen in our family."

"It's not a problem, *M'sieur*. I was glad to help. But it is strange."

"Yeah. Strange is the word. So, have you still got the envelope?"

"Yeah, it's here." Johnny pulled a crumpled ivory C5 envelope from his charity jacket pocket and gave it to Ralph.

"It's got my name on it!"

"Yeah. How did they know, Dad?"

Amanda nearly dropped her mug and failed to stifle a little "Oh!"

"Well, the best thing you guys can do is forget about it. Why don't you go and see what's on TV?"

"No, Dad, I want to see what's in the envelope."

"I don't think that's a good idea. Please."

Johnny knew that look, that tone. He realized he wasn't going to get anywhere by insisting. "Ok. But let us know. Promise?"

"I promise. But it may not be straight away. Now, go on."

"Come on Laurent, let's go upstairs."

"We can try again your PSP?"

"You still won't beat me!"

Ralph turned to Amanda once he'd seen the two boys leave. He waited a moment, listening for their steps on the stairs. They both heard the boys reach the landing and go towards Johnny's room.

Amanda got up and stood behind Ralph, putting her arm round his shoulders. He held her hand and looked at the envelope. She put her head next to his.

"I suppose I'd better open it."

"Shouldn't we call the police?"

"No. If anything, I'll get hold of Lyle. Let's see what's in it."

He peeled open the flap that sealed the envelope as if it was an unexploded bomb. There was a sheet of matching A4 paper inside. He pulled it out and unfolded it. It was printed in capitals on one side - looked like dot matrix rather than laser, the kind you could get anywhere and impossible to trace. They both read the words.

STOP NOW OR SOMETHING WORSE WILL HAPPEN TO
YOUR FAMILY
YOU KNOW WE ARE WATCHING

# 20

GIANNI COULDN'T UNDERSTAND why 'Viaggiatore' was not responding. He had talked with Maria the night before, and all was well. Now, as he and Sabina approached the island of Symi from Rhodes, he couldn't raise Giorgio, the ship's captain, on the radio. Sabina tried Maria's mobile, but it just reverted to voicemail each time.

She spoke over the helicopter's intercom: "D'you think there's a problem?"

"I can't see that there would be. There's nothing to worry about. She's safely in harbor, not going anywhere. Perhaps they're shopping for supplies."

"Could be. I did ask Maria to get me some more sponges before we leave. It's not far now, anyway. I'm so looking forward to getting back."

They sat in expectant silence as the helicopter ruffled its way across the Aegean. Gianni had dressed typically in navy cotton chinos and a pale blue polo shirt. He was wearing the diver's watch Sabina had given him for his fortieth. A choice of gift that seemed to run in the family. She was comfortably chic in a raw silk overshirt and trousers she'd bought years ago on a trip to India. The light played the green fabric so that it was now olive, now almond.

Soon the rocky outcrop of Symi came into view ahead. Sabina looked down at the sea bed. One of the things she liked most about Greece was water so clear you could make out the ground rising from the continental shelf like the sides of a mountain until it broke the surface. From the air, each island was a dry brown summit surrounded by white surf, sitting on top of vast undersea foothills that spread far out in every direction.

"She's not there!" exclaimed Sabina.

"I can see. She's not in Emborio either, where they might have moved her. I'll call Theo." Gianni flicked the switch on his transmitter. "Harbormaster Symi, Harbormaster Symi, this is 'Viaggiatore', come in please. Over." There was the sound of static and then a distorted voice.

"Viaggiatore this is Harbormaster Symi. State your position please. Over."

"Harbormaster Symi our vessel's position is unknown. Theo, this is Gianni returning in the ship's helicopter call sign India Sierra Delta Victor Nine. We cannot locate 'Viaggiatore' or contact her. Last known position was docked in Yialos harbor. Over."

"India Sierra Delta Victor Nine, Γειά σου -Yassou Gianni! 'Viaggiatore' left Yialos harbor Symi at 02.00hrs this morning, en route to Rhodes. Over." Sabina stared wide-eyed at Gianni, her hands gripping in tight fists of anxiety.

"Harbormaster Symi we have just flown from Rhodes and have had no contact with 'Viaggiatore'. Request permission to land on helipad. Over."

"India Sierra Delta Victor Nine permission granted. Helipad is clear and ready. Over."

"Roger. Thank you. Out." Gianni turned the transmitter off. "Did you hear all that?"

"Yes, I don't understand. Giorgio wouldn't go anywhere without asking you or me."

'No,' thought Gianni, 'Viaggiatore's' captain may not have had a sense of humor, which was hard at times, but at least he was reliable.

"We'll have to see if Theo can throw some light on it." Gianni brought the helicopter round in a slow arc towards the helipad, just to the north east of the Harbormaster's office.

Theo Mastorides' family had lived on Symi for generations. Like many Greek islanders, he was warm, friendly and a generous host. Theo was also of generous proportions, bulging out of navy trousers and a double-breasted jacket with braided cuffs. His right arm held the front of his jacket down and a naval cap was in his other hand as the wind created by the helicopter spun his dark hair upwards. He half closed his eyes and tipped his head away from the whirling dust.

The whine of the jet engine diminished and the rotor blades slowed from a blur to flailing arms which gradually came to rest, flopping with exhaustion in the heat that was already burning. Gianni switched everything off and went through his post-flight check as Sabina unbuckled her seat belt. She stepped out and greeted Theo, who brushed his hair back and fitted the cap at a low angle, shading his eyes.

"Καλημέρα Θέω - Kalymera, Theo!"

"Καλημέρα Κοντεσα - Kalymera, Contessa!" She took his outstretched hand, which almost crushed her delicate fingers and smelt faintly of hair oil.

"Τι κάνετε -Ti kanete?"

"Καλά, ευχαριστώ - Kala, eucharisto. Και εσείς - Kai eseis?"

"Καλά, ευχαριστώ πολύ - Kala, eucharisto poli."

Having established that they were both well, the two walked towards Theo's office.

"How can I help you, Contessa?" Theo asked, as if the conversation in the helicopter hadn't taken place.

"Well, I'm not sure really. I can't understand it. We left 'Viaggiatore' here and now it's gone."

"We did request that the ship be moved round to Emborio two days ago - to make room for a large private charter, and then the log shows that she left early this morning, bound for Rhodos. I was not on duty, but the entry is clear."

"Does it say who advised you that she was leaving?"

"No." Gianni came into the office just as Theo was offering Sabina a seat, which she declined. The room was large and plain, with three wooden chairs and a long work surface under the windows that looked out over the pretty harbor, even more attractive in the early morning haze. Detailed Admiralty charts on the rough-painted walls showed the waters all around Symi's coast: a deeply indented outline of headlands and coves with the occasional shingle beach.

"Can you put out an alert?" asked Gianni.

"Surely you don't think it's serious?" countered Theo.

"Yes, I do. It's never happened before. Maria always answers her phone and Giorgio would never move the ship without permission."

"Very well. You want to come back in an hour, see if anyone has reported sighting 'Viaggiatore'?"

"Yes, thank you," Sabina said, looking at a chart of the west coast. "That's a good idea. We'll go and get a coffee." Gianni moved to open the door, but Sabina turned back to Theo. "Actually, I don't think I can wait. Gianni and I will take the helicopter round the island - we can cover all the places she might have gone if she's still here. At least then we'll know one way or another."

"That's good. You will do that quicker than I could. I'll concentrate on the area between here and Rhodos. I'll call the port

116

there first, see if they have any record of her arriving. Tell me as soon as you sight anything."

"We will, Theo. Αντίο - Andio!"

"Αντίο Κοντεσα - Andio Contessa!"

Sabina and Gianni decided to head to starboard as they flew out of the bay - that was the direction any boat would take going south, and as whoever was commanding 'Viaggiatore' had told the Harbormaster's Office they were bound for Rhodes, they would have gone that way so as not to arouse suspicion. Gianni and Sabina were both now thinking that something was badly wrong and were beginning to assume the worst, though neither acknowledged their fear to the other.

Gianni found it hard to concentrate on flying. He felt an overwhelming sense of responsibility towards the Contessa. After all, it was she who had engaged him and Maria two years ago when they were out of work and had no references. Their previous employer had been a tyrant who fell out with everyone - the PA to a famous rock diva who was notoriously picky about everything, impossible to please. In the end, Gianni had been glad to leave - the constant criticism was a kind of bullying that had been affecting their health - but it left him and Maria vulnerable without any income. Still, they both took pride in their work and they had their principles.

Sabina had taken them on trust and her faith in them had been rewarded by total loyalty and impeccable service. She had become almost family - or was it the other way round? But they were careful never to cross the line, never to be over-familiar with her. The three had developed a kind of unconscious co-dependency that none had spoken about but was no less real. For her part, Sabina had always been generous.

Gianni was also distressed by the silence from his beloved wife, Maria. Where was she? Was she all right? Had she been hurt?

Had she tried to call him? He felt physically empty at the thought of losing her. They had a son, Umberto, who lived in Ostuni. He was clever, had done well at University in Lecce and was now practicing as an ophthalmic optician. But they had little contact - it was difficult when they were at sea most of the time - and had drifted apart over the past few years. Gianni was suddenly filled with love for the boy and resolved to go and see him as soon as possible. They would have lunch at the Osteria Piazzetta Cattedrale, which would be a real treat for all of them.

"Agia Marina is clear. Nothing in Pedi either, apart from the water tanker," said Sabina. She had a chart on her lap and was following their progress with her finger. Not that there would have been room for 'Viaggiatore' to anchor in either bay. How stupid it made her sound! She'd only spoken out of nervousness. She decided to keep quiet and concentrate. She could sense that Gianni was on edge, and that was hardly surprising. Oh, Maria! Sabina offered up a silent prayer, desperately hoping that they would find her well, that it had all been some terrible confusion.

The water was almost transparent - a light glaze of aquamarine over the rocky sea bed. Sabina spotted the tiny chapel on the small island off Agia Marina before they rounded Agios Nikolaos and banked towards the next bay - Agios Georgios Disalona.

Nothing.

It was still early. The first ferry from Rhodes would be arriving soon with its payload of trippers, followed shortly by the hydrofoil. People who stayed on the island for their holiday would already have made for the more remote beaches - the day visitors would not be able to reach them and return in time for the ride back. Sabina could see the black-hulled 'Triton' puttering along below, making for the next bay - Nanou. The season had only recently begun, and just a handful of people were sitting on its

118

wooden benches, looking forward to a swim and lying in the sun while the crew prepared a barbecue. Later they would be washing down grilled fish and chicken with local white wine - 'rocket fuel' served from jerry cans - and Χωριατικι - Horiatiki, the classic peasant salad of tomatoes, cucumber, red onion, green pepper, feta cheese, herbs and Kalamata olives. On the way back, they would be offered a free glass of Metaxa or Ouzo, which would go straight to their legs and make natural sailors of them all, rising and falling with the waves, arriving in Yialos at one with the world, the happy sound of Greek music filling their heads.

Sabina thought how different their two worlds were as the helicopter's shadow passed over 'Triton's' white awning - below, carefree, above, tense with worry and anticipation.

Past Nanou and Marathounda, they saw the long jetty that served Panormitis Monastery, tiny blue fishing boats bobbing quietly at their moorings. Their work had been done many hours before and octopus were already drying in the sun behind a bunch of dark-skinned men in faded clothes who sat untangling great mounds of bright yellow nets. A few island kittens tentatively explored the area between the wheels of a parked moped and a stack of shallow fish boxes.

"Look, there!" shouted Gianni. A cloud of milky-white eddied out on the water from behind the next headland. Sabina and Gianni gave each other a fleeting look, then concentrated on the scene in front of them.

Flying past Agios Vasilios, they could see the source of the pollution in the distance. It was coming from Skoumisa, a scruffy little cove right at the end of a large bay on the island's west coast. Sabina remembered that only goats ever went there - the stony beach was littered with rusting machinery, broken fishing boats, a large, empty cable drum, plastic bottles and other debris.

At first they could see nothing unusual apart from the widening stain that clouded the sparkling water. But, at the same moment, before they could speak, they were both kicked in the stomach by the realization that their lives would never be the same.

It was a nanosecond, but in that sliver of time Sabina and Gianni saw the radar mast of 'Viaggiatore' sticking out of the water at a crazy angle - unnatural as the bone of a smashed leg. They flew closer, the hull of the ship gradually becoming visible underwater. She was heeled over on one side - port - facing away from them. The upper decks were just below the surface, the helipad half out of the water.

"Oh my God! No!" screamed Sabina, her hands to her mouth, the chart slipping to the floor.

"Maria!" shouted Gianni, tears forming behind his shades, twitching momentarily at the controls and dipping the helicopter before righting it straight away - as if the machine itself was bowing in sympathetic grief.

The white stream gave way to a dark slick of oil bleeding from the ship's side. Gianni brought the helicopter round and hovered so they were looking at the ship's bows below the steep cliffs.

"We have to get down there! Is the diving kit still on board?"

"Yes, it's behind your seat. But it's too dangerous! *Oh, il mio dio!*"

"No, we can't wait. What if someone's still alive?"

"I'll call Theo. You can't do anything."

"Call him. I'll get the stuff on."

Gianni saw it was pointless arguing and there was no time to waste. "Harbormaster Symi, Harbormaster Symi, this is India Sierra Delta Victor Nine ..."

Sabina unbuckled her seat belt and turned to fish out the diving equipment stowed behind her seat. She was glad she was wearing decent underwear, although it wouldn't have mattered if she had had nothing on. She had to get down there. Pulling out the single oxygen tank, she turned the valve to check that it was full. There was no point messing about with the wetsuit - she pulled off her overshirt and trousers and reached for the fins and mask. She decided against the weight belt - which probably saved her life.

"Theo's sending a patrol boat round now. I've given him the coordinates, but he won't have any trouble finding us." He glanced sideways at her as she wriggled her feet into the fins, her head dangerously close to the controls. "Are you sure about this?"

"If I can ski out of a helicopter I can dive out of a helicopter," Sabina responded, glad now of those two years at Aiglon College in the Alps - not the usual stereotype of a Swiss finishing school, which she would have hated. Sabina was properly feminine, but although privileged she was no helpless airhead, no pampered doll who flapped when things went wrong. "How low can you go?"

Under normal circumstances, looking at Sabina wearing very little and squirming into the aqualung, Gianni might have made a risqué remark in response to her question, but it never occurred to him: his focus was absolute. "I'll try, but there'll still be quite a drop."

Sabina grabbed the mask and crouched by the door. They were fifty feet above the surface. Gianni moved the helicopter forward and then flew away from the ship. Sabina looked at him.

"I'm sorry, it's difficult so close to the cliffs. I'll come round and lose height that way." He managed to sweep the machine away from the land and brought it down in a gentle slide until they were hovering just a few feet from the water. Sabina opened the door and looked at the sea stirred up by the downdraught. She confirmed that the straps of the aqualung harness were tight and stepped out, her heels just holding her, one hand on the door handle. She closed her eyes and jumped, away from the helicopter, which jerked upwards as the balance shifted.

The shock of the water was harder than she expected, nearly ripping the mask out of her hand and knocking the air from her lungs. She went down, down, further than she wanted, kicking with the fins to reduce her descent. Taking her thumb and fingers away from her nose, she pushed with her hands, desperate to end the dive. Her legs stung from the impact and the water grew colder as she plunged deeper. Then she kicked strongly and shot upwards, gasping for breath as she broke the surface.

She trod water and looked up, waving to Gianni and giving him the thumbs up. The helicopter moved away and hovered further out in the bay so as not to disturb the water where Sabina was swimming. She spat into the mask and rubbed the inside of the glass to keep it from steaming up. Pulling it onto her face, she took hold of the mouthpiece and tried a couple of breaths. Satisfied that everything was working, she dipped under the surface and cleared the mask, blowing hard through her nose and just lifting the bottom edge of the rubber so the water could be forced out, checking all round that none of her hair was breaking the seal.

She looked down, arched her back and dived, kicking with the fins once she was completely submerged. Breathing steadily, she glanced left and right to get her bearings. The portholes of the main saloon were below her and she swam deeper until she could run her hand along the metal sides of her ship. The water was calm and there was no danger of her being banged against the vessel by any waves or tidal flow - just the gentle pull of the current away from the cove, the current that was carrying the oil and milky ooze out into the Aegean.

# 21

GENERAL SEYMOUR LYLE was seriously out of sorts. Dressed in an unseasonably warm brown herringbone three-piece suit, he sat in his stuffy oak-paneled London office staring at a portrait of Sir Francis Walsingham, Queen Elizabeth I's spymaster, on the far wall above a small chesterfield sofa.

The building creaked a little, all the time. It wasn't the Ministry of Defense, as Barford might have expected, but a black-bricked house in Petty France, put up in the reign of Charles II. There was no indication from the outside as to its purpose, which was how Lyle liked it.

Lyle's desk was solid as a tank trap, its combat green leather top broad enough to have sat eight people round - had there been any room for their knees. As it was, the long sides bristled with drawer knobs, and the area immediately in front was guarded by two brass lamps.

He was discomfited by the fact that that bloody man Billington still hadn't called him about the success of the raid on the ship, and thoroughly pissed off by Barford who seemed to be even more useless than he'd feared. Open in front of him an envelope and letter that had arrived via the internal mail, having been posted in Rochester the day before. The words shouted at him:

STOP NOW OR SOMETHING WORSE WILL HAPPEN TO
YOUR FAMILY
YOU KNOW WE ARE WATCHING

He had reassured Barford on the phone that his family would be protected - not that he was promising him anything new, as he already had Barford under surveillance, but it would cover him if any member of the team was spotted. What worried Lyle was that he didn't know the source of this warning, or how anyone else knew that Barford was involved. His concern was that whoever it was might also know about Lyle. He couldn't care less about the Canon- - huh, the loose Canon - but he needed to know if anyone was on his case.

Perhaps it had been an error of judgment to bring the man on board. This was all getting too messy for Lyle. He liked to be in control. He liked to have everything feeding into everything else. He admired the principles of the Lucidi - the way they used disease, war, debt, drugs, religion, corruption, environmental disaster, crime - anything that would increase fear and make it easier to launch their world government. Bloody hell, when he thought back, just in his own lifetime, the idea had gone from comic book fantasy to genuine possibility. Every US President who mentioned the phrase 'New World Order' in his inauguration speech was merely acknowledging that the Lucidi had put him there, that he was there to do their bidding, and how many times had we heard that recently?

He loved the fact that every Lucidi strategy fed itself and multiplied. Take drugs - or rather, don't take them, because a golden rule was never to fall for the methods they used, one of the reasons he despised Billington, who was known to the authorities in Kenya and Thailand for interfering with small children - but look at the example. The Lucidi made money out of drug production and distribution; drug users destroyed their own lives and those of their families; crime increased exponentially to feed victims' addictions; local and national resources were squeezed in the fight against drugs and drug-related problems; generations of bright, enquiring individuals dropped out of university, out of responsible jobs, out of life. Every stage was to the Lucidi's advantage, a virtuous circle - though nothing had ever been less virtuous.

The same was true of war - make money out of arms manufacture; create unrest; multiply fear; oversee genocide; force governments to spend money on aid that was conditional on buying more weapons, start another conflict: another perfect circle. Disease - gain sufficient control of the global pharmaceutical industry; create pandemics like AIDS; decrease population; raise fear levels; sell antidotes; create new sickness. Apparently, one of the items he'd missed at the recent Beychevelle meeting was an announcement about various mutations of common 'flu that would bring the next wave of disease upon the world.

His department was religion. Well, science, belief and religion really. Which is why he still posed as a military man - excellent camouflage. For Lyle, what people believed was the most powerful motivator on the planet. Look at the hundreds of millions who had died as a result of Communism which, for all its tosh about religion being the opiate of the people, was a belief-system if ever there was one. He was fond of quoting Steven Weinberg, Nobel Laureate in physics: "Religion is an insult to human dignity. With or without it, you'd have good people doing good things and evil people doing bad things, but for good people to do bad things, it takes religion."

The General stood up and walked over to the near window. He looked down on the heads of people passing by. Most would be on their way to lunch somewhere - perhaps sandwiches in nearby St James's Park, or one of the many small restaurants between here and Victoria. How little they knew about who was really in control of their lives! How fondly they imagined that they were free to think and do just what they liked! And these were just ordinary people. What about the fundamentalists and fanatics who murdered, raped and destroyed all in the name of their god? People who, as Weinberg pointed out, may think of themselves as good but who do bad things?

He reckoned the history of the Christian church demonstrated that time after time. Well, once Constantine had decided to make Christianity the official religion of the Roman Empire. The man had turned it into a political force with wealth and temporal power. Before then, it had been unstoppable because it was driven by men and women of faith who would rather die than compromise their beliefs. There's nothing you can do in the face of that kind of sacrifice, he felt. Lyle was reminded of the trouble Ghandi had caused - and what he had achieved - with his peaceful protests. He thought of his own garden at the country house in the Cotswolds - and hacking away at nettles - the more you did it, the stronger they came back. The more people died for their faith, the more the faith advanced. Lyle's own studies of the persecuted church in the twentieth century proved it - the faith grew like wildfire under regimes that tried to suppress it. The General reckoned that was a huge tactical error. The key to rendering Christianity toothless was to tolerate it, to make it mainstream. And that was Constantine's great contribution. Not many centuries later, the church had so lost sight of its original purpose and values that it launched the crusades - a politically motivated slaughter that totally contradicted the basic tenets of the faith as outlined in the New Testament. It was that faith that worried Lyle the most - and the book it was based on.

Anything that gave the Bible credence was a major headache for Seymour Lyle. Especially the first book, Genesis, which was almost totally at odds with modern science. This Noah business was the worst thing he'd had to deal with. Imagine - the actual treasure looted from graves that looked likely to belong to Noah and his wife, not far from where the fossilized remains of the ark had been found. Precious little he could do about that except blow it up, but until now he hadn't worked out how to do that without it being traced back. No, he had to get the treasure. What was Billington messing about at? And Barford! He looked at the note again and a thought crossed his mind.

Perfect! If Barford got too close, became a real problem, he could just have him bumped off, and then use the note to confirm that he couldn't possibly have been involved. It was covered in the Barford family's fingerprints. It clearly hadn't come from Lyle, but some common enemy. It wasn't a problem, it was a possible solution. Or, even better, attack him through his wife - he was the kind of man who might not mind suffering himself, but he wouldn't last long if his wife's life was in danger. It was amazing what people would do when their loved ones were threatened.

Lyle stood up. He was so pleased, he'd forgotten that his real concern was that someone knew he was on the trail of the Noah treasure. This perfect cover for killing Barford or his wife had clouded his judgment. But with that murderous thought in his head, he was feeling much better. Time for lunch. Time to go in pursuit of something raw.

He left, in search of Sushi.

# 22

SABINA COULDN'T FIND MARIA anywhere and she was running out of air. She could taste the rubber of the mouthpiece and was beginning to feel cold. She'd searched both saloons, the four cabins and her own suite. Her study was wrecked - not that the whole ship wasn't in a terrible state. Whoever had come on board must have tried to scuttle her and misjudged how shallow the water was here. Everything had tipped over and there was a jumble of furniture, beds, china, pictures, drink, food - piled up on the port hand side of each space. Much of it had already been damaged beyond repair by the force of the explosion that blew great holes in her hull and by the sea water flooding in.

They had managed to open the safe with more charges that had shattered her desk into so many splinters of wood it was unrecognizable. The Bridget Riley was gone, shredded by the blast, and the jewelry nowhere in sight. Not that it mattered - Sabina's concern was for the people, and the stuff wasn't real any way. Her mother had always insisted that nothing valuable be kept on board (apart from the most precious thing they owned - and Alex had already taken that) and Sabina knew that her proper jewelry was all intact at the castle or safe in deposit boxes deep underground in the vault of a Zurich bank.

The combined effects of panic and physical exertion were making her tired. She wasn't thinking straight. She needed to work out where everyone would be. She had to find them.

Sabina headed for the wheelhouse. The door was jammed shut and slightly out of line but she didn't need to get in to see what had happened. All four of her crew - who had joined her so recently she still hadn't mastered their names - were floating up by the ceiling, obviously dead. One had his leg pressed against the window. She wanted to cry, but knew that would be disastrous, taking up the last of her vital oxygen supplies and making it hard for her to see. She had to keep a control of herself. But if they were dead, what of Maria and Giorgio?

She was shivering now and she knew she had to surface soon or she would get cramped and drown. Really, she had stayed down much too long already. She had to make one last effort. She had to think. Think. Where could they be?

If they were below then they would be dead by now. She should search parts of her ship where there was some possibility of survival. But there had been no pockets of air in any of the places she had been into that might have enabled them to last this long. What would they have done? They hadn't managed to prevent the safe being blown and they weren't in the wheelhouse. Where were they?

Sabina was starting to feel dizzy and she needed to get out. She swam up to the submerged sun deck. The sauna was tipped at an acute angle, pointing to where bubbles of air were rising from a mangle of sunbeds. She looked down and thought she saw something. Then she passed out.

*

MARIA WAS NOT a strong swimmer. It took all Giorgio's strength to keep her head out of the water and make progress towards the shore against the prevailing current. She must still be alive because she kept shouting at him - and he shouted back, telling her to save her energy.

She slipped under and the water went into her mouth and nose which was painful - it made her sinuses ache and she choked. Her coughing and thrashing around was so strong Giorgio almost lost his grip on her. They recovered, but they had lost ground. Giorgio kicked out, his left arm across Maria's chest, looking towards the shingle and refuse of Skoumisa behind him.

She blinked water out of her eyes and stared at the azure sky. She was in shock, arms bruised from where the men had held onto her and her jaw aching from where she had been punched. It had all started just after midnight.

Maria had been disturbed by something; the merest scraping sound. But after Alex's visit and with both Gianni and Sabina away, her senses were alert to anything out of the ordinary, however slight. She had got out of bed and was moving towards the crew's cabins when she heard a loud crack above her head followed by a thump. She found out later from Giorgio that it was one of the crew being struck on the head by a heavy wrench and collapsing. They had been boarded.

Before she knew what was happening, she had been grabbed by powerful hands from behind, one clamped over her mouth, and bundled back into her cabin. She couldn't see her assailant, but his hand smelled of petrol. Whoever it was held her face down on the bed where she could just catch sight of an accomplice carrying out a sweep of the room. He picked up her mobile phone and smashed it against the ship's intercom system. The man holding her saw that she had turned her head to look - and punched her in the face. The door was locked, leaving her battered, alone and out of communication.

An hour or two later she felt the throb of the engines and knew that 'Viaggiatore' was under way. She must have dozed off, because when she woke it had begun to get light. As she was rubbing the sleep out of her eyes, there was a huge explosion and the whole ship rocked. It threw her back on her bed and she cracked her skull against the wooden headboard.

She opened her eyes and saw that the shock had burst open her cabin door. She waited a while and then cautiously stepped out into the corridor. There was a great deal of shouting coming from the direction of Sabina's suite, and Maria guessed the raiders must have blown up her safe. She didn't know what to do or where to go. She was no match for these men and it sounded as if they had got what they'd come for anyway. Soon they would be leaving. She had to find somewhere to hide.

There was more noise and heated exchanges between several men who seemed to be speaking in English. She thought they sounded American. The engines started up again and 'Viaggiatore' began to move, nearly throwing Maria off balance. It was clear that Giorgio was not at the helm. Or if he was, he was under duress.

She could see the side of a hill through the nearest porthole and guessed they must be in one of Symi's many coves. Her only thought was to get off. She didn't know why - it was a purely instinctive reaction. She made for the stairway and eased her way up, keeping a lookout for anyone who might come by.

Maria stopped halfway and put her head just above the level of the deck. There was no-one around. She panicked, and ran up the rest of the steps, going towards the stern where the boat garage was, with no idea what she was going to do. She could see the sea and a shingle beach in the distance and she just kept going.

Someone shouted and a shot was fired. She reached the stern and jumped into the water.

It was colder than she'd been expecting and she waved her arms around uselessly for a moment before calming down. Her dress was heavy with the seawater. The ship had already moved some way ahead and she was very much on her own. She caught sight of a man in black standing on the aft sun deck but he hadn't seen her.

\*

GIORGIO WAS PACKED into the wheelhouse with four crew, all dead, and a masked diver who looked as if he was made of solid muscle. He had a gun pointed at Giorgio's head.

"Just keep on this course, ok, and someone will see you sooner or later," the man shouted in a nasal accent as he stepped out of the wheelhouse. Giorgio's hands were bound to the wheel with plastic cable-ties. He was shaking uncontrollably, wondering what had happened to Maria, alarmed by the deaths of his crew members. The man returned and looked straight at Giorgio. "No funny business!"

He left abruptly. A few minutes later Giorgio saw a powerful orange and gray RIB speeding out to sea with four men dressed in dark wetsuits. He knew they'd all gone, that he and Maria were alone on the ship and there was nothing he could do.

He tried to free his hands but the plastic just bit into his wrists. He bent down with his teeth and started to chew at the strap. After a while he realized he was getting somewhere. He kept at it, gnawing away like a rat until the tie snapped and his right hand was free. He cried with relief.

He reached into a drawer to his side and found the knife he was looking for. With both hands free, he started to think more clearly. There were no boats ahead or to either side. He sniffed up the snot that was dribbling down his nostrils, mixing with tears to bring a salty taste to his mouth, then wiped his nose with his arm. Why should he head out to sea? Why not stay here, anchor the ship and radio for help. Theo the Harbormaster would respond and everything could be sorted out.

Giorgio swung the wheel and the ship shuddered round to port. He would wait until he had secured her before trying the radio. The far side of the bay came into view, moving rapidly from left to right as Giorgio steered the vessel back towards Skoumisa.

Suddenly he was pitched off his feet, smashing his right eyebrow bone on the wheel and slithering to the deck. There was a huge tremor throughout the ship, accompanied by the loudest noise Giorgio had ever heard. He was lifted off the deck and thrown into the side of the wheelhouse, banging into two of the dead crew. As he landed, two more lifeless bodies flew at him and pinned him to the bulkhead. He blacked out.

When he came to, Giorgio felt wet. At first he thought it was his own blood, but it was water, seawater, churning around, pushing him up towards the ceiling. He scrabbled around, unable to get a foothold, and reached out with his hands. He saw that the window in front of him was broken. Holding onto the ceiling, he kicked the glass and it fell away, carried off by the surging water. He managed to get out feet first, which was not his plan, just what happened. He was outside, bobbing around, being pushed against the superstructure. It was dangerous and he had to swim away. He struck out against the current into the water in front of him.

A few minutes later, clear of the ship which had now sunk so that only the radio mast was above the surface, he found Maria facing the shore and making breast stroke motions but going nowhere. He swam over to her and told her to lie on her back. She was close to exhaustion but still full of life. '*Ringrazi il dio!*' he thought, pulling her through the water.

After a while he let his legs swing down and they touched the rocky seabed. He walked the rest of the way, and even Maria was able to stumble the last fifty meters until they both sat, completely worn out, on the hard shingle beach surrounded by years of flotsam and jetsam.

Before they had time to catch their breath, a couple of goats came and bothered them, hoping they might be tourists with food. Giorgio suggested they shelter under the shade of the large wooden cable drum and wait for help. Sabina and Gianni were due back any moment, and it couldn't be long before they were found.

\*

GIANNI WAS SURPRISED at how quickly Theo had been able to get a boat out to Skoumisa before he saw the bold white markings 'P287' on the light gray hull and realized that it was a Greek navy patrol vessel. The 29 meter 'Diopos Antoniou' was on routine tour of duty in the Eastern Aegean when its sonar picked up the explosion that sank 'Viaggiatore'. Gianni established radio contact and the Captain sent a fast launch to search all round the sunken ship. Between the port side of 'Viaggiatore' and the cliffs that came down into the water, they found Sabina floating unconscious. She had only just surfaced and it was not long before one of the sailors had revived her. Wrapped in a survival blanket, she was rushed on board the patrol boat and attended to by a naval medic. The launch set out again in search of the crew. Gianni decided to have a closer look at the land on three sides of the cove, and it was he who spotted the sleeping Maria and Giorgio, sheltered in the lee of the cable drum, half hidden by brown, black and white goats grazing on what they could scavenge.

# 23

RALPH STOOD IN THE LARDER staring at objects on a pine wooden shelf in front of him, about chest height. It was lined with red and white checkered plastic. There were last year's jars of jam and chutney. Bags of flour, sugar, rice and pasta. Tins of this and that. Custard powder. A fruit cake Amanda must have baked for some occasion that escaped him.

He wasn't normally absent-minded, but he had no idea what he'd come in for. Ah! Eggs. Of course. He saw the two trays stacked on top of each other. What was that gray mush they were made of? Pressed out of? He reached for a coupe of large brown ovoids and stopped, arrested by a flush of panic that almost lifted him off his feet.

Ralph remembered when he'd first had that sensation. Climbing out onto the highest level of the Eiffel Tower at the age of twelve and thinking he was going to die. The distance between him and the ground nearly a thousand feet below made him not just dizzy but sick with fear. Before that moment, it had never occurred to him that he was anything other than a whole being, but he was suddenly aware that there were different parts to him - and they all seemed to have come unglued. Worse, they were trying to fly away from each other - his brain going one way and his organs another. Steadying his mind in the wind that swooshed round his head was impossible, especially as he could see straight through the metal grid walkway beneath his feet. It wasn't until they were safely at the bottom, and walking on terra firma, that he began to recover, that the various elements that constituted 'Ralph' reassembled themselves. He had to hold onto something - something solid, and his parents' sympathy grew to frustration as he sat on a public bench and clung to its wooden slats with his teeth clamped shut until he felt sufficiently reconnected to carry on.

He was shaking inside for hours afterwards, and now he was reminded of that same sense of impermanence, of falling apart, of having come dangerously close to a yawning black hole that threatened to swallow every fragmented piece of him before he could gather himself back together again.

It was a huge relief that Lyle had told him he wouldn't be needed anymore. That meant the threat of anything happening to his family had gone away - if he was no longer involved, there was no reason for the person who issued the warning to be interested in him. He couldn't bear the idea of his son's life being at risk. Worse, the concept that Amanda might be a target. And Lyle had promised protection, even though it wouldn't be necessary. Still, it was comforting to know...

What had really hit him was the thought of not seeing the Contessa. It was not a clear deliberation. A percentage of him was grateful that he would never again have to go near this woman who was mixed up in a life and death drama. And who belonged to an entirely different world - universe. But a disturbing amount of Ralph's inner self wanted to see her, wanted to know more.

It was profoundly unsettling for Ralph - faithful, loving, committed, decent Ralph - to realize that in a very short space of time, a fleeting encounter, he had... Well, what? Been attracted? That wasn't it. Not deep enough. Felt that he'd touched someone he'd always known. Oh, Lord! Better not to think about it, not to give his feelings any kind of form or shape or... Discipline, that was

136

it. He just had to shut it out of his mind. It wasn't going to happen anyway, so no point going there.

He knew it wouldn't be that easy - but that was no reason not to try, not to fight, not to resist what everything inside told him was wrong.

Yet was a fact.

Stop! Stop right now.

He picked up the eggs. As he was passing them to his other hand in order to gather more, one fell to the ground.

"Shit!"

Far too strong. Goodness - it was only an egg! There were plenty more.

For a moment, it looked as if it hadn't broken. The egg still seemed perfect, whole. But then a thin, sticky liquid seeped out from underneath and began to form a gelatinous pool around it on the hard stone floor.

"Are you all right darling? I thought I heard something?" Amanda called from the kitchen.

"Yeah fine. Just dropped an egg."

"Oh, never mind. D'you want a piece of kitchen roll?"

"Thanks, I'll get it."

Never mind! No, never mind. All would be well.

All would be well.

Keep saying it.

All would be well...

# 24

THE CASTELLO DI SANTA MARIA NOVELLA had commanded the highest point on the road between Florence and Siena for nearly a thousand years. Set in a landscape of rolling hills punctuated by exclamation marks of dark green cypresses, its polygonal walls surrounded a tranquil inner courtyard. Although views from the castle were panoramic, it was sometimes hard to see it from below, and the entrance was usually missed by those driving past.

Alex parked his Bentley in the late afternoon shadow cast by the main entrance tower and got out. He was wearing loafers, dark jeans and a blue and white gingham check shirt. A scarlet cashmere jumper hung over his shoulders. He checked the large yellow envelope in his hand and looked up at the battlements fringing a deep blue sky above rows of arched renaissance windows. It was still a fortress, protected not just by high stone walls but an elaborate security system. He pressed the intercom on a wooden post by the massive studded doors.

"*Pronto!*"

"*Buon giorno. Aleksander Kovalaneko per vedere il Contessa.*"

"*Momento per favore.*"

Alex straightened up and glanced to the east, where he could just make out the towers of San Gimignano. Each prosperous medieval merchant had sought to outdo the other, expressing wealth and success in ever higher stone towers that created a Manhattan skyline six centuries before the World Trade Centre was flattened by aviation fuel and intolerance. Alex could not be sure of the extent of the Lucidi's involvement in 9/11, but they had certainly capitalized on the sea change it generated. He scratched his Tsarist beard, reflecting that he had noticed parts of it graying recently, which was worrying.

A squeak of iron told him the postern gate - a small hinged flap cut out of the main door - was being opened. A white-gloved hand beckoned him in.

Alex stepped over the sill and into the darkness of the gatehouse. He could see nothing apart from straight ahead, where buildings at the far end of the castle were framed by the short tunnel of the entrance archway. Arranged in a circle on the cobbled courtyard were enormous, pale terracotta pots from Impruneta, filled with oleanders.

Having been here before, he was prepared for the next experience as his feet crossed a trembling wooden floor - a form of drawbridge that could quickly be swung out of the way to make ingress to the castle almost impossible. Coming into the light-filled quad he turned to see that his host was standing behind him.

"Sabina! That was a good trick!"

She laughed. "Ah, I thought I might get away with it!"

Alex pecked her on both cheeks, noticing the scent - something by Guerlain, he thought - and taking in the denim miniskirt and Pucci print top.

"But your hand!"

Sabina held out the gloved hand, turning it over and back again. "It's mending. I shredded it on something underwater - no idea how. My hands were so cold by the end I couldn't feel a thing!"

"But you look well." In truth, Alex thought Sabina looked fragile. She appeared to have lost weight - weight she couldn't afford to lose, and she seemed slightly shrunken. Her legs and arms were skinny rather than slim, accentuated by the clothes she wore.

"Yes, I'm getting better. Now come, let's have a drink." She led the way to a table and chairs that had been set out where the lengthening shadows would not reach for an hour or two. As they neared the white metal table, Maria came out of a doorway with an armful of pistachio-green cushions. "You see, we haven't quite got things organized yet. It's been a bit of a shock having to move back here. *Grazie, Maria.*"

"*Contessa.*" Maria was dressed as usual in a low cut, white shirt dress and her magenta hair was highlighted by the sun. But she gave Alex what could only be described as an old-fashioned look as she placed the cushions on the chairs and he put the envelope on the table. She would never trust him again after the way he deceived her in order to remove the most valuable contents of 'Viaggiatore's' safe. And who was to say that he was not in some way to blame for what had just happened?

By the time the drinks had arrived - a vodka tonic, ice and lime for Alex, a prosecco for Sabina - her habitual wariness towards him had returned. She had initially been pleased with the idea of him coming to see how she was. Possibly because she was not fully recovered, she had forgotten what a snake he was. And she had felt quite alone. But actually being with him made her realize that he would not have come unless there was something in it for him, and she needed to find out what that was.

Sabina picked up a date while he helped himself to an olive. The silence was growing awkward, and the mood was only saved from terminal decline when they both put their stones in an empty bowl provided for that purpose at the same time.

"So, I wanted to be sure you were still in one piece," said Alex, not certain whether this concern for her welfare had convinced her. He was not a psychopath - he could empathize from time to time - but his upbringing in a family devoted to organized crime, (against a background of Communism in which everyone looked out only for their own interests in order to survive), led him to accept without hesitation that if someone stood between you and what you wanted, you simply removed them. If that meant killing them, then so be it. There was no real concept of the sanctity of life in Alex's universe. And yet this woman! She was a potential obstacle, but she also seemed to have got under his skin, through a gap in his armor that he didn't know existed.

He wasn't there to reassure her - he had come to warn her off. He couldn't afford to have her involved. She was too clever, too persistent and he didn't want to have to kill her. He thought that if he could persuade her he only had her best interests in mind, she'd relax and let him continue with his ambition to join the Lucidi. But she could so easily get in the way.

"Thank you. I'm touched. As you can see, I'm fine." She took a sip of the cold bubbles and looked up as a bird of prey - she thought it was probably a buzzard - circled far overhead. "So, what else brings you here?"

Alex put another olive in his mouth in order to provide some thinking time. He didn't feel comfortable with someone who was intelligent and whom he also found physically attractive. It confused him. He wasn't good at respecting women: another casualty of his education - well, the extra-curricular part at least. Too many Russian mafia girls - mostly from the Ukraine, Odessa, Kiev, Nikolaev - who would have been truly beautiful without the needle-marked limbs and dead eyes. He had a way of being with females that was normally easy, confident, relaxed, superior. But with Sabina he could not afford to lose focus. He took the olive stone out and concentrated on the machicolations that ran round a corner tower of the castle's defenses.

"I thought it would be a good idea to warn you about something - someone, actually."

"You could have done that on the phone."

"It's not secure."

"Oh, that kind of warning?"

"Now, don't misunderstand me. You remember I told you I'd removed the Noah from 'Viaggiatore' for your own safety?"

"Yes, but I'm not sure I believe you."

"Not even after what happened earlier this week?"

"Well, it was a little extreme, yes."

"Extreme's not the word for it. I doubt you'll ever get her back."

"No. The salvage company's initial report doesn't look good."

"I know."

"How? How do you know all these things, Alex?"

"I have some very good people. It's my business to know these things. You should be grateful that I'm looking out for you."

There was a lull in the conversation. Sabina was unconvinced that Alex was motivated by concern for her. But she didn't want to rattle him.

"I'm sorry. I interrupted."

Alex drew a deep breath. He took a swig of his drink and held onto the glass. The ice clattered. "I told you that if anyone ever found out that the Noah was on board 'Viaggiatore', you would be in serious danger. Can you imagine what would have happened to you if you'd been there when the raiding party arrived? You would not be alive now. It is a miracle that Maria and Giorgio survived, but they are only pawns. You are the Queen, and you would have died for that."

Sabina looked at him. It was the first time she'd really tried to connect with his eyes, see what was inside. Although he sounded genuine, her intuition told her that she still couldn't trust him. Alex reached for the envelope.

"I've got something to show you." He took out a set of A4 color photographs and passed them to Sabina. "These are satellite images taken at dawn on the day of the raid."

"How did you...?"

"Just look at them." Sabina studied the first photo. It showed a ship in a cove on the left hand side of a land mass. She recognized the coastline of Symi. "This is Viaggiatore?"

"Yes, anchored off Skoumisa."

The next picture showed 'Viaggiatore' on her side. "And this is after the explosion?"

"The one that sank her, yes. When you see the whole sequence it seems that your captain headed back into the bay."

"Yes, Giorgio said he managed to free himself and turn her round."

"When they noticed what he was doing, the people who hijacked 'Viaggiatore' must have triggered the explosives they'd laid to scuttle her, but I imagine they'd planned on doing it in much deeper water. If you look carefully at the far left hand side..."

"Oh, there's a little boat!"

"Yes. The raiding party." Sabina looked at the next shot of the same scene but zoomed out.

"What's this?"

"P287."

"What - the patrol boat? The one that picked me up? That had P287 on the side."

"Yes."

"But what's it doing by the raiders' boat?"

"It picked them up. At least, it tried to, but they opened fire. They managed to interrogate one who remained alive, but he died of his wounds soon afterwards."

"You mean, their bodies were on board when I was...?"

"Yes."

"Alex - I'm not going to ask." Sabina picked up her drink and swallowed a bigger mouthful of prosecco than she'd intended.

"It's probably best if you don't. I'm showing you these because I want you to understand what's at stake here. These men were sent by someone in the US."

"Maria and Giorgio said they thought they were American."

Alex paused. He had decided to tell her about Billington, but he knew it was a risk. On the other hand, if he didn't give her something concrete, she'd just keep on tenaciously and he had to stop her, had to show her that this was work only for professionals.

"They were sent by someone called Billington, Henry Billington. He's a United States Senator."

"My God, Alex!" The glass of prosecco suddenly felt cold in her hand, and she put it down.

"I know. I want you to let me handle this. It's too deep for you. Just before you interrupt, I don't mean because you're a woman. It's high level stuff and lethally dangerous."

Sabina sat back, holding the photographs so loosely in her left hand Alex thought she was going to drop them.

"May I?" He held out his hand. Sabina returned the pictures and Alex tucked them safely back in the envelope.

She stared again at the blue sky bordered by the castle walls. There were a few bars of cloud edged with gold from the late sun, like sand ripples left by the tide. She supposed she shouldn't have been surprised. It had always been clear to her and her parents that they were the guardians of something so potentially explosive that if it ever came to light... But even so, the reality of what Alex had just told her was stunning, like a body blow.

"There's something else you should know." Sabina looked at him. "You shouldn't be working with Canon Barford." This was beyond belief! How could Alex have found out about Ralph Barford? "I know about Milton Keynes. I've warned him." Sabina felt numb. Alex observed a change in her and realized that he had won. He had achieved his goal. She would not be a problem now. He thought about asking how she'd got on with the Aston Martin, but that would probably be too much. The realization that he was aware of her visit to the shopping centre - and what she wore - would be more than enough. Time to ease, as it were, off the throttle...

But Sabina was not totally defeated. She wanted something to hold on to. "You are so far ahead of me, Alex, that there's nothing I can say. I'll leave it to you. I don't feel that great right now, anyway. But I do have one favor to ask, one thing that will put my mind at rest."

"What is it?"

"I'd like to see the Noah - the real one. Just to know that it's safe. Then I'll drop it, I promise. It'll be just your responsibility."

"Sure, why not. When you're strong enough, come over. You know where I am - I'll be at the vineyard for the next few weeks, unless I'm called away, but it would only be for a day or two at most."

"I should be fine next week. Is Wednesday any good?"

"I'll check, but I don't think it'll be a problem. You'll come in the helicopter?"

"Yes, it's a long way to drive for lunch!"

Sabina felt light-headed - whether it was the wine acting on her exhaustion, or that she felt she'd scored some kind of point, or both, she didn't know - or care. At least she now knew the Noah was in France, at the Château Roüet-la-Dauphine. She'd seen the strong room there before, and she looked forward to hearing the steel door squealing open again, and the glorious sight of her precious inheritance.

# 25

AS HE ROSE AND FELL in the saddle of his 17.3 hand dark bay gelding, 'Hugo', the General was trying hard not to think about Billington.

Sunday mornings in the country were all about a good hack - he didn't hunt anymore, didn't have the time, and he hadn't shot since leaving the army - but he liked to trot down familiar lanes and canter across his fields. He loved this part of England - deep Cotswolds, east of Stow-on-the-Wold and the Swells, between Guiting Power and Naunton. The gentle valleys, rolling views, dry stone walls, hamlets, farms and woods formed a timeless landscape. On the left, he passed the solid urn-topped pillars of a gateway to his neighbor's estate, protected by three miles of stone walls and a thick belt of ancient deciduous trees, all now in full leaf. He could see down the drive for a moment, although the house was well-concealed. There had been some good parties in Sunny Beauchamp's time, but the new owners (from Qatar) kept themselves to themselves and were hardly ever there. Over the hedge to his right he recognized the cluster of farm buildings, grain silos, tithe barn and cavernous metal shed with combine, tractors and power harrows that meant he was nearly home.

Later, he would go into the village - not to the church, although that was socially expected of him - but to pick up the Sunday papers and show his face. From a professional point of view, he attended the odd service during the year - just to make sure that the place was still as dead as the bones in its yew treed graveyard. Even here, he thought, a world away from the threat of suicide bombers, it was clear to him that fear of militant Islam had neutered what was left of the Church of England.

He wasn't bothered himself by radical Islam. In fact, it played right into the Lucidi's agenda. Unlike early Christianity, Islam had spread through battle and conquest, and held sway often via brutal intimidation. Oh, there were millions of wonderful people who were Muslims - caring doctors, brilliant lawyers, sincere academics. That wasn't the point for Lyle. Islamists had redefined martyrdom, turning it from a selfless surrender of life to a devastating suicide that murdered as many innocent bystanders as possible and was motivated by the promise of paradise that was expressed in what Lyle thought owed more to adolescent male fantasy than anything lofty.

Right now though, he didn't really care about religion of any kind. The thought of a bath and a stroll to the shop before a stiff drink spurred him on towards the stables that formed a separate quadrangle to the right of the manor house that he'd bought twenty six years ago. He liked the village - the sight of its traditional, oolitic limestone houses was reassuring - and he enjoyed the clearly marked seasons and way of life steeped in the past. It was the perfect antidote to the General's other world of control through terror and indoctrination.

Lyle unzipped his leather half-chaps while Joy the raven-haired stable hand sorted out Hugo's tack. There was little conversation - the man could hardly be described as a 'people-person' - and he left her filling the hay net in Hugo's stall. Joy was invaluable - a twenty-three year-old BHS II riding instructor whose parents lived in Upper Slaughter, she looked after all five of his horses in return for very little money and the chance to ride every day, practicing her dressage in the manège and giving private lessons.

He came into the house via the Muck Room, where he pulled off his Jodhpur boots and padded in yellow socks through the kitchen. Mrs Jenkins, his housekeeper, was busying herself with preparations for lunch - roast chicken - and nearly missed him.

"Ah, General, there you are, back from your ride I expect."

"Er, yes, as you can see."

"Be about half past one - is that all right for you?"

"Yes, that's fine." Lyle gazed at the woman: thin, with hands that looked gray from cold, even though it was a warm day, wearing a dark floral tabard apron, maroon nylon slacks and shoes that reminded him of the peat bog man.

"Oh, there was a delivery while you was out."

"A delivery? On Sunday?"

"Yes. I didn't see no-one, but I found a big envelope on the mat. I've put it on the hall table for you."

"Thank you Mrs Jenkins."

Lyle took the envelope with him upstairs. He leant over the bath to turn on the taps and sat on the closed wooden seat of the loo to examine it.

When he saw the satellite pictures of 'Viaggiatore' off the coast of Symi, and the Naval Patrol Boat, and the RIB, he nearly passed out. His reaction was too strong to internalize - he shouted: "Arsehole! Billington, you stupid arsehole!"

The photos hadn't been sent by the Senator, that was clear. The Lucidi had ways of communicating these things. No wonder he hadn't heard from him. The raid had obviously been a failure. He'd call him straight away, time difference or no time difference. The man was history.

# 26

IT WAS EERILY QUIET at the Château Roüet-la-Dauphine.
Sabina stood in the cobbled *cour fermée* enclosed by pale stone walls
and ornate wrought iron gates. Waves of heat rose from the
motionless rotors of the helicopter parked on a wide lawn by the
main drive: Gianni had shut down the engine and was walking
towards her. She looked past him at the surrounding vineyards,
across the rocky landscape of Châteauneuf-du-Pape, where rows of
vines combed the pillowy hills.

The stillness was broken by a plaintive cry: "Ai-yow! Ai-
yow!" The grating call of peacocks from the formal garden, where
they were allowed to roam freely amongst the parterres, gave a
disturbing substance to the silence. Gianni joined Sabina by the
shallow stone steps that led up to the glazed front door.

"*Niente?*"

"*Niente.*" She flicked an imaginary stray thread from her
highly fitted pink satin trouser suit, feeling vulnerable and bit rock-
chick for the occasion. It was unlike Alex not to have someone
answer the door. At this time in the morning, she would have
expected people to be working, a bustle of activity somewhere.
Turning, Sabina clacked on her narrow heels towards a small gate
between the château and the wall of the *cour fermée*. Gianni followed
her through to the next courtyard where she could see that the door
to Alex's office was open.

Sabina pushed the door wide enough to step in and instantly recoiled in horror, clutching her throat with her gloved right hand. Alex lay face up on the small hexagonal terracotta tiles near his desk in a pool of blood.

He was dead. The skin of his face framed by his beard was a bluish-white and his eyes were locked in a fixed stare. Gianni pushed past Sabina and knelt down by the body, keeping his distance as there was a great deal of blood. A sharp knife was clenched in Alex's right hand. There was blood on the jagged blade.

"We should call the emergency services," whispered Sabina.

"*Si.*"

She found it hard to move, hard to take her eyes off the sight of Alex crumpled on the floor, powerless, his body slightly twisted, completely immobile. His feet were splayed and she could see the hair on his legs above his charcoal gray socks. It was not a dignified pose. A tear fell down her cheek and she realized that for all his apparent duplicity, she had been close to him. No, close implied a connection that wasn't there. They had been linked by some kind of bond, although she would never have acknowledged it had he still been alive. And he certainly would not have mourned her. She wiped her hand under her eye, which absorbed the tear completely.

Sabina noticed that a drawer was open in Alex's desk and the chair that normally stood behind it was over in the corner on its back. With whom had he struggled? What had happened to his assailant?

"I'll see if I can find a phone." She left and walked slightly shakily along the side of the courtyard to another door. It was unlocked - she was surprised that it opened when she turned the handle. Sabina found herself in a dark passage with doors leading off it. The first one she tried was a store room full of bulk cleaning supplies - pallets of toilet roll, paper towels and detergent; a floor

150

polisher, brooms, a metal bucket and mop; and shelves of smaller tins and bottles. The second contained two chest freezers, old baskets and a cupboard with enamel bowls piled on top. At the end of the corridor was another door that took her into the main kitchen. It was surprisingly modern in its equipment, contrasting sharply with the old walls and curved stonework of an ancient fireplace above the commercial cooking range. There was a phone on the windowsill which she used to call the police and an ambulance.

As Gianni explored the courtyard, a high-clearance 'Bobard' vineyard tractor, capable of straddling a tall row of vines, turned in and stopped. Wearing the traditional blue cotton jacket and trousers of the French agricultural worker, Henri climbed down from the cab and was just going towards the *chai* when Gianni hailed him.

"*Mi scusi!*"

"*Oui?*"

Henri stood still, forcing Gianni to jog over to him. Gianni had very little French, and tried to take Pierre's arm, pointing towards Alex's office. "*Urgente! Venite subito! Patron - mal. Mort.*"

Henri raised his eyebrows and shrugged, but he understood that something was very wrong and followed Gianni to where Alex lay.

Perhaps less used to such sights, Henri rushed out and was violently sick into the gutter that ran along the bottom of the outside wall. Sabina was just in time to see him wiping his mouth with a mustard yellow handkerchief as Gianni came out to check that he was all right. He stood staring at the ground, supporting himself with his left hand against the masonry. She called to him:

"*Alors, M'sieur!*"

Henri looked sideways at her. "*Oui, Mademoiselle?*"

She explained to him that they had found Alex dead and called the emergency services, who were on their way, and asked

151

him to look out for them. Sabina added that she and Gianni had called to collect something and would just be a few moments while they picked it up. Henri was slightly confused by all this, but nodded anyway and stood watching blankly as they went towards the door she had found. Sabina halted.

"*Gianni? Momento.*" Sabina had a change of plan. She headed right out of the courtyard, past the tractor and onto a lane that led to the vineyards. Going left, she opened a wooden door in the side of a large cart barn. Shafts of light fell from innumerable gaps between the roof tiles supported by huge beams and dusty rafters. There was space for about five cars, and Alex's black Bentley was right by the door. But apart from a rack of tools above a workbench and a biscuit colored Citroen 2CV that didn't look as if it had been anywhere for years, the place was empty.

"What were you looking for?" asked Gianni.

"I don't know. I just wondered. I don't know. Come on, let's go back inside. I must check the strong room."

They slipped out and back round the *chai* into the château by the door Sabina had found. She led the way into the kitchen. There was a door at the far end that she hadn't seen last time, which opened onto the main entrance hall.

For a moment they just contemplated the fine stone staircase that swept up three flights to the first floor. The walls were decorated with enormous frescoes of battle scenes from the Napoleonic war against Russia. Above the door were two decaying regimental flags protected by fine mesh net. Across the checkered black and white marble floor, a tulip wood veneered table held two large Sèvres vases in dark blue, and a rococo gold clock. A large pier-glass above it reflected light from outside.

Gianni gathered his thoughts and said: "Won't it be locked and alarmed?"

"Yes. I was wondering how we would get in. Let's start by finding it. I remember that it's underground somewhere."

"There must be cellars."

"There are. But not off here, or any of the main rooms." A siren sounded outside. Sabina went over to the main door and looked through its square-paned glass. "It's the ambulance. The police will take a little while. But we can't waste time..." She stopped and stared at the ornate clock. "There's a lift."

"A lift?"

"*Un elevatore.* Not here. Just from Alex's room on the first floor and down to the strong room. It's the only way. *Acceso!* - come on!"

Sabina went up the stairs two at a time, holding tightly onto the shoulder strap of her Chanel bag. When she reached the galleried landing, she paused to get her bearings. To the left, the metal balustrade that looked out over the hall: ahead, the archway leading to the next flight of stairs up to the second floor; to her right, three large doors with highly carved surrounds, painted in pigeon gray. Gianni caught up with her just as she launched herself at the middle door.

She had remembered correctly. Alex had a study here with windows that overlooked the fields of the vineyard. To the left was a large marble fireplace with an Empire desk in front of it. On the opposite wall was a set of dark umber painted doors that looked like a built-in wardrobe. Sabina went over and pulled the faceted glass knobs to open them. There was the stainless steel door of the lift. For a moment she stared at the keypad to the right of the metal frame.

"Do you know the code?"

"I think... I think it's his birthday and then something. Third of February, but no zeros." She punched the numbers with her index finger: 321956 and then added #. Nothing happened. She

153

tried again: 321956 and *. There was a whirring sound and the steel doors slid to the left. Sabina looked at Gianni, unable to suppress a girlish grin of delight at having got this far.

The door closed and they waited inside the metal chamber. Gianni pressed the lower of two illuminated green arrows, pointing downward, and the lift descended. It slowed and bumped to a standstill. The doors opened.

There was very little room, just a space to one side and the stone vault of the strong room in front. A wall of bars separated them from the vault, with a door framed by two much thicker vertical bars in the middle. The strong room was lit by a bulkhead lamp in the ceiling, and they could see stone shelves on each side. But what struck them most was the fact that the barred door was open.

Sabina stepped across the flagged floor and inside the vault. She knew immediately that the Noah wasn't there. She searched the shelves but there was nothing the right size.

# 27

RALPH LOOKED ACROSS his fellow passenger on flight BA2602 from Gatwick to Pisa at the scene through the small Plexiglas window. The outskirts of the city flipped towards them as the plane banked sharply on its final turn to the runway. Sunlight bleached the terracotta roofs and scrubby fields of the outer suburbs. A tower, patterns of streets with cars and scooters, a small cupola, traffic lights, power lines, a galleried walkway and an old church seemed so close they could be touched. His stomach pulled as the pilot leveled the plane and extended the flaps to slow their descent. Ralph could hear the electric motors whirring and glanced towards the cabin crew, seat belts fastened, facing the passengers.

He missed Amanda. Throughout the flight he had been preoccupied with thoughts of her and whether he was doing the right thing. But he couldn't have stayed away after the Contessa's phone call. He was in too deep. He owed Ariq and he was aware that finding the Noah was critically important. He just hoped that Amanda's hospital appointment didn't come up while he was away. She was amazing. He guessed she knew him well enough not to insist on him staying. It was the same as when he wanted to go to Baghdad. She had never stood in his way, always supported him.

It was liberating to know that the man who threatened him - and the lives of his family - was now dead. But still Ralph agonized over his decision. He knew that coming to Italy was the right thing to do but he felt uneasy. Was that just fear? How sure did he feel that he was...? He stopped, realizing that if he went on like this he'd be no use to anyone. The main concern was his feelings for the Contessa. He'd just have to be objective, detached, do what he had to do and come home.

The jet engines changed note and he could feel the plane appear to rush forward. He glanced at the in-flight magazine and laminated safety instruction card filed in the pocket below the folded gray plastic tray and the white anti-macassar of the seat in front. Full reverse thrust roared and then the tires bumped once, landed again, rumbled, settled and the plane was connected to the ground once more, decelerating fast.

Gianni was waiting with a board marked 'CANON BARFORD' which Ralph thought unnecessary and rather embarrassing. The two men recognized each other straight away and met with a firm handshake and good eye contact. The air was warm, and everything smelt different - full of coffee, smoke, disinfectant and the odor of people. Gianni wore shorts and deck shoes, his shirt tails outside. Ralph wondered if he could get away with wearing his shirt out, but thought it would just make him look as if he was trying too hard to act younger than his age. His cream linen jacket and Panama hat had seemed quite cool when he put them on in England, but now he felt like a vicar at a church fête.

All around him was the chatter of relatives greeting each other, lovers kissing and crying, families pushing trolleys of luggage to the glass exit doors, business men checking their mobiles. Police in high-fronted peaked caps patrolled in twos. An African group - the women in immaculate loud dresses and matching turbans - was arguing about something in a language Ralph had never heard, surrounded by piles of huge cases wrapped in cling film.

From the Aeroporto Galileo Galilei they took the Strada Grande Communicazione Firenze-Pisa-Livorno, turning right at

Empoli onto the SR429 towards Siena. As before, Gianni said very little, and Ralph soon gave up trying to make conversation, deciding that the man was naturally taciturn. He sat back in the passenger seat of the big Audi and enjoyed the Tuscan scenery saturated in bright sunshine. It had been raining in the UK when he left that morning. Now - far from the wet black runways of Gatwick - rolling green hills of pasture, vineyards and olive groves topped with small villages, woods and cypress trees all paraded past him in harmonious succession, while nearer the roadside he caught sight of wayside shrines, large wooden barns and rough stony tracks leading over the next rise to meander up valley flanks.

Passing through Certaldo, he remembered that Boccaccio had escaped the plague to write his Decameron there. As they approached Poggibonsi, he was appalled at the sheds and discount warehouses of the *Zona Industriale*, preferring to fix his eyes on the thirteenth century Castello di Strozzavolpe which dominated the skyline on his side of the car. Here, they went left onto the SR2 signposted 'San Casciano' and 'Firenze'. After Barberino they arrived in the centre of Tavarnelle Val di Pesa. Gianni stopped to buy cigarettes and Ralph took advantage of the break to stretch his legs. The tree lined square was charming, and he was tempted to go and get a drink of water, but Gianni returned at that moment and they headed off up a small side road to Marcialla and the Castello di Santa Maria Novella.

*

AS HE STOOD IN HIS ROOM IN THE CASTLE, he felt overawed. The place itself was remarkable, but it was the account of recent events that the Contessa had told him that left him breathless. Even the long bath he'd just had didn't seem to have soaked away the drama of it all. If he had worried about coming to

Italy, now he had every reason to go straight home. What was he, a Canon in the Church of England, doing helping this woman recover something her family had stolen in the first place? And not just any old thing, but a priceless treasure that, in all honesty, belonged to every human being? It was such a part of world history, no-one could claim it for themselves.

He gazed out of the renaissance window wrapped in a thick green towel, realizing for the first time how high up he was. The view stretched for miles across cultivated countryside to distant hills and towns. Beyond the far ridge was another line of hills, and behind that another and another, growing paler until they fused with the evening sky. Between each fold of hills a mist was forming, so that the crests were separated like headlands in a sea of cloud. It was a magical panorama that soothed his feverish mind. A mind that was gradually coming to terms with the situation: gaining focus, sensing direction. In the end, the archaeologist and theologian in him convinced Ralph that he had to continue, if for no other reason than to regain the Noah and see it in good hands. That would be his contribution.

He dressed - chinos, blue, green and white striped shirt and navy cotton jumper - and tied the laces in his suede brogues. The leather soles were a bit slippery on the spiral stone stairs and he held onto the thick braided rope that hung from iron rings on the way down. He stepped across a hallway with an unusually dark blue and blood-red Turkish rug and a few animal head trophies on the walls towards the door that the Contessa - or Sabina as he was now to call her - had indicated earlier.

Ralph was immediately taken with the painting at the far end of the south drawing room and went over to examine it closely. Sabina had not arrived and he had a chance to look round the room. White sofas, two glass side tables on metal frames, with lamps and family photographs, a monumental fireplace, Venetian mirrors, three windows along the outside wall, charcoal sketches of horses, a black lacquered chest with a tray covered in bottles, glasses and mixers. The floor looked as if it was made of polished bricks and a fine Aubusson rug in faded pinks, fawns and ivory connected the sofas and hearth. His eyes went back to the painting that seemed to be the focal point of the entire room.

"So, do you feel refreshed?"

Sabina appeared distractingly beautiful in white trousers and emerald green collarless top. Her hair was done up and she wore a necklace of large gray freshwater pearls and gold beads. Dark make-up emphasized the shape of her cat's eyes - again her regal, vibrant frailty seemed to belong to another world.

"Yes, much better, thank you." Rather than trip over a compliment, he pointed to the picture.

"That's a Bridget Riley, isn't it?" he asked.

"It is. How clever of you to notice."

Ralph felt slightly patronized and attempted to make his position clear: "Oh no, it's just that my wife studied her. She's an art historian and works with ceramics. She wanted to do Riley for her thesis, but the college felt she was too contemporary and Amanda worked on Cezanne instead."

"Cezanne! I love Aix - have you been?"

Again, she leaped ahead of him and he was unsure how to respond. He was trying to remember whether he knew Cezanne lived and worked in Aix-en-Provence. Of course, it wouldn't normally be a problem, but right now but he couldn't be certain: "No. No, it would be great to see it."

"What am I doing - you haven't got a drink! What will you have?"

"Oh, um, a gin and tonic would be nice. Thank you." Sabina moved towards the chest and opened a bottle of gin. Ralph tried to steer the conversation back to the picture: "But the painting is exceptional. It's quite early, isn't it?"

"Yes. 1964. My mother bought it from a gallery in New York. Ice and lemon?"

"Yes please. It reminds me of the landscape round here - hills and colors fading into the distance."

That seemed to have had an effect: Sabina looked up at the painting, glass in one hand and tonic bottle in the other. "Hmm... I see what you mean. I've always liked it because it made me think of the sea. I had a copy on my ship, but it was destroyed with everything else."

"It must have been horrendous!"

"Horrendous? Yes, I still can't quite believe it." She brought Ralph his drink.

"Thank you. I can't imagine what it must be like to lose so much." Sabina poured herself a tomato juice.

"You think I have so much to lose?"

Ralph felt he'd wandered into a trap: "Yes - no, I didn't mean it like that."

"People often think I have everything, but things don't matter. They might look at you, Ralph, in comparison - you seem to have nothing, to be a pauper, and yet you have everything."

Again, he felt that she had put him down, but the way she did it made him feel that it wasn't meant unkindly - just her perspective. He was beginning to understand her a little. "I am very fortunate. I have my wife and son and we live well. I love my work." There was an awkward pause. Perhaps he had been premature in thinking he had the measure of her. "I didn't mean to offend you."

"No - I am just a little, how would you... um - touchy."

He tried to defuse the tension with a compliment. "Your English is excellent."

"It should be. I was at boarding school in England. Tudor Hall near Banbury. You know it?"

"No, I don't."

"Please sit." Ralph looked behind him and stepped back to one of the large sofas. Sabina settled herself on the one opposite. She raised her glass and he raised his. They nodded to each other. Not knowing any Italian, he tried French:

"*Salut!*"

"Cheers!"

How did she do it? Every time he thought he'd met her on her own ground, she seemed to shift position. He decided to let her talk for a moment. "It was like a prison at first. Then it became a kind of game - escaping from the dormitory at night. I liked to ride - we were able to go most afternoons, or at least it seemed like we could. And plays. We put on plays. I enjoyed dressing up - it helped me keep my sanity." They both sipped their drinks. Ralph glanced at the painting and then out of the window. He tried a new tack:

"So, is this home for you?"

"Home? What is home?" she asked.

"Well, where you belong, I suppose."

"I don't feel I belong anywhere. I've traveled so much, lived in so many places."

There was a pause. Ralph felt that he just wasn't able to be true to himself. For him, home wasn't a place, it was with Amanda. They'd been at home in Baghdad just as much as in Rochester, or Cambridge, or any of the other places they'd lived. But he wasn't going to correct himself as Sabina appeared very single and he didn't want to open up another difficult topic of conversation.

Sabina looked at him. She liked him a great deal. He was so transparent, so honest. And not bad looking. She worried that he found her so attractive: she was used to dealing with male attention and could tell from his nervousness that he was trying desperately to please and ending up saying things he wasn't happy with. She decided to be a little less hard on him.

"I was born here. But I haven't felt comfortable in this place since my parents died two years ago."

Ralph took a risk and decided this was something he could empathize over: "I'm sorry."

"Why should you be? Actually, I think they were killed."

"Goodness!"

"It was a road accident. I was away at the time - in America. The J Paul Getty Museum in Santa Monica."

"Ah, one of my favorite buildings,"

"Me too! How extraordinary! You must tell me why."

"I will, but you were talking about your parents."

"Yes. They crashed not far from here - Fonterutoli."

"Ah, the Chianti border."

"How do you know that?"

"I like my wine. I was fascinated by the legend of the black cockerel - the Gallo Nero. You know, how they ended the constant fighting between Florence and Siena."

"Yes, of course. Something about them sending out riders? Remind me."

Ralph was more comfortable now - at last he knew something she didn't, or she was being gracious. Either way, his confidence slowly returned. He started using his hands to illustrate what he was saying: "They just couldn't agree where one province ended and the other began. They got fed up with always being at war with each other and decided to end it with a competition. They agreed that when the morning cock crowed in each city a horseman would start riding towards the other, and where the two riders met would be the border."

"Ah, yes," interrupted Sabina, "and the Fiorentini tricked the Sienesi. Really, if it was fair, each rider would have covered about the same distance. But while Siena chose a healthy white cock and fed it up in preparation for the contest, Firenze picked a scrawny ill-fed black cock. The black cock woke up hungry well before the sun rose and crowed while the white cock was still fast asleep."

Ralph continued the story: "The Florentine rider got to within ten miles of Siena before meeting their rider. So the boundaries were drawn and Florence got the better deal - and Chianti became part of the Florence Republic."

"That's right. Why didn't I think of that?"

"Sorry, I don't suppose it's important."

"No, I think it's very important. I think you've just solved a mystery that's been bothering me all this time. I always suspected Alex, who also likes - liked - his wine, of arranging the 'accident'. It fits. Typical of him to stage it in a vineyard - the Mazzei in Fonterutoli. I'm sure he wanted the Noah for himself."

"But why?"

"I think it was his entrance ticket to some strange group he was connected with. Or at least, he wanted to be. He mentioned it once. He saw the Noah as something powerful, something he didn't value for itself but which he could trade with for something that he thought was priceless. He - well, we'll never know. What worries me is that Billington now has both the copy and the real one."

"You think he killed Alex?"

"Who else? The police have no idea. The fact that the Noah has gone is the most obvious motive - not that they know that. They're completely in the dark."

"You didn't tell them?"

"No, of course not. I have to do this for myself now, and I don't want them involved."

"So what will you do next?"

"Go to America."

"To Billington? You can't confront him on your own. You know what he's like."

"Exactly. I was rather hoping you'd come with me."

"Won't you take Gianni?"

"Oh yes, and Andreas will fly us there. But my plan requires at least one more person, preferably a man."

# 28

THE CHOCOLATE BROWN UPS VAN cruised east in the dry Connecticut afternoon on Highway 1 - Westport Avenue. Its driver was anything but calm - David Adler felt uncomfortable in the dark tan uniform and his hands were sweating in their leather gloves against the hard plastic of the oversize steering wheel. He was a jeweler, not an assassin, and he had been regretting his decision ever since the journey began.

But each time he considered turning round, he was reminded of the way his father Reuben had been killed, of watching him die in front of him, and his resolve returned. The sun was past his right shoulder now and he didn't need the shades, but he felt stronger behind them and if he was going to confront Javier Mendoza he needed all the help he could get. Plus, with the cap covering his hair they helped disguise his features.

Sooner than he expected, the white security gates of Henry Billington's farm materialized on the left. He parked up and got out, attempting nonchalance. As his feet hit the ground, he started to shake and had to hold on to the large wing mirror to steady himself. He stared at the black work boots on the gravel and pressed his knees to stop them juddering. A wave of heat passed from between his scalp and skull down to his soles and socks. He felt nauseous and faint, and hoped his obvious fear wasn't starring on a CCTV screen somewhere inside the property.

Adler located the intercom but found it hard to focus. He took off the shades and wiped his eyes with the back of his right sleeve before putting them back on again. He pushed the buzzer. There was a long interval. He tried again. A man's voice responded, charged with impatience.

"Yes?"

David hoped he could trust his ability to speak without giving away his nervousness: "UPS. Delivery for Mr Mendoza." There was another pause. He looked away from the lens of the camera that was probably scanning him. He heard a man clearing his throat before speaking:

"Mr Mendoza's out. He'll be back tomorrow."

He wasn't prepared for that, but adrenalin had started to kick in and he wasn't backing out now: "Just needs a signature."

Another delay. Then the gates drew back and he jumped into the van. What was he going to do? Binyamin had given him a spare UPS handheld computer - the kind customers are presented with to sign on delivery. It was coated with thallium and an accelerant that Binyamin's guys had concocted - the same poison Mendoza had used on his Visa card to kill Reuben. He had it ready in a plastic bag and he'd been careful to wear brown leather gloves. He planned that Mendoza would hold it long enough when signing for the parcel for the thallium to take effect. But he couldn't use that now. The contents of the package - an anonymous pair of women's briefs - were also steeped in the stuff, but if Mendoza wasn't going to open them until the next day, there was a possibility the poison wouldn't be toxic enough to finish him off. And yet, he'd come this far...

Senator Billington was waiting in the drive as David Adler pulled up. He looked miles away. Almost shell-shocked. David wasn't to know about the raid on Sabina's ship and how it had gone disastrously wrong. Or the phone conversation with Lyle. A small tail of blue chambray shirt was sticking out of the back of his high-waisted jeans and he was blinking. David guessed that he'd disturbed the man's afternoon nap.

He grabbed a regular handheld device that he hadn't treated in any way and swung out of the van with greater ease this time: "Thank you, sir. Appreciate it. Means I don't have to come out all this way again tomorrow."

Billington just stared at him. David thought he'd sounded pretty dumb - after all, that was a UPS delivery driver's job, wasn't it? What does a courier do, for goodness sake? He made his way round to the back of the van and unlocked the rear doors. There was a selection of parcels and packages of varying sizes, some tipped over on the ribbed metal floor where he'd taken a corner too sharply. He hoped Billington wouldn't notice, but the old man hadn't moved.

He picked up a small scarlet box addressed to Javier Mendoza from 'La Petite Coquette' - a lingerie store in Greenwich Village. Binyamin had done his research and found out Mendoza liked his women. The head of security at Haretz Diamond LLC had got one of his associates - a man who owed him big time - to buy the 'gift', paying cash so it could never be traced to his boss. David closed the doors and walked back to the Senator, noticing a wisp of white hair at the back of his head sticking straight up like a tufted duck. He'd been right about the nap.

"Sign here please, Sir."

Billington took his left hand out of his pocket. The middle finger was missing above the first knuckle. He balanced the proffered machine in his left hand and held the plastic stylus in the other. The surface of the screen was hard and Billington's signature wasn't much more than a squiggle. Not that it mattered - Binyamin had made sure it wasn't transmitting and no record of the delivery would ever be found. The Senator handed the device back to David, who gave him Mendoza's package. The box was unsealed and the lid didn't fit that tightly - it was only held together by the white satin ribbon tied round it.

"Thank you. Have a good day now!"

Billington mumbled something and turned away. David hopped into the driver's seat. He put the handheld computer on the passenger seat before starting the engine. 'Sandy' - the Senator's ancient Golden Retriever - had come out to see what was going on and David waved as Billington looked up.

He hoped the man hadn't suspected anything.

# 29

"WHO WAS THAT, MUM?" asked Johnny Barford, walking into the kitchen clutching his acoustic guitar by the neck.

Amanda was looking through her reading glasses at a Nigella recipe book, both hands covered in flour. A bowl stood on the wooden work surface with a whisk sticking out of it.

"Who was what, darling?"

"On the phone just now?"

"Oh, that was Dad."

"How's he getting on? Any chance of a cup of tea?"

"Fine. He's fine. You can put the kettle back on if you like. It's only just boiled." Amanda wasn't really reading the recipe anymore. She'd almost forgotten what she'd been wanting to cook. She was trying not to cry and wished Johnny hadn't come in at that precise moment. The story Ralph had told her was truly alarming and she just wanted him home. Johnny put the guitar against the wall in the corner by the garden door. Oblivious to her mood, he lifted the AGA hob lid and slid the kettle across.

"Oh, Mum!" Johnny noticed the wallphone had flour and butter on it. He picked a sponge from the windowsill above the sink and wiped the handset. She turned to look at him, dusting her hands on the heart printed apron and taking off her pink reading glasses.

"Thank you! He's all right. He's loving Italy, says it's amazing. It sounds fantastic. The Contessa's got some castle between Florence and Siena - and an original Bridget Riley! Imagine."

"Cor. Wish I was there!"

"Yea, me too!"

"Wow. Lucky Dad."

"Yes, well, don't get too jealous. She's had a terrible time and it's not over yet. Now he's off to America."

"What? But your appointment. Isn't he coming back for that?"

"No, darling, he isn't."

"Why not?"

"Because I didn't tell him."

"Didn't tell him?"

"That's what I said. Kettles' ready. I'll have a cup too, please, while you're at it."

Johnny lifted the kettle off. "D'you want proper tea or that hot cardboard?"

"Hot cardboard?"

"You know, those pips."

"You mean my fruit tea? No, I'll have Lapsang, thank you."

Johnny busied himself making a cup of tea for Amanda and a mug for himself.

"I don't understand why you didn't tell him? How're you going to get to hospital tomorrow?"

"I didn't tell him because he'd have felt duty bound to come back, and I know he really needs to go to America. I can get a taxi."

"I'll come."

"Thank you darling. I hoped you'd say that." Johnny saw his Mum moving in for a hug - he put the mug down and went to pick up his guitar.

"D'you want to hear my song?"

She stopped and stood by the table. "Another one?" She saw the disappointment register in his face. She hadn't meant to put him down.

"No, it's the same one I wrote last week, but I've changed it. It's much better."

"Ok, yes."

"Well, you might sound a bit more interested."

"Sorry. No. Er - play it."

"No, I won't bother now. If you don't want to…"

"No, Johnny, please. Play it. I'd like to hear it."

Johnny sat on a kitchen chair and leant over the guitar. He didn't understand what was happening. His Dad was away and his Mum - well she seemed even more distant. Parents! He'd never understand them.

Amanda knew she'd upset him. She was so preoccupied with what Ralph had told her, with the idea of him spending time with that woman, with the danger his life was in. Like most Mums, she was normally good at caring deeply for each member of her family, but right now she seemed to have run out of capacity.

# 30

HENRY BILLINGTON PRESSED THE RED 'START'
BUTTON and the 5.5 liter V12 Ferrari engine fired up. It was a
sound he'd never tire of, the powerful motor growling like a
container of starved carnivores.

He eased the *Canna di Fucile* (gunmetal gray) 456M out of
the garage and pressed the remote control to close the up-and-over
door. He noticed that his Golden Retriever was sitting on the front
step - didn't he lock the house? Really, he'd been feeling strange this
past hour.

He listened to the glorious opera of the engine for a
moment longer before pulling the door handle with his left index
finger. It had grown strong in the forty years since he'd lost the
middle one in a farm accident. The heavy driver's door swung wide
and he started to shift out of the Bordeaux red leather seat, but he
suddenly felt very tired. What was wrong? He'd had a nap. He was
raring to go just a while back. He didn't want to get Sandy's hairs on
his trousers - he was dressed to impress. Black tuxedo and crisp
white shirt, no tie. Very hip. Especially for someone who'd had
them both replaced, he mused.

As an international banker, he viewed sex as a commodity,
and he had an excellent broker called Ros who kept him supplied
with a series of beautiful girls willing to do almost anything for
money. The idea of a new young model from Brazil was thrilling

and the Senator was looking forward to the evening. Well, night - it was already 8pm and the sun had set. The hotel was south of here - not too far, he'd be there before nine. And then…

He put his left foot on the drive. It seemed to him that it was getting dark quicker than usual, so he flipped on the headlights. Sandy's head moved slightly at this, and the dog stood up slowly, shaking himself. Billington smiled. He wondered who the hell had sent Javier those briefs. God, they made him excited! It was quite a mystery. There was more to the man than he'd realized. Perhaps that was where he was tonight - perhaps it was a signal, delivered too late…

It had been just too tempting - the scarlet box with the sexy white lettering, what was it? 'La Petite Coquette'. I'll say! It was too easy to slip off the ribbon and have a peek inside. He'd not been able to stop there - he'd taken the briefs out and had a good look at them. There was no note or card, but an intoxicating smell. He'd held them to his face and breathed in deeply. Whoever she was, it seemed to the Senator that Javier was a lucky man. Yes, sir, a lucky man!

Sandy wandered towards the car. Billington watched. He was finding it hard to focus. What the hell was wrong with him? He hoped he'd put the briefs back all right. They'd looked OK on the tissue paper and he didn't think Javier would notice. Closing the box and retying the ribbon hadn't been difficult. Anyway, he could always blame it on the clumsy courier if anything was said. But he doubted Javier would want attention drawn to it…

He thought of Lyle. How he hated that smug Brit! It wasn't his fault the Noah hadn't been on board, or that the Greek navy had been snooping around just then. Lyle seemed to think he'd deliberately withheld the information - fact was, he hadn't a damned clue what had gone on.

Time to get out of the car and secure the house. If the door was open he couldn't have set the alarm. But his legs wouldn't move. They felt numb. His hands began to tingle. Too late, it dawned on Henry Billington III what must have happened. But before that thought was complete, his heart had seized and he was dead.

Reaching the Ferrari, Sandy rubbed his molting coat on the black trouser leg of his master's tux. The dog looked up at the man, his frozen expression clear in the glow of the car's interior light as Billington's upper body sagged forward. His right temple came to rest on the steering wheel and his mouth dropped open.

The only prints on the murder weapon belonged to Billington - and Krystal, the shop assistant who'd gift-wrapped the briefs.

# 31

IT WAS THE THIRD TIME they'd had to stop to refuel Sabina's small Learjet, but they were very close to the target. With a range of around 1800 surface miles, she'd explained to Ralph that they couldn't just fly straight to North America in one hop. He had no idea where they were, only that the last two places had been extremely cold, but as they took off for the fourth time he was aware from Gianni and the Contessa that their visit to Senator Billington was next on the night's itinerary. Not that Ralph thought the man was likely to be awake at that hour in the morning.

Andreas had begun the flight from a small private aerodrome in Tuscany just before 8pm and the four of them had been in the air - off and on - for nearly twelve hours. They had flown via Scotland, Iceland and Labrador, having filed a flight plan for Washington DC to distract attention from the fact that their real destination was the small airstrip on Senator Billington's farm. Andreas, who, like most Dutch people Ralph had met, spoke impeccable English, had confirmed that at 900 meters the strip was just long enough for them to land on and take off from, but it would require all his skill to achieve this in the dark.

Ralph felt sticky and tired, his clothes were crumpled and he could have done with some space to stretch his legs - the cabin was only one and a half meters high. The food Maria had provided had been good, but he was exhausted - and bored. It was a relief when

Gianni produced a large rucksack that contained a navy blue tracksuit, T-shirt and black trainers for him to change into. He had a quick wash in the lavatory at the back and sat down again on one of the six pale leather seats with a new light in his eye. Sabina remarked on it.

"You look better, Ralph."

"Yes, thank you. I'm sorry, I'm not used to this sort of thing.

"Neither am I!" laughed Sabina. "Not long now."

The plan was to land as unobtrusively as possible. Sabina, Gianni and Ralph, all dressed in the same dark clothing and wearing a rucksack each, would jog the half mile to the main house, avoiding the pony paddocks. As far as they knew, all the staff lived off site apart from the Senator's driver and general factotum, Javier Mendoza. Sabina was counting on Gianni's experience in COMSUBIN - the elite Special Forces of the Italian Navy - to get them into the house and subdue Billington and Mendoza. A few days before, she had arranged for Mendoza to receive an invitation to a free dinner, room and breakfast at a nearby hotel which offered 'in room services' but there was no way of knowing whether he'd gone for it. The whole plan was risky, but she had decided that this was their best chance, and she couldn't leave the Noah a moment longer in the Senator's hands - it had to be recovered at all costs. Gianni's expertise would also come into play when they found Billington's safe. The contents would be transferred to the rucksacks and onto the plane.

In the cockpit, Andreas leveled out at 45,000 feet and switched to autopilot. He wore dark green trousers and a white short-sleeved shirt with button-down pockets and epaulettes. Beside him on the co-pilot's seat was a green jacket and peaked cap. He had smooth, sallow skin and bushy hair that was prematurely gray.

Recently, he'd grown his facial hair a little, so that he looked more than unshaven but not quite bearded.

With the Learjet settled on the correct heading at 500 knots, he went over the approach for landing one more time. He would fly the last few miles manually, using the VSI - visual speed indicator. From the satellite pictures he'd seen, there were no power lines or other obstacles in the way and he'd plotted a course that allowed him to adopt a very low altitude trajectory. The problem was that he had to slow the plane sufficiently to make sure he didn't overshoot the short runway, which meant that if there was any kind of problem, he wouldn't have enough airspeed to abort and climb again. The thought of it was making him perspire - unusual for Andreas who, as a 46 year old ex-KLM pilot, had a reputation for being cool under pressure. He wondered what his much younger girlfriend, Hanneke, was doing right at that moment. On her way to work, he imagined, cycling the flat three kilometers to the elementary school in Sliedrecht where she taught a class of 10 year olds.

The other issue was getting in and out of Billington's place and on their way before air traffic control noticed the deviation. Since 9/11, the authorities in the area had become much more watchful for any plane that moved off its expected course. But it was 1.50am, there were no obvious terrorist targets in the vicinity and Andreas would be flying the last leg very low so that he stood the best chance of not being noticed or remarked upon.

An hour later he brought the jet right down, reduced groundspeed to 190 knots and called Sabina:

"T minus ten, Contessa."

"Thank you, Andreas," she replied. "Ready Gianni?"

"Ready, Contessa."

"Ralph?"

"Sabina, I'm as ready as I ever will be." He made an attempt at levity, but it came out as too casual in an atmosphere that was growing increasingly military.

"Good," she smiled, taking the edge off his anxiety for a moment.

The lights in the passenger cabin dimmed and all three checked their seat belts. They didn't meet each other's eyes, but stared blankly at some fixed point.

A few minutes later they could again sense the plane slowing and descending, though not as rapidly as the dive they'd just experienced. Outside it was dark apart from the odd lamp by a barn or house, but the moon gave enough radiance for larger buildings to throw shadows. The sodium orange avenue of lights marking a highway passed just under the plane and they banked to starboard.

"T minus five."

All three hearts skipped a beat. Ralph was aware that his whole body had tensed up. A fear was creeping over him that manifested itself in slight cramp and a metallic taste in his mouth. The Learjet seemed to suddenly lift and fall like a car going over a humpback bridge and Ralph felt his stomach lurch uncomfortably. He looked out through the porthole: the ground seemed very close and they were still traveling extremely fast.

"T minus one."

The engine note diminished by a couple of tones. Andreas was trying to land with a minimum of noise, which meant slowing gradually rather than maintaining speed until the last minute. He could see Billington's place ahead now. The big red barn was over to starboard, right where it should be. But where was the landing strip?

Just as he was thinking he was going to miss it, the plane's landing lights caught sight of a windsock and the surface of the strip showed up as a pale band of reflected moon light. Andreas eased the throttle as much as he dare. At 110 knots the stick shaker activated, accompanied by an automated audio warning, "Stall, stall, stall." Andreas held his nerve and the plane floated slightly ahead of 100 knots - stalling speed.

Ralph, Sabina and Gianni experienced a collective shock as the aircraft sank abruptly. Before they could gather themselves, the jet's undercarriage struck the tarmac and they were thrown forward. Andreas reversed the engines and braked the wheels gently, gently. The end of the landing strip rushed towards him and he slowed the plane as rapidly as he dare, but he reckoned then that they were probably going to overshoot.

The Learjet stopped. All Andreas could see in front of him was grass and an unlit set of airfield ground lights. It was too dark to detect any sign of the tarmac on either side. He began his post-landing check.

"We're here, folks."

A sigh escaped from Ralph, sounding as if he was blowing out a candle. He looked at Sabina and Gianni and felt embarrassed. Andreas spoke again:

"Gianni, could you get the door and see if we've overshot?"

"*Si*, Andreas." Gianni moved out of his seat and to the forward entry door on the aircraft's port side. Opening it, he engaged the stairs and climbed down. The wheels were a few meters from the end of the landing strip. Andreas had only just made it - but he would be able to turn the plane round, taxi to the other end and circle 180 degrees ready for take-off into the wind.

Gianni leaped back up the stairs and popped his head into the cockpit:

"You've got a few meters. You should check it before you go anywhere!"

"Thanks, Gianni, that's great."

Sabina was already standing with her rucksack on: "OK? Shall we go? Half an hour, Andreas - we should be back by 03.35."

"I'll be ready. Don't be late - the longer we're on the ground the more Air Traffic Control will give me a hard time."

Sabina gave the others a pair of disposable gloves each and made sure they put them on. They were to leave no fingerprints. She left the plane first, followed by Ralph. Gianni grabbed a small toolbag and followed. Once they were clear of the plane, Andreas maneuvered himself out of the tight cockpit to inspect the ground.

Their eyes adjusted quickly to the moonlight as they ran with their empty rucksacks towards the main house. The first hundred meters were fine, but Ralph soon realized that he was not as fit as he had been in his rugby-playing days. Gianni was the same age but in much better shape and Sabina - well, she was coasting along. The air in his throat was dry and he was worried that he'd let them down.

Gianni looked round and slowed until Sabina and Ralph had passed him.

"Are you OK?" he asked Ralph.

"Yes. Just not used to running anymore."

Sabina vaulted over a white-painted fence onto a lawn that led to the main drive and disappeared. Ralph clambered over it, resting on the top bar, losing time, and Gianni took it like a steeplechaser. The two men nearly ran into the back of Sabina as they rounded the side of the house. She held her hand up.

Before them was an extraordinary scene: a dark gray sports car parked by a garage, with its headlights on and engine running. A dog lay on the gravel by the open driver's door, and the interior light showed that someone was sitting slumped over the wheel. Gianni put his index finger to his lips, motioning the other two to stay where they were, and crept over to the car. Sabina ignored his instruction and followed.

The Golden Retriever growled quietly and Gianni stepped back while Sabina went on. She made a downward gesture with her hands, speaking quietly to the animal.

"Shh, it's ok."

The dog looked at her and then at the ground. Sandy yawned and settled his head between his shoulders, one eyebrow up. The driver's left leg was out of the car, a black tasseled loafer flat on the gravel. There were white and blond dog hairs all over the wool trousers. She saw the hand with the missing middle finger, then crouched to look at the man's face. She turned to Gianni.

"It's Billington!" she whispered.

"*Siete sicuro?*"

"*Si, certo.* Just like the photo I saw. And his middle finger's missing."

"*È guasto?*"

"*Si.* Very dead. For a long time, I think. Shall I turn it off?"

"*No, lascilo,* don't touch anything."

Ralph walked over to join them. He had heard the conversation and was shaken by the discovery, but there was no time to waste. "If Mendoza were here he'd have noticed this by now."

"You're right," agreed Sabina. "He must have taken the bait. Good. Let's try the house."

Gianni led the way to the front door. "Please do not upset the stones," he cautioned. He didn't want to leave any sign that they'd been there, if possible, and the gravel was easily disturbed. They walked as lightly as they could, making an effort not to roll their toes and heels. Close up, the house appeared tall and forbidding in the dark, but to their amazement the door was slightly ajar. Gianni stopped by the steps and pulled a large torch, two flashlights and three sets of elasticated shoe covers out of his toolbag. They put the clear plastic covers over their trainers and gingerly moved to the door. Sabina pushed it open and Gianni switched on the torch. At that moment Sandy ambled past them into the house, giving them all a fright.

Gianni handed Sabina and Ralph a flashlight each and issued instructions in a deep whisper: "OK, we stay together. We do each room. We look for a safe - behind the pictures, no matter where. It must be at least this size," he gestured with his hands a shape about half a meter square. "Keep your body away from the furniture, try not to move anything. We start here, we go left, we do all this floor, yes?"

"That's fine, Gianni. Lead on," encouraged Sabina, speaking as quietly as she could. The first room off the entrance hall was a small cloakroom. Gianni backed out before the others had a chance to go in. He shook his head and moved on. Next was the kitchen and he signaled that they should not waste any time in there. He crossed the corridor and entered the dining room. Moonlight reflected off the glazed doors of the china cupboard. Putting his finger to his lips, he turned to the others and pointed to the walls. Ralph went to the far end while Gianni and Sabina stepped left and right. There was a door leading to a sun room which Ralph decided would not be a place to find what they were looking for. Sabina and Gianni lifted all the pictures but there was nothing behind any of them apart from the occasional cobweb. On their way out Sabina bumped into one of the twelve English Hepplewhite dining chairs that were set round the narrow yew wood dining table. It scraped slightly on the parquet floor but she held onto it straight away and the sound only lasted a second. They all waited: the house remained silent.

Gianni retraced his steps to the central hall. He flashed his torch up the carpeted stairs and then across to the other side. The first door led into a music room. Again they checked behind all the pictures with no result. A sitting room was next, but that yielded

182

nothing either. At the end was a study where the walls were taken up with book shelves. There didn't seem any chance of a large enough safe being in there. Sabina found a painting of a military college but there was just smooth painted plaster behind it. Gianni pulled a few books back to see if any of them were false, but they all looked normal. He swung his torch round the room just to check, but there was nothing out of the ordinary. As they were leaving, Ralph noticed a dull gleam in the moonlight and aimed his flashlight.

"Look, here!" he hissed.

Behind a desk were two piles of aluminum cases - three in one and two in the other.

"What is it?" asked Sabina quietly.

"I don't know. Some cases. It might be worth a try."

Gianni peered across. "You have a look. We will search upstairs. Join us when you can." He and Sabina left the study and moved quickly towards the staircase. Time was passing and they needed to be out of there soon.

Ralph focused his flashlight on the top case on the pile of three. It was locked - the combination was set at '0000'. He could be there all night trying to find the code. Perhaps Gianni was good at that sort of thing. He moved the wheels one digit to '9999', but it made no difference. Then he had a sudden thought: if it was what they were looking for, there might be a clue to the numbers. He didn't know anything about Billington that would help. He racked his brains. He tried '1234' - no good. Then he had an inspiration. He tried '2345' - the year the earth tipped off its axis and the most likely date for the great flood. The lock clicked. He was amazed, elated. Ralph didn't think it could have been Billington's idea. No matter: he pressed the handle and the case opened, although he could only lift the lid a little because it was right next to the bookshelf. He reached inside and pulled out a soft roll of cloth that had something hard inside. He knew what it was - what it had to be.

He unrolled the cloth in his hands. Immediately, the rays from the flashlight bounced off a set of gold discs and bright, flashing gems. It couldn't be the real Noah - that was far too valuable to be left lying around like this. It was more likely to be the fake - which from what Sabina had told him was probably worth less than Billington's set of dining chairs.

Ralph put the jewels back into the top case and secured it. He found the handle and lifted the case carefully, trying not to scrape it against the one underneath. It was heavier than he had expected and as he swung it clear he nearly banged it on the floor.

He tried the next case and the same combination '2345' worked. It opened all the cases. As he was securing the fifth case, he heard a muffled cry from the floor above. Ralph went and stood at the bottom of the stairs but there was no further noise. He walked silently up the carpeted steps. As he reached the landing, Gianni and Sabina were coming towards him.

"Anything?" he asked.

"No, nothing, *niente!*" responded Sabina, clearly upset.

"It's not here," added Gianni.

"We've looked everywhere. We found a safe but it just had the usual things - documents, some cash, account books, a little jewelry." Sabina sounded slightly hysterical.

"You didn't have to blow it up?" asked Ralph.

"*No, era facile,*" said Gianni, dismissing the simple task as if anyone could open a safe. "It's closed again - no-one will know. Now, we must go." He started down the stairs.

"Did you find anything?" Sabina asked Ralph as they followed Gianni.

"Yes, I've found the fake Noah."

Sabina's hands went to her face. "Oh!" she gasped. Gianni stopped at the bottom of the stairs.

"Come and have a look. I thought it might be the real one at first, but no-one would be that stupid." Ralph led the way back to the study, opened the top case and held out a roll of jewels to Sabina.

For a moment, she was stunned. "Yes, this must be my mother's copy. We should take it anyway," added Sabina, looking at Gianni.

"There is so little time," objected Gianni.

"I think Sabina's right," argued Ralph. "Look, it won't take a minute to unpack these into our rucksacks."

"OK," said Gianni. "Contessa, turn round."

Swiftly Ralph opened the cases and the two men loaded Sabina's rucksack with the contents of the first one. Ralph and Gianni divided the rest between themselves and replaced the aluminum cases as they had found them, setting all the locks to '0000'.

"We must go," said Gianni. He checked his watch - the one Sabina had given him. "It is 3.30. *Siamo in ritardo.*"

Gianni reached the door first, opened it wider with the side of his foot and went out. Ralph followed Sabina out of the house. There was no sign that they had been there, or that anything was missing.

The three crunched over the gravel with their feet as flat as possible, but the rucksacks were heavy and it was hard not to make an impression. Once they reached the grass at the side of the drive, Gianni stopped and slipped the shoe covers off his trainers, cramming them into his pockets. Ralph was glad to stop. He wasn't looking forward the journey back to the plane with such a weight on his back.

It was easier to make progress without the slippery shoe covers, but after a few hundred meters they were all aware of the load in their rucksacks. Ralph looked up and was relieved to see that the Learjet was waiting at the nearer end of the landing strip. He was close enough to read the identification I-SDV7 on the tailplane. Gianni reached the plane first and opened a door under the port engine so that they could stow the rucksacks in the baggage hold.

Back on board, doors closed and seat belts fastened, the three remained anxious, perspiring and breathing intensely.

"All ready?" asked Andreas.

"Yes."

"Absolutely."

"*Si! Avanti!*"

Andreas had entered new "V" speeds for the additional weight of the fake Noah and set the flaps at eight degrees. He advanced the thrust levers three detents to the takeoff position, released the brakes and the plane surged down the airstrip, lifting off well before the tarmac ran out.

Rotating to 13 degrees nose up, with a positive rate of climb, Andreas brought the landing gear up. Within seconds, he was hauling the thrust back and leveling off at 1,000 feet and rolling to port, bringing the plane round on course for Washington DC. Once he'd reassured Air Traffic Control that all was well and been given clearance, he'd climb to their cruising altitude of 45,000 feet.

Sabina, Ralph and Gianni rubbed their arms, flexed their hands and looked at each other. There was a mixture of elation, shock and distress. Elation because they had got in and out without being caught and, as far as they knew, without leaving any obvious trace of their visit. Shock at Billington's death - was it natural or had someone murdered him? Distress because the real Noah was still out there somewhere.

All roads had led to Billington and now they were at a loss. If Billington had taken it, had his killers stolen it from the house? Who were these people? Where were they now? And if Billington hadn't taken the real Noah, who had?

There were too many unanswered questions. And too many people were dead.

# 32

IT WAS JUST AFTER MIDDAY when the nurse asked Johnny Barford to leave the 'Talbot-Butler' ward at Medway Maritime Hospital near Rochester. He wore a gray cotton jacket over a white T-shirt, black drainpipe jeans so low they defied Newton in staying on - certainly the wide studded black leather belt wasn't making any difference - and gray sneakers. The Law of Gravity was further challenged by his blond quiff.

The smell of hospitals always upset him, and now a stale odor of fish, boiled vegetables and jam sponge added a piquancy to the usually balanced aroma of antiseptic and eau de bedpan.

"Are you sure you'll be all right, darling?" asked Amanda, propped up in the metal framed bed with three crisp white pillows.

"Of course, Mum. I got to Paris and back didn't I? A night at home's a doddle in comparison."

"I know, I know. You won't forget your supper's in the fridge…"

"And there's beer in the larder, the alarm code is 4242, Mrs Mee will be in to clean at 9.30 tomorrow morning but she has a key and I'll come and see you at lunchtime."

"Yes, ok, I fuss too much."

"Don't worry, I'll be fine. Just you be all right."

"I will. See you tomorrow. Love you."

"I love you, too, Mum." He pecked her on the cheek. "'Bye!"

"'Bye my darling."

Johnny's heel squeaked on the vinyl floor as he turned and walked out. The nurse, in a sky blue uniform dress and a name badge that read 'Sara Blake - Medway NHS Foundation Trust', watched him leave and turned to Amanda.

"All right Mrs Barford? Are you comfortable?"

Amanda sat back into the pillows and looked at the woman - five feet six, she reckoned, neat chestnut bob framing a rather attractive young face. Slim, with large eyes and small moles on her face and arms. She wasn't at all comfortable in the Liberty print nightie she'd chosen - it felt far too sensible and grannyish, but it was a mixed ward and she didn't want to attract attention. Reading the 'Inpatients - What to Bring' list had reminded her of going away to boarding school: 'two sets of nightwear; dressing gown; slippers; bath and hand towel; toiletries; box of tissues; reading and writing materials; small change'. Packing without Ralph had been the hardest part - it was the first time in their marriage that she'd filled a suitcase to go somewhere without him.

She wasn't comfortable about not telling Ralph where she was, and she wondered what he was up to in America, how he was getting on with Sabina, whether he was safe. And she wasn't looking forward to the treatment - it always made her feel exhausted for days afterwards. She checked the clip that was holding her long blonde hair in place and smiled for Britain:

"Yes, I'm fine thanks. Perfectly fine."

"Good. You just let us know."

"I will."

Sara Blake moved along the ward to the nurse's station and sat down. She had a load of paperwork to attend to. Amanda reached for her cheap pink reading glasses and opened the copy of

'Kent Life' that she had bought herself as a present, but her eyes skated over the pages and she soon gave up.

# 33

AS NEIL DROVE THE METALLIC GRAY JAGUAR up Shooter's Hill across Blackheath on its way east, Seymour Lyle was in the back staring out of the window, musing about various highwaymen who had terrorized travelers on that stretch of the old road from London to Dover. He wore a charcoal suit with a bold pinstripe, light pink shirt and Royal Green Jackets regimental tie - dark green with thin red and black stripes. The whole effect was slightly intimidating, which was intended.

To his left was Greenwich, and he realized that they were crossing the meridian. He turned his head, glancing at the bunch of flowers on the other side of the seat, and gazed at the back of the headrest in front of him. Lyle was surprised he hadn't been completely overjoyed that Henry Billington was dead. The old man had been an obstacle to Lyle's progress and he was finally out of the way. He'd also lost his grip and been compromised, unable to control his sexual appetite - or tastes. But the General supposed the death of anyone you've been close to at some point reminds you of your own mortality, and he was feeling a bit maudlin.

A heart attack, so Javier Mendoza told him. Lyle wasn't particularly taken aback - the man had hardly been young. He had called to discuss their next step. Mendoza was terse on the phone and Seymour hadn't been able to work out from the tone of his voice whether Billington's driver was more upset by the death of his boss or having to speak to him. The two had never got on that well, but since his last visit to the Senator's farm, Mendoza had been positively poisonous beneath a veneer of professional politeness.

Perhaps the man was feeling guilty because he was away when it happened, but Lyle doubted that. Still, it must have been a shock to return from a night out and find your employer dead in his car on the drive. There were no signs of foul play and the funeral was being arranged by his estranged daughter. Lyle assumed (was that a mistake? he wondered) that Billington had been scrupulous in leaving no evidence of his involvement with the Lucidi - at least, certainly not where it could be discovered. There was nothing he could do about it from his end, however, and a trip to Connecticut would only arouse suspicion where none currently existed.

What he did do was to make sure Mendoza disposed of the fake Noah, which was no good to him. As a collection of objects it was practically worthless, but as a copy of something priceless and inflammatory it could cause a major headache if anyone came across it. It had, after all, been stolen from the National Museum of Iraq in a clandestine operation that could implicate a number of Lucidi colleagues. All Lyle's ambitions would be vaporized if that happened. He knew Mendoza had some idea about the contents and would understand the need to destroy them. Even now, as Neil shifted his gray-suited bulk in the driver's seat and slowed the Jag for the Prince Charles roundabout, Mendoza was preparing to take the locked cases to a breaker's yard in Norwalk, where they would be crushed and melted down along with scrapped cars and other metal waste.

The General was headed for Rochester - unannounced - to put pressure on the Canon's wife, who was in hospital. He knew Ralph had gone to Italy - his passport had been checked at Pisa's Galileo Galilei airport four days beforehand. He suspected that Barton had somehow contacted or been contacted by the woman

192

on the ship - the Contessa di Volturara. If true, then she hadn't been killed in the abortive hijack made by Billington's raiding party. The last thing he wanted was the two of them working together.

# 34

JOHNNY BARFORD WAS JUST A LITTLE DISTURBED to find that his mother had moved beds and not mentioned it. Rather typical of her scattiness, he thought. He was sure he had the right time - around 12.30pm - and the right bed, but Amanda was no longer there. He went to find a nurse on Talbot-Butler ward.

Sara Blake of the Medway NHS Foundation Trust wasn't sure what Johnny was doing there. She recognized him from the day before, although he looked different in his dark suit, white shirt and striped tie - the King's School sixth form uniform. He felt less self-assured but the nurse was impressed by his initial confidence.

"Your mother was discharged before I came back on duty this morning," she informed him, walking towards the nurses' station. She consulted the register. Sure enough, Amanda Barford had checked out at 20.07 hrs the night before.

Now he was very disturbed. It was like a sick joke, like something surreal. "No, that can't be right," said Johnny. "She didn't come home. She wasn't meant to leave - she'd only just been admitted. Her treatment was supposed to begin this afternoon."

"I know. It does seem strange. It's very odd that you haven't seen her."

Panic started rising. "We should call the police!"

"No, I don't think they'd be able to help. It's not twenty four hours since she left."

"No, this is ridiculous. I'm sure something's happened." Johnny was angry with the nurse for being so calm, but all she saw was the distress of an adolescent boy.

Sara Blake half laughed. "Seriously, I don't think you should worry. Maybe your mother's just gone to see a friend. Perhaps she got cold feet and didn't want to worry you."

By this point Johnny had no further interest in Nurse Blake, who clearly wasn't going to help.

"No, Mum wouldn't do that. And even if she had, she'd have called me. I'll try her now."

He pulled out his mobile and dialed the number.

"You can't do that here. It should be switched off."

"It's an emergency." He paused. "She's not answering anyway - it's gone straight to voicemail."

"Is there someone else you can phone - outside?"

"Yes. I'll get hold of my Dad. She might have spoken to him."

"Don't worry. I'm sure it's all just a little misunderstanding."

'Yeah, right,' thought Johnny, but he didn't say anything other than, "Thank you." He left, and later regretted being so abrupt.

Outside in the polished vinyl corridor that seemed to stretch for half a mile, with its fluorescent lights, shiny metal plates protecting the corners of every doorway and pale blue and white signs for 'Oncology', 'x-Ray Department', 'Pediatrics', 'Way Out', 'Cafeteria', Johnny took out his phone again and called his Dad. He was glad it was still set for international calls since his time in Paris, especially as he had no idea where he was - probably still in America. He just hoped he wasn't on a plane somewhere with his mobile switched off.

Ralph was in the back of the Audi with Sabina when Johnny called. Gianni was driving them back to the Castello di Santa Maria

Novella after Andreas had landed the Learjet less than an hour before. All three were exhausted.

They had stayed over in Washington DC in order to reduce suspicion: it was a long way to go in such a small plane, and to have returned immediately would have been commented on. Ralph had been fascinated by the city. He loved the fact that no buildings were taller than ten or twelve stories. He knew it meant the city was more spread out and rents were high, but the benefits were clear to any visitor - glorious, uninterrupted views of some of the world's most iconic buildings.

He was also smitten with the Metro. His immediate thought was that it couldn't have been designed by committee - it had to be the work of one person. It was too harmonious, too well-realized. He discovered afterwards that he was right - the creator was Harry Weese, who had studied under Finnish architect Alvar Aalto at MIT. Ralph would never forget that first escalator ride right down onto the centre of the platform. The relative darkness, the lack of advertising, the plainness made it feel as if he was going into a cave. Magnificent vaulted ceilings dominated the space. Weese had insisted on few materials to maintain the integrity of his design. All was concrete, steel and glass. There was no graffiti - the platforms were built away from the walls, and the far walls were beyond the live rail. Genius! But the best bit for Ralph was the round glass panels let flush into the platform edge. Most of the time, they were unlit and passengers were unaware of them. But as a train approached, the panels would start to glow slowly on and off, growing in intensity as the train grew closer so that by the time it arrived they were permanently illuminated.

"Johnny! How are you?"

"Dad! Mum's not at the hospital!"

"Well, I know that. What's wrong?"

"Oh, no, she didn't tell you did she?"

"Tell me what? Johnny, what is it? Calm down."

"No, no, you don't understand. Mum got her appointment. She didn't tell you because she thought you'd come straight back and she knew you needed to be there."

"What? Oh, goodness! She shouldn't have done that."

"Well, she did and she went in yesterday with me in a taxi and she was supposed to have her treatment this afternoon and I just went to see her at lunchtime like we'd agreed and she wasn't there. The nurse said she'd checked out last night just after eight."

"Hang on. You mean you haven't seen her since yesterday and she's not there now?"

"No. Have you heard from her?"

"No. No I haven't."

"So I think we should call the police but the nurse said it's not twenty four hours yet."

"Yes, she's right, they wouldn't do anything. But I agree with you, we should let them know as soon as we can. You've got the details. Are you up to calling them?"

"Yeah, of course."

"And are you all right for everything? Johnny, I'm so sorry. This is all my fault."

"No, Dad. Mum should've told you."

"Yes, but I said I wouldn't leave while her appointment was coming up. I'll get there as soon as I can."

"When?"

"I don't know. We've just got back from the States. I'll call you in a bit."

"Ok. I'll phone the police."

"I'm really proud of you, Johnny. Stay strong and I'll get back to you as soon as I can."

"Thanks."

"Bye now. Take care."

"And you. Bye."

Ralph put his mobile away and sat back in the seat. He had looked tired - now he looked white, drawn, older. Sabina wasn't sure how to react. From what she understood, the news was terrible. She was also fascinated by the conversation between father and son. She envied him.

"Ralph, I couldn't help overhearing. I'm so sorry."

"Yeah, thank you. It's typical Amanda to do that - to go into hospital without telling me. I don't know what to do - other than get home as fast as I can." He sighed. "What d'you think? Has she just wandered off or has someone taken her?" As soon as he asked the question, he realized that Sabina couldn't possibly know the answer.

"Would she just wander off?"

"No." Ralph thought about the situation for a moment. He knew what he wanted to say, but worried that saying it would escalate the problem. "So we have to assume that something has happened to her." He sighed again. Sabina waited before continuing.

"Well, it can't be Alex, he's dead. And it can't be Billington, either." She paused. "The thing is, if someone has taken her, they'll have done it for a reason. I can't help thinking that it's connected with our trip to America."

"Me too. If it's another warning, we should hear from them, shouldn't we?"

"Yes, I guess so," Sabina agreed.

"You guess so?"

"No, you're right. From what you've told me, she wouldn't just disappear. So someone else must be involved. And we'll hear from them sooner or later. The most important thing is for you to get back to England. We can pick up your things from the castle and Andreas can take you there tonight."

"Oh, no, that's too much. I'll go back on the flight from Pisa."

"There's only one regular flight that I know of, and we'd never make it. Besides, at this time of year it's likely to be full. I insist."

"Sabina, thank you. I'm too tired to resist. It's very kind."

"No, it's the least I can do. Andreas was going home to Holland tonight anyway."

She'd done it again. Not told him the answer, but asked the questions that enabled them to work out what to do next...

# 35

WHEN HE HEARD THE DOOR UNLOCK just after 6pm Johnny hoped it was his Mum. He was surprised that his Dad had been able to get home so quickly. He was even more taken aback when Ralph introduced him to Sabina and Gianni.

"Johnny!"

Johnny couldn't believe himself as he held onto Ralph. What was he doing? He didn't care, he was just so glad to see his Dad. It was all he could do not to cry.

"Oh, Dad. Thank God you're here!"

"Yes. It's good to see you, too." He went to ruffle Johnny's hair, then realized that his son was too old for that sort of thing anymore - and disturbing the quiff would have been a big mistake. He took in the tight black jeans, pointed boots and bright T-shirt. "I've brought a couple of friends along. Well, actually, they insisted on coming to help us. Meet the Contessa di Volturara."

"Sabina, please!" She beamed at Johnny, noting how like his father he looked. She shook his hand. "I'm very pleased to meet you, Johnny. Your Dad's told me so much about you." Johnny colored. He just stared at Sabina. She was wearing a delicate ivory blouse above ivory pleated trousers, an ivory cashmere jumper knotted round her shoulders. She was more than beautiful, she was lovely and glamorous and - he was behaving like a puppy. Ralph rescued him.

"And this is Gianni."

"Johnny," Gianni said enthusiastically, shaking hands - his grip was considerably more forceful than Johnny was expecting.

"Gianni. Thank you." Johnny noticed Gianni's navy cotton chinos, deck shoes, striped green and white polo shirt and blazer, then looked back at Ralph. His Dad looked tired, but different. The navy shirt and khaki chinos really suited him. Johnny was less sure about the blue sneakers. He'd have to have a word with him when they were alone.

Ralph took control. "Well, the first thing is supper. Johnny, I don't suppose you've eaten?"

"No, not since this morning."

"Right. The quickest will be to order Pizzas. I hope that's ok with everyone. Can I leave you to do that? There's a menu by the phone. Find out what everyone wants. I'll have a Four Seasons."

Johnny showed the menu to Sabina and Gianni and got onto the phone. Ralph took his case upstairs and showed Sabina and Gianni to their rooms. Although the Barfords were a small family, the grace and favor house had five bedrooms and there was plenty of room for everyone, even if it was not quite what Sabina was used to.

"Oh, Ralph, please, it's fine," she reassured him.

After they had eaten, Johnny offered coffee, but they were enjoying the wine and declined. He cleared the plates and fetched himself another beer.

"So," said Ralph, "Amanda's missing, the police won't do anything yet but at least they know she's gone and we suspect that she's been taken against her will. Thank you for doing that, Johnny. The only person I can think of to call is General Lyle."

"Lyle?" asked Sabina.

"Yes - why, do you know him?"

"No, but I think I've heard the name. I can't be sure."

"He's supposed to have someone watching the family. I think he should know - if he doesn't already."

"I'm not sure, Dad," objected Johnny. "You said that you and Mum don't trust him. And his protection obviously didn't work."

"Well, yes, there is that. But…"

"I still think it's something to do with that man in Paris," Johnny added.

"What man in Paris?" asked Sabina.

Johnny explained the incident near the Place des Vosges - and the subsequent business with the envelope and motorbike in Rochester.

"That's strange," she mused. "I know Alex has - had - a house in Paris, but it's nowhere near the Marais. I mean, we know Alex ordered those two warnings. Could you find the house again?"

"Yeah, think so," nodded Johnny.

"But what is the point? Since Alex is dead - we both saw it - then there is no-one to make it happen," interjected Gianni.

"Perhaps," said Sabina, "perhaps this man and woman are acting on their own?"

The conversation went round and round. It was impossible to know what to do for the best. There was no clear path, no obvious solution. The one thing all were agreed on was that it was intolerable just sitting around and waiting. They decided not to tell Lyle just yet, but planned to visit the house in Rue du Parc Royal at some point. Everyone hoped that Amanda would turn up any moment, and failing that, anticipated that a good night's sleep might bring some clarity in the morning.

# 36

RALPH SAT AGAINST THE WORN, buttoned headboard catching up on his post. It was hard to concentrate. The sheets smelled of Amanda and a dent in the pillow next to him showed where her head had last laid. Being in their bed somehow made the fact that she was missing so much more unbearable. Her dressing table was just as untidy as ever, with pots, bottles, beads and small boxes on top; all sorts of tights, sleeves, straps and bits of clothing hanging out of the half-open drawers. She was there but not there.

The last few days had been a maelstrom of activity - even though there had been long hours of waiting and interminable traveling. Looking back, the highlights were easy to recall - actually hard to push away - while the dull times receded and vanished. Ralph's head and heart were revving hard, boosted by the twin turbos of feelings for both women. One he missed more than he was capable of articulating: the other's presence under the same roof - this particular roof - was profoundly unsettling.

There was a connection with Sabina that had been ignited by an electric spark of first contact with someone from another world and developed into a friendship that was deeper than either was prepared to acknowledge. Ralph had feared that such a thing would happen, right from the first moment that he heard her voice. Even his Milton Keynes experience hadn't been able to dilute the concentration of his regard for her. She was the sum of all his fantasies made real. And she was such a nice person. If she'd been just sexy or coarse or vulgar he could have dismissed all flights of imagination. But it was not so simple. Could a man love two women at the same time? Did he love her - surely it was far too soon to be asking such a question? And even as these thoughts snapped to and from the synapses in his brain, waves of guilt over Amanda and the fact that she was in danger threatened to engulf him. He needed to pray and recover his peace.

The phone went off in his right ear like an IED.

"Hello?"

"Barford. There you are. Lyle here. You back from your travels?"

"General Lyle. Er - yes."

"Good. Heard you'd been in Italy. I hope you haven't been talking to the Noah family."

"What? What do you mean?"

"You know what I mean, Barford. I suggest you drop the case. It's far too sensitive. Sorry I got you involved in the first place. Don't worry, we've got things under control. I also hear your wife's gone missing."

"How did you know that?"

"I told you I'd keep an eye."

"Yes, but it doesn't seem to have made any difference. She's still missing."

"Indeed. And that's why I think it's best if you stay put for now, old man."

"Stay put?"

"Yes, no more jaunts abroad for a while."

"What are you saying?"

"We're following a few leads and I think it'll only make her situation worse if you stick your oar in. I'm afraid I'm going to have to insist that you don't leave the country. Until further notice."

"But that's ridiculous!"

"Well, nothing you can achieve that we can't do better. And you don't want to put her life in danger now, do you?"

That sounded more like a threat than wise advice, but Ralph was completely discombobulated by Lyle's knowledge of the situation. "No, of course not."

"Good. I knew you'd see sense. We're obviously watching all the borders for her and her possible abductors - ports, airports, that sort of thing, so don't do anything silly."

"No."

"I'll be in touch. Hope it's good news next time. Goodnight."

"Goodnight," responded Ralph, but the phone had already clicked off. He put the receiver down as if it was contaminated. The post slipped to the floor. He turned out the bedside lamp but didn't move. There was no point in waking the others - it could wait until morning.

Streetlights shone though a crack in the curtains onto the opposite wall, sealing the bedroom door with a vertical bar of orange tape.

# 37

EVEN SAUSAGE, BACON AND EGGS couldn't lift the mood at breakfast. Ralph's news of his phone call from Lyle had come as an additional blow. Sabina kept asking questions and then drifting off into a world of her own.

"Johnny, what are you doing today?" she inquired.

"I've got school this morning, games and study periods this afternoon. Why?"

"Oh, I was just thinking. So, you'd be able to get back here for when?"

"Well, if I didn't go to games, I could be here for lunch."

"Is games a problem?"

"Not really. I'm not much of a cricketer and there's no third XI practice. I could bunk off."

"Yes," said Ralph, "I suppose you could. Or I could send you in with a note."

"If you like. They're not that fussed."

"Well, I'm not sure I like the sound of that, but right now it might suit us. What do you have in mind?" he asked Sabina.

She continued in thought for a moment. "Lyle doesn't want you to leave the country."

"Correct."

"Why? Why is that of any interest to him right now?"

"I've no idea. Seems bizarre."

"You must be a threat. He's not the kind of man who wastes time or energy on things that don't concern him."

"That's true. And he knows I was in Italy. Must have a link to passport control."

"Well, yes, if he's able to watch the UK borders, he could probably do that, too. Unless that's just a bluff. But I don't think so, somehow."

"Nor do I," added Johnny, not sure why he felt that, but wanting to be part of the conversation.

"What time do you have to leave?" Gianni asked Johnny, ever the voice of reason and practicality.

Johnny looked at his watch. "About five minutes ago."

"You'd better go," said Ralph. "We'll catch you up on everything when you get back. But I'm right in thinking you'd be happy to join us in whatever Sabina is planning?"

"Oh, yes!"

"Good. We'll see you at 12.30."

"Before if I can."

"OK. Bye darling."

Ralph had never called his son 'darling' before, but neither of them missed a beat. "Bye Dad - Sabina, Gianni."

They all joined in wishing him a good morning and telling him not to worry. It was a much brighter Johnny Barford who walked to school that day. Apart from anything else, he couldn't shift the image of Sabina in her jeans, boots and Versace biker jacket at breakfast. That would stay with him forever.

"So," said Ralph, spooning ground coffee into an empty cafetière, "more coffee?"

"No, thank you. We Italians like to start the day just with a little shot, you know. Not your great English mugs!"

"Not sure how to take that, but I'm having some anyway. Now, what's on your mind?" he directed his question to Sabina.

"As I said, Lyle doesn't want you leaving the country. And he doesn't want you working together with me either. That's right, isn't it?"

"I'm sure that's what he meant by 'the Noah family'. The big problem is, we don't know just how much he's aware of. Hang on."

"What?" asked Gianni.

"Lyle told me the Noah stolen from Baghdad was a fake. How could he have known that if he wasn't in contact with Billington?"

"True," Sabina nodded. "I wonder if he was aware of Alex's involvement."

"We can't know that," said Ralph. The kettle had boiled and he refilled the cafetière.

"No," agreed Sabina. "And I got the impression that Alex was operating on his own. He warned me against Billington. He may have warned me against Lyle, I can't remember. But I don't think he was working with them. If anything, he was ahead of them."

"But we still don't know who killed Mr Kovalenko - Alex," added Gianni.

"No," agreed Sabina. "Oh, it doesn't really help."

"Well, how about this," announced Ralph. "The only thing we do know is that there's a question mark over this house in Paris, and Lyle doesn't want me to leave the country. I don't know about you, but all I can think of is going to find the place and having a look. I can't see that we'd be harming Amanda's chances by doing that. And you never know, she may be there."

"That's what I was thinking as well," said Sabina. "And we can easily get you out. Can you divert your phone calls to your mobile?"

"Er, yes, I think so. There's a number I have to dial. Why?" asked Ralph.

"Well, it might just convince Lyle if he calls again. It's worth a try. If we get Andreas to pick us up from Rochester airfield, where we landed last night, they may not check our passports. And even if they do, I don't imagine Lyle expects you to fly off in a private jet - no offence. Lyle doesn't seem to know I or Gianni are here. If he's watching the place, he's not doing too good a job, but we can't take any risks. We just need to think of a legitimate way of getting ourselves out, and you and Johnny away from the house without arousing suspicion."

Ralph plunged the cafetière and poured himself a mug of coffee, deep in contemplation. Was he mad? This time, they really were stepping out into the unknown. Should he just stop right now and calm down and wait?

No, he couldn't sit around while Amanda was missing and the real Noah was still out there somewhere. He had to follow this through. And he was incensed by Lyle's behavior.

\*

THE FIRST THING Johnny noticed when he came home at 12.25pm was that Sabina and Gianni had gone. Nothing tangible, he just knew she was no longer there.

"Hi Dad! Where are Sabina and Gianni?"

"Gone ahead. We have a plan. Can you get changed? You'll need something that doesn't matter too much. I'm ready when you are. We'll pick up sandwiches on the way. Oh, and don't forget your passport."

"I've got some Euros left over as well."

"Excellent. You've got five minutes. Oh, I hope you don't mind - I've packed an overnight bag for you and given it to the others with mine. It was just too risky taking them ourselves."

"No, ok - depending on what you found!"

"Oh it's just pj's, washbag, that kind of thing. We can always buy more stuff if I've forgotten anything."

Ralph and Johnny made no attempt to disguise their exit. It was a clear, early summer day and the trees in the Cathedral Close were bright with new green growth. Sabina and Gianni had left via the garden gate into a lane that ran behind the Cathedral precinct an hour earlier.

As Ralph fastened his seat belt in the silver Mercedes C class estate he had owned for years (ideal for carting all Amanda's pottery stuff and pictures around), Johnny asked him where they were going.

"Shopping." That was the last thing he was expecting. "Don't worry, you'll see." They waved at Gerald who was on the barrier and moved off into the traffic. A dark blue Ford Mondeo parked down a nearby side street indicated and cut in, three cars behind them. Ralph didn't notice, although Johnny was aware of it, but he wasn't concerned.

They made their way to a large Waitrose on the outskirts of the city and left the Merc in the south car park. The Mondeo halted some distance away, its two occupants - Derek and Stuart - watching Ralph and Johnny as they entered the superstore by the front doors and headed for the sandwich counter. It was peaceful for such a busy place, with wide aisles and carefully arranged products. Large windows at the front of the store let in natural daylight, and the mood was set with a color scheme of cool white, gray and green.

Lunch bought, father and son went deeper into the fruit and vegetable aisle and then left towards 'Prepared Food' and 'Ready

Meals'. Across the back wall were large white letters on a white background, announcing 'BAKERY', 'DELICATESSEN' and other departments. Here, there was another exit facing the north car park.

Gianni spotted them first and started the mushroom-colored Honda Civic he and Sabina had hired that morning. He drove round by a bank of cash machines and stopped next to Ralph and Johnny, who hopped into the back.

"Ok?" asked Sabina.

"Yes, fine, thanks. We can go," responded Ralph.

Gianni headed for the north exit, which led onto a roundabout near the 'Deliveries' entrance of the store, well away from the view of Derek and Stuart in the Mondeo, still on watch duty in the south car park.

"Were you followed?" Gianni inquired.

"I don't think so," said Ralph.

"Well, we might've been," added Johnny. "There was a blue Mondeo that joined just behind us soon after we'd left and it's parked the other side."

"Why didn't you say?" demanded Ralph.

"I didn't want to worry you, Dad. Anyway, you said you had a plan."

"Yes, and so far, so good. Now, Rochester airfield."

# 38

SEYMOUR LYLE WAS INCANDESCENT with rage. He had his jacket off, which was always a bad sign. He had snorted into the Petty France office like a rhino with a hangover. Everyone was keeping well out of his way as he charged through reception and ran up the stairs.

In the Ops Room next to his study, two men wearing suits - Niall and Colin - and a woman in a formal skirt and blouse - Emma - were looking at each other with eyebrows raised, braced for the General's entrance. All in their late twenties, they sat at oversize gray laminate tables equipped with computers and desk trays. The walls were banked with filing cabinets or papered with maps and photographs; a heavily curtained window looked out onto the street; one door led into the room from the landing; the other gave access to Lyle's wood-paneled study.

His words preceded him, bursting like water through a dam as he followed into the room and stood his scotchgrain leather brogues on its stained gray carpet. "Does no-one know where they are?" He threw his arms in the air like a mad inventor. It would have been comical, but nobody laughed. "The whole department beaten by a vicar! Absolute bloody shower, the lot of you!" he roared. When he said 'shower', it sounded like 'shah'.

Lyle's afternoon - a long lunch at a very good restaurant in Mayfair - had been interrupted by a call from Derek and Stuart, the two men in the blue Mondeo. They had waited half an hour, then Stuart had gone into the Waitrose store they were watching. It took a while to search the aisles, even just walking along the ends of all the rows by the tills. There was no sign of Ralph or Johnny, but their car was still there.

"Where the bloody hell could they have gone? Come on, I want everyone checking bus routes, taxi firms, car hire - think! Did they walk? How near is the station, where do the trains go, what about ferries? Where are they going? You've got half an hour to come up with some ideas. And they'd better be good!"

He stomped into his study, threw his double-breasted blazer with the regimental buttons down on the small chesterfield and stared at the buildings on the opposite side of the street, knuckles on the windowsill.

Bringing Barford in on this had definitely been a mistake. Now it was a question of damage limitation. How had the man made the connection with the Contessa? There was a link somewhere but he couldn't think what it was. Italy? No, that's where she lived now her ship was sunk. But she was vital - she knew where the real Noah was. By following her, Lyle would find it, sooner or later. Those kids next door had better find where Barford was, and fast!

# 39

"I THOUGHT WE WERE GOING TO PARIS," said Ralph, pulling open a box of roast chicken salad sandwiches as the Learjet cruised 30,000 feet above the English Channel.

"We are," explained Sabina, sitting opposite with a Michelin road atlas on her lap. "But I want to go to Château Roüet-la-Dauphine first. It won't take much longer. Did I tell you Alex has left it to me in his will? Sorry, I didn't get a chance. There was a letter from his lawyers when we got back, but in the middle of everything I didn't really take it in."

"That's brilliant, isn't it?" asked Ralph.

"Yes. At first I couldn't understand why me - I'm not related or anything. But then I realized it was because of what was stored there. He must have done it very recently. Anyway, back to the plan. The thing is, I kept thinking about the house in Rue des Quatre Fils. If your wife's being held there, we can't just break in. And it would be stupid to get there and walk up and down outside, unable to find a way in. Then I realized that Alex kept a remote control for his houses in his car, which is at the Château. If the Marais house in Paris does belong to Alex, the remote will open the big vehicle entrance Johnny mentioned. If not, we haven't lost anything - just a bit of time perhaps."

"Well, I trust your judgment," Ralph mumbled through a mouthful of bread and lettuce. Johnny kept looking at the inside of the cabin with its pistachio walls and vanilla leather seats, lit by frosted white lamps. A cream carpet ran down the aisle and the fittings were in brushed stainless steel. It was more practical than it looked - which was very Italian. He thought it extremely cool, just like its owner. He turned his head and gazed out of the porthole by his seat, mesmerized by the experience of flying in such a small plane. Sabina smiled at him.

"Not hungry?"

"No. I mean, yes, but - this is all so amazing. Thank you so much."

"Well, Ralph risked his life for me - I couldn't do any less."

"So how do we get into Paris?" asked Ralph, using his tongue to move compacted bread off his teeth. "I mean, we can't exactly land in the Champs-Elysées!"

"No - we can't. Look," she said, opening the road atlas and turning it round so Ralph and Johnny could read it. "Henri, who works at Alex's - my - vineyard, will meet us at Caumont, which is the airport at Avignon here, and drive us to Roüet-la-Dauphine, which is in Châteauneuf-du-Pape, only about twenty kilometers - twelve miles - north here, to pick up Alex's car and the remote." Sabina pointed the route out on the map. "I'll take everyone back to the plane in the Bentley, then Gianni will go to Italy with Andreas to collect the helicopter. The three of us will drive towards Paris and meet Gianni just outside, here." She put her finger on the symbol of a chateau near Melun, a few kilometers south of the capital.

"Vaux-le-Vicomte?" said Johnny.

"Yes, why, do you know it?" she inquired in an animated tone.

"I went there with Laurent recently. It's amazing."

"Well, it belongs to a relative of mine. I called her earlier and she doesn't mind us parking the helicopter for a few hours, though she took a bit of convincing. She's away at the moment, so it shouldn't be too much of an imposition!"

"I don't understand. Why aren't we flying the plane to Paris?" asked Ralph.

Gianni took over. "It's too risky. If General Lyle is watching the airports, once he realizes what we're doing then Paris is a very obvious place for us to go. Remember that he knows about the house in the Marais district and the threat to Johnny - you told him the whole story. By filing a flight plan for Avignon, we will have put him off the scent, but we don't know for how long. Then we have to get your wife back to England and it will be much easier to do that in the helicopter."

"And this way, we can land somewhere privately, which would be difficult in France with the Learjet. It's not like America!" added Sabina.

"Ok. You've obviously thought it all through. So we drive into Paris at night?" he asked Sabina.

"Yes - it'll be after midnight I think by the time we reach the house. It's a very long drive, but will make it much easier, being dark and relatively quiet." Sabina looked at Johnny again. "What sandwiches do you have?"

"Er, BLT. D'you want one?"

"No thank you. But if you don't eat them soon I think Gianni might!"

"How many seats are there in your helicopter?

"Four. So once Gianni, you, Ralph and your mother are in, I'll drive back to Avignon and Andreas will take me home - to Italy."

"Oh, so after he and Gianni have got the helicopter, Andreas will fly back and wait for you in Avignon."

"Exactly. Very good. You have a bright boy here, Ralph."

Andreas spoke over the intercom: "We'll be landing at Caumont in one hour, Contessa."

"Good. Eat up! You'll get a great view of the city as we come into land. It's a beautiful sight," added Sabina.

# 40

NIALL FERGUSSON KNOCKED ON Lyle's study door and hovered with his head slightly down and hand a few inches from the paneled wood, poised for a reply. There was no response. A square-shouldered graduate of Trinity College, Dublin, he had once been trialed for London Irish and still played Centre for a local club side. He looked back at his colleagues, Colin and Emma. His orange hair and freckles were complemented by a neat blue suit, pale shirt and green tie. When he smiled, a light came into his bright blue eyes and also revealed crooked teeth.

The door suddenly opened and Lyle stood holding the handle, his expression full of expectation.

"Well?" he barked.

"It's Avignon, sir."

"Avignon? What's at Avignon?"

"No idea, General."

Lyle paused and changed his mind about something. "Well done. How did you find out?"

"Car hire company, sir. Rented a Honda Civic to a Miss Volturara this morning."

"That's her. They're driving to Avignon? How do we know that?"

"No, sir. The firm have trackers in all their hire cars, which she obviously didn't know about. We traced it to Rochester airport, where it's parked. Her plane - call sign India Sierra Delta Victor Seven - took off at 13.45hrs bound for Caumont which is the international airport at Avignon in the south of France."

"I know where Avignon is, thank you Niall. But this is good work. How do we get there?"

Emma Gregory turned from her computer screen and talked to Lyle. Her long, light brown hair was streaked with blonde highlights framing an oval face with full but narrow mouth, snub nose and wide eyes: "There's an evening flight from London City Airport to Paris Charles de Gaulle that connects with a flight to Avignon, or we could take the Eurostar to Lille. It's only four hours from there to Avignon by TGV. The train would be quicker."

"No, we need to be able to get around while we're there. What if Avignon's a decoy, just a stop on the way? There's no telling where they may go after that. Can't we use the chopper?"

Colin Rigg answered: "We don't have the budget for it, sir. The cost would be prohibitive."

Lyle stared at Colin's short, greasy black hair, pale face, brown suit, white shirt and Technicolor tie. "What do you mean, we don't have the budget for it? We're on the tail of a woman with a private jet and we have to what - give chase on push-bikes? Bugger me, Colin, get on the phone and clear the budget. We need to be in the air within the next hour. In the meantime Niall, Emma, come in here and let's look at everything we've got."

# 41

SABINA WAS AT A LOSS. There was a blank space on the cracked cement floor of the cart barn where she had last seen Alex's Bentley Continental R.

"Oh!" she exclaimed, standing in the doorway.

"What?" asked Ralph, from behind, unable to see past her.

"The car's gone," she said, speaking into the void in front of her.

"Ah. So what's Plan B then?" Ralph wasn't sure why he'd made a joke of it. He was worried about bringing Johnny along and he couldn't stop thinking about Amanda. What if they'd made the wrong decision? What if they should have waited in Rochester? Worst of all, what if taking action had put her life in even more danger?

"Plan B? I think it's Plan G by now isn't it?"

"Probably," he responded.

"Hang on, there's something else here." She stepped into the barn, followed by Ralph, Gianni and Johnny. It took a while for their eyes to adjust to the dim light.

"That's it!" shouted Johnny, pointing to a black saloon parked next to the biscuit-colored Citroen 2CV at the far end. "The Beemer. The one in Paris."

They all moved quickly to examine the car. It was indeed a 5-series BMW with dark tinted windows.

"It's a Paris registration," remarked Sabina. "See, it ends with '75'."

"I will ask if Henri knows where the keys are," suggested Gianni.

Sabina tried the driver's door, which opened. The sound of the lock being released and the door hinges moving was amplified by the high wood-beamed space. "Don't worry, they're in the ignition. I wonder if there's a remote." She sat in the car and tried the glovebox. There was the remote control she had been looking for. She held it up, shook it and shouted, "Got it!" She put it back and settled into the seat, turning the key in the ignition. The BMW's 3.5 liter engine fired and rumbled into life. It sounded deep and powerful, rather like a boat. She checked the fuel level - half a tank - and switched off.

"Well, I guess that's Plan G then? Paris in this?" asked Ralph.

"Looks like it," agreed Sabina, climbing out.

"The good thing is, we now know the house is connected with Alex or this car wouldn't be here. And we know we can get in," reasoned Ralph.

"Now I know where Johnny gets it from," teased Sabina.

# 42

GENERAL LYLE WAS HAVING A BAD DAY, a terrible day, and it had just got worse. Niall had told him that they'd missed Sabina's plane by twenty minutes. Still in his blazer and gray flannels, Lyle stood looking out across the tarmac of Caumont airport to the perimeter fence, its metal mesh illuminated by cones of light shining from the top of each concrete post. Although the sky was now dark with evening cloud, apart from the occasional claw-slash of Mediterranean blue, the place was well-lit and he seemed to have at least four shadows.

It wasn't a large airport and there was very little activity. In fact, as low-cabbed service vehicles, motorized tugs and tankers tractored to their sheds - and doors rolled shut with a metallic clang - it seemed to be closing for the night.

Behind him the gray military helicopter that had taken Ralph to meet Ariq Tafisi rested in the glow of powerful lamps mounted on the roof of a cavernous hangar. He sipped a cup of black coffee that Niall had brought back with him from a machine in the departure lounge.

Late rush-hour traffic drove past on the road outside the airport. Lyle watched without interest. Coming out of his daydream, he asked Niall: "What else do we know? Where are they heading for now?"

"The flight plan for India Sierra Delta Victor Seven would suggest a private airfield in Tuscany, sir."

"Italy! Why didn't they just go there? Why stop here?"

"To refuel?"

"No, they've got plenty of range."

"The thing that's odd is that there were only two people on board."

"What? Why didn't you say?"

"I was coming to it, General."

"Which two?"

"I don't know, but one must be her pilot, Andreas Schumann. He's Dutch."

"So where are the others? Have they stayed here or gone on somewhere else?"

"The only place in France that's connected is Paris, sir. You know, the house in the Marais district that Barton's son mentioned. Where he was threatened that first time."

"Paris? But that's miles away." Lyle pondered the conundrum a moment. "They wouldn't fly there - it's too risky. I warned them I was watching the airports."

"Are they driving?"

"Well, it's a good six and a half hours to Paris from here, which means they wouldn't get there until 23.30 at the earliest."

"But it's possible, sir?"

"It's possible. But if you're going to do that and send the others off to Italy, why fly so far south?"

"To put us off?"

"You might have a point. See if you can get hold of our people in Paris. It won't do any harm for someone to keep an eye on - what was the name of the street?"

"Rue des Quatre Fils, sir."

223

# 43

AMANDA COULDN'T UNDERSTAND why the nurse didn't come. She'd called for her often enough. The thing was, she couldn't open her eyes, no matter how hard she tried. She pulled her cheek muscles down and moved her jaw but it made no difference. All she could see was orange and green with stars moving past and some branch things like a map of a river delta. She tried again. 'Blara Sake!' That wasn't her name, was it? 'Blara!' She called again. 'Bloody Blara. For Blara's sake!' she cried.

No one came. It was hot. Amanda was floating in heat, like a bath. No, more like chocolate. A pool of hot chocolate, melted chocolate. She could feel the mattress for a moment and then it was gone again. Perhaps it wasn't chocolate. Mud - that was it! She was having a mud bath. In Turkey. The sun was shining. She was on holiday, covered in mud, floating around in the sun. She giggled.

The mud was drying. It crept up on her. She was trapped in it. She squirmed and the mud oozed with her, but heavily now. It was hard to move her arms and her legs had stopped working. There was a flash and she thought she saw a curtain blow in from somewhere. Voices from downstairs. Or was it in the street outside?

She rose up with the mud, like a huge wave. No, it was clay. She was clay. She landed on something hard and flat. It knocked the air out of her. Then she was going round. Faster. The ceiling had beams. Then hands came round her and squeezed. She was going up. Round and round. She was feeling giddy and wanted it to stop. 'Blara stop! Stop!' she screamed.

They were making her into a pot, she was sure of it now. Round and round on the wheel, hands pushing in, shaping her. It was exhausting. She didn't like it. Someone grabbed her arm and it felt like they were tearing it off. Then a sharp stab. A rush like bruise. 'What is bruise?' she thought. 'What is bruise made of? How does it travel? How does it move up my arm like a big rush of ache?'

Then she was free. Floating like a balloon. The water was still there, but it felt like sky.

# 44

THE AIRE DE DARVAULT SERVICE STATION on the A6 at Nemours, 77 kilometers south of Paris, was a good place to stop. Sabina, Ralph and Johnny were tired and hungry. They'd filled up the car just outside Lyon, but that had been hours ago. The red 'Autogrill' sign promised a half-decent supper after living off sandwiches and snacks since cooked breakfast in Rochester over fourteen hours beforehand. It seemed a lifetime ago.

Sabina took the exit and negotiated her way past a 'Norbert Dentressangle' truck to park in front of the cafeteria. It was one of many names they had read to themselves time and again as they traveled on the autoroute. Freuhauf. Spedition. Logistics. Trasporti. Salvesen. Maersk. Mammoet. All three were stiff-limbed as they climbed out of the black BMW. They might have moved more quickly had they known that Gianni was already waiting for them at Vaux-le-Vicomte.

As they sat over small cups of coffee after devouring their trays of food - a Salade Niçoise and San Pellegrino for Sabina; pork casserole and rice for Ralph; pizza and Orangina for Johnny - they smiled at each other. It was a moment of much-needed relaxation in a day wired with tension. Sabina asked Johnny about the best part of his visit to Vaux-le-Vicomte.

"I think, coming out the other side of the house and looking across the gardens, right up to the statue in the distance. The scale of it was awesome. And then, when you walked, the end seemed to get even further and further away."

"Yes. The gardens were designed by Le Nôtre - a friend of Fouquet who had the place built. He was very clever, especially with perspective - he went on to create the gardens at Versailles. I'm afraid you won't see much in the dark!"

"Never mind," added Ralph. "Another time, perhaps. When all this is over. Shouldn't we be getting on?"

Gianni had heard a car approach and was very glad when its headlights appeared from the left. He stood next to Sabina's helicopter on a tight carpet of grass in front of the château of Vaux-le-Vicomte. Its dark lawns were quartered by bone-white gravel drives. The building's great mass, high roof and enormous dome seemed magnified in the moonlight behind him. He had spent the last hour pacing up and down, at one point walking past the moat to stand on the south terrace - watching the pewter reflection of the ornamental ponds, listening to a clock chime the hours; and the fluted flight of owls; and foxes fighting in the surrounding forest, sensing the burning odor of hot aviation fuel in his head give way to the coolness of woods and the unmistakable tang of water.

He was dressed for action and had brought a change of clothes for the others - the same as they'd worn that night in Connecticut.

*

THE BLACK BMW 535i approached Paris from the N6 via the Bois de Vincennes just before 1am. On the way in they saw knots of young people hanging around on corners or outside fast food joints, while vagrants huddled asleep in doorways. Streetlights illuminated grand avenues of plane trees in full leaf; traffic was sparse and couples were strolling past shuttered shop windows and closed pavement cafés. Gianni was driving, much to Sabina's relief. At Place de la Bastille with its futuristic opera house he took the Boulevard Beaumarchais and turned left down Rue St Gilles. By day, the Marais was full of chic bars, fashion boutiques, patisseries, bookshops, antiques showrooms, restaurants and crêperies: now it was quiet.

They were very close.

"Cross over Rue de Turenne into Rue du Parc Royal," advised Sabina, who was navigating with a street map in her hands and trying to watch for traffic at the same time. She felt responsible for everything. "It's a one way street. It leads to Rue de la Perle and then becomes Rue des Quatre Fils - where Johnny's house is."

"It's not my house!" Johnny objected.

"No," agreed Gianni, "but I hope you can show us where it is. Can you remember if it's near where we are or further away?"

"Yes," interjected Sabina, "it's quite a long street."

"I'm pretty sure it was this end," said Johnny.

"We must leave the car and see. Johnny and I will walk to find the house and check that no-one is watching."

"You think Lyle will have someone here? How could he?" asked Ralph, keen to be involved. He had noticed that Gianni was far more talkative than he used to be. Perhaps it was something to do with Johnny being around. Ralph knew the man missed his own son, Umberto.

"We must be very careful. He will work it out sooner or later. He is not to be underestimated."

Gianni found a spot to park the car in Rue de la Perle. When he turned off the engine, it was suddenly very still. To the right, the green neon sign of a pharmacy flashed on and off, the bars of light filling from the outer edge to the central cross and emptying back out in a steady rhythm. A hooded boy on a scooter buzzed past like an angry hornet. Everyone looked round, aware that they were minutes away from their goal. All four doors opened soundlessly. Gianni and Johnny crossed over and moved down the street; Sabina walked round and sat in the driver's seat; Ralph closed the rear doors quietly and settled into the front next to her. Neither spoke.

After a few meters, Johnny touched Gianni's arm and they both stopped. "I was wrong," Johnny whispered. "It's here in the Rue de la Perle. I don't remember seeing this street sign - just the next one."

"Which house?" asked Gianni.

"Over there," pointed Johnny. It was a typical seventeenth century town house of dressed stone and brick, five stories high. The front door was set in an ornate portico of rusticated stone pillars. To the right was the arched courtyard entrance barred by high wooden doors that the black BMW had come out of that day Johnny and Laurent had ambled by. What a different mood there had been then! And how strange for Johnny to be coming back in the very same car that had threatened him! They were close enough for Gianni to be able to read the circular warning notice: '*PRIERE DE NE PAS STATIONNER - SORTIE DE VEHICULES*'.

"Good," said Gianni. Now we must go to the end. Look for any car or van that has lights on or people in."

They stepped along the pavement, avoiding dried dog excrement and concentrating on the cars parked down the far side. They were all facing away from them, and if Lyle had sent anyone, Gianni and Johnny had the advantage, as they would be behind those watching.

That street was quiet, although they could hear all around them the hum of a capital that was far from asleep. Over in the centre, a laser beam flickered in the cloudy sky above some hidden attraction. Crossing Rue Vieille du Temple they saw a middle-aged man and a younger woman locking up a restaurant. The boom of a disco vibrated not far away. Johnny could smell French tobacco and drains, powerfully recalling memories of his recent stay in the city.

This time it was Gianni's turn to halt Johnny in his tracks as he spotted two men in a dark blue Citröen saloon twenty meters ahead.

Patrice and Philippe had been sitting watching Rue des Quatre Fils for more than four hours. Earlier, they had both dozed off, but a shot of caffeine from Philippe's thermos flask, topped up with a can of Red Bull, had fueled them with adrenaline. They were alert, looking in front and behind, windows open. Patrice opened the driver's door and got out. He bent down, nodded to Philippe and then strolled away from Gianni and Johnny down the street. Gianni swung Johnny round by the arm and headed back the other way, round the corner into Rue Vieille du Temple and out of sight.

As the two men reached the BMW, Sabina and Ralph could sense their excitement - their movements were charged with tension, barely containing the drama of their discoveries. Gianni and Johnny got into the back. "He's found it," said Gianni. "And Lyle's sent someone. The good thing is, they're parked in the next street, so if we're quiet, we should be all right."

"Well done, Johnny," said Sabina.

"Brilliant!" agreed Ralph. "So, do we go?"

"Yes," Gianni breathed decisively. They got out and Sabina locked the car, giving the keys and remote control that operated the vehicle entrance doors to Gianni.

"You'd better look after these," she whispered. "And here's the remote."

They crossed Rue de la Perle and stood against the wall of a building. Ralph and Sabina adjusted to the night air. All four felt the cold grit of stone through their clothes - and a combination of urgency and caution in their wired limbs. Gianni led the way forward. They walked past the front door of the house and just beyond the high wooden doors, where there was an area of shade from the streetlights. Their minds were filled with what they might find. Each in their own way yearned for Amanda to be there and hoped her abductors might be asleep. Gianni pulled the remote from his pocket.

Their optimism was abruptly punctured by a light going on in a window above the front door. Although they knew they could not have been seen, they froze in fear. Nothing had happened, yet in that moment they thought they had failed. Ralph beckoned Gianni with a sideways shift of his head and all four moved further down the street, out of earshot.

"So, what's the plan now? We know someone's there, which could be good, could be bad," hissed Ralph.

"We have to go in through the doors. We don't know what we will find," whispered Gianni.

"Do we wait until the light goes out?" asked Sabina.

"That could be any time. We are here and we should go in," decided Gianni.

"Ok," said Ralph, moving back towards the house. All followed and stood again by the doors. Gianni held out the remote and pressed the button.

The automatic mechanism engaged with a thunk and the doors cracked open. An amber light flashed from the courtyard within. It was too late to worry about the disturbance - they were committed.

Gianni pushed impatiently through the widening gap, followed by Ralph, Sabina and Johnny. Eventually the wooden doors stood fully open and the flashing light went out. Gianni turned to Sabina - they'd both seen the Bentley at the same time.

"I want to have a look at the car with Johnny," said Sabina. "Take Ralph and see if you can find a way in."

Gianni nodded, signaled to Ralph and crossed the courtyard to a half-glazed door.

Sabina tried the driver's door of Alex's Bentley. It opened. There was dried blood on the ivory leather seat and both could see that the pale carpet was stained dark red. They glanced at each other, disturbed by their discovery. Sabina moved to the back of the car and tried the trunk. It swung up. She was not entirely surprised by what she saw, but still taken aback.

There, on the sand-colored carpet, were her two Louis Vuitton cases that contained the real Noah. Johnny came up beside her. She smiled at him with the widest beam, overwhelmed, tearful, unsure how to react to the explosion of emotions coursing through her. She was just wiping her eye when the trunk lid slammed and the two were faced by a man aiming a pistol at them.

Harutyun waved the gun, stepping backwards and opening the passenger door. "Get in!" He moved the electric-powered seat forward so Johnny could climb into the back. With his gun trained on Sabina, he pushed the button that sent the seat back again and closed the door. He motioned for her to follow him round the hood of the big car. The driver's door was still open and he pushed her in. "Move over!"

Sabina shuffled across into the passenger seat, avoiding the automatic gear stick, aware that the pistol was trained on her head all the time. Harutyun took some keys out of a trouser pocket with his other hand and sat behind the wheel. Johnny and Sabina both noticed that he was moving stiffly, wincing from time to time as if in considerable pain.

The lights started flashing again and the wooden doors began to close. Harutyun fired up the engine, engaged 'drive' and lurched the car to the right: the first stage of a lunging three-point turn. He braked and reversed, aligning the Bentley for an exit. Stretching across, he pulled open the glovebox and searched for a remote. Sabina thought about fighting him for it but could see he was desperate. White-faced, wild eyed and obviously wounded, he was terrifying. It was the work of a nanosecond for her to realize that this man who had worked for her parents - and then Alex - was Alex's killer.

Gianni and Ralph had broken in and searched the ground floor. The kitchen was chaotic, pans and plates piled in the sink, a bin overflowing with tins and plastic trays from microwave meals. They were on their way to the stairs when they heard the car start and saw the amber light flash.

Harutyun pressed the remote and the doors stopped closing. For a moment nothing happened, then they started opening again. Gianni burst out of the door on the other side of the courtyard and shouted. Harutyun opened the electric window and fired at him. Gianni was knocked down by the force of the shot. Ralph appeared, took in the scene and ducked back inside the doorway. Harutyun fired again, put the car in gear and accelerated, scraping the right hand side of the Bentley on the wooden door that had not fully opened and bouncing off the cobbled pavement into Rue de la Perle.

The car gathered speed at a frightening rate. Philippe looked up from the passenger seat of the Citröen as it flew past and called on his mobile to Patrice, who was patrolling the far end of Rue des Quatre Fils with the car keys in his pocket.

Ralph rushed forward to Gianni and helped him sit up. "Are you ok?" he asked.

"Yes, just my arm," muttered Gianni, holding his right upper arm with his left hand.

"Can you walk?"

Gianni stood up. He was dazed. Ralph looked him in the eye. "Give me the keys!" Gianni went to move but his arm hurt too much.

"Right pocket."

Ralph reached into Gianni's right jacket pocket and fished out the keys to the BMW. "Stay here," Ralph shouted, running towards the doors. Having reached the end of its time delay, the amber light came on again and the doors twitched, beginning to close. Ralph raced through the gap and up the street towards the BMW. He pressed the key fob on the way, the car's indicators flashed at him and he grabbed the driver's door.

In his panic he couldn't fit the key into the ignition lock. He took a breath and tried again. The car sprang into life and he roared off down the street, pulling his seat belt on. As he passed the Citröen, Patrice was running towards it.

Harutyun's driving was insane. Sabina and Johnny both put their seat belts on as the huge machine thundered across Rue des Archives without stopping to see if anyone was coming.

"So, it's you!" he grunted in Armenian.

"What?" she asked, totally astounded to hear him address her in a language she had not heard since her mother had died.

"You. His granddaughter. You know, Razmig Assadourian?"

Sabina, already in fear of her life, was struggling to comprehend. "How do you know that?"

"Ha! I worked for him. The graves."

Sabina stared at him. "You worked for - you were one of the..."

"Yes, the only one alive. It's mine."

Sabina knew without asking. It was one of those awakenings where it would take her much longer to explain to someone else than to understand for herself. It all made sense. This man had robbed the Ararat graves on her grandfather's orders; had killed Alex for the treasure; had probably been involved in the death of her own parents. She knew him, of course. She recognized him as

Hari. It was so strange to hear him speak in Armenian. How had he reinvented himself as an Italian? But there was something else even more pressing she needed to find out as they crossed the next street without slowing.

"And what have you done with Amanda?"

"Amanda?"

"Canon Barford's wife."

"I don't know what you're talking about."

"The woman in the house?"

"There's no woman in the house."

Distracted for a moment, demented with vengeance and drained of blood, Harutyun slammed the Bentley into a line of parked cars in Rue Michel le Comte. Nearly two and a half tons of speeding machinery crushed the first vehicle, pushing it into the one in front. The shockwave passed through twelve cars before it dissipated and the Bentley stopped moving forward, though the rear wheels continued turning for a few moments while Harutyun's foot was still on the accelerator, squealing and smoking, making the car judder and kick like a dying animal. Airbags and seatbelts had saved Sabina and Johnny, but Harutyun's head was halfway through the driver's window and he was stone dead. Sabina was unconscious: Johnny was trapped in the back, unable to operate either seat back and free himself.

Ralph slowed at Rue des Archives but decided the Bentley had probably gone straight on. He didn't know where it was and once he started turning off the one-way system he wouldn't know where to go. As he approached the next crossing he could see a car ahead on the left with its lights on and smoke pouring from its rear. Halfway down Rue Michel le Comte he came across the Bentley, stuffed into a car made unrecognizable by the impact, engine still running, half-hidden by a dispersing cloud of burning rubber. He came to a standstill in the middle of the street and ran over.

Lights were on in the upper stories of flats and houses on either side of the street. An elderly couple looked out of a bedroom window, discussing the accident and what might have happened. Several of the local inhabitants had called the emergency services.

He could see Johnny in the back and tried the driver's door, but it was jammed shut, having taken much of the force of the collision. At the sight of Harutyun's bloodied head he felt a shock of nausea but pushed it down, dashing round the other side and managing to pull open Sabina's door. She was alive but out cold. He reached over and turned off the engine before undoing her seat belt. It was unexpectedly quiet, though the smell of burnt rubber was appalling and made him want to gag. Sabina flopped out towards the street and he only just caught her in time.

Ralph dragged Sabina out and onto the tarmac. He laid her gently down and pressed the seat back button to release Johnny.

"Are you all right?" he asked his son.

"Fine, Dad. Thanks for coming along."

"Who was that maniac?"

"I've no idea, but he and Sabina knew each other."

"Help me get her into the car." The two lifted Sabina carefully and managed to place her on the back seat of the BMW. "Get in!"

"There's something we should bring," said Johnny.

"What? We need to go. We've got to get Mum."

"She's not there, Dad."

"How do you know?" Ralph asked.

"He said so."

"And you trust him?"

"Honestly, he didn't know what we were talking about. But there's something in the boot. It's very important. Sabina was crying when she saw it."

Ralph paused. He was worried about Gianni, anxious for Amanda's safety, keen to get away from Lyle's men and concerned that the police would be along any moment. "Show me!"

Johnny went back to the Bentley and opened the trunk. Ralph stared. "Bloody hell! Is that what I think it is?"

"I don't know, but I think we should take it," answered Johnny. The two men struggled with the Louis Vuitton cases, dragging one each across to the BMW. They only just fitted in the German car's trunk, which was considerably smaller than the Bentley's.

"We should close the lid," said Johnny, looking at the wreck of Alex's car.

"Ok. Get in the back and hold on to her!" shouted Ralph. He ran to the Bentley, slammed the trunk shut and jumped into the BMW. Driving off down the street, he asked, "Any idea?"

Johnny turned his head away from Sabina and looked out of the windows. "I don't recognize it. Laurent and I never came down this far."

"I'll go left and left, see if we can get back where we started." Ralph stopped at the end of the street and turned into Rue Beaubourg, which was a much wider road. The next left was a cul-de-sac so he waited and took the Rue des Francs Bourgeois. "Anything?" he asked.

"No, not yet." They drove on, crossing Rue des Archives. "I'm sure we crossed that street."

"Yes, so am I, just now. Let's keep going." As they went over Rue Vieille du Temple they heard a siren and saw the blue flash of police lights in the distance. "We need to get out of here!"

Patrice reached the Citröen and leaped in.

"*Allez, Patrice, allez vite!*" shouted Philippe.

"*Ou?*" asked Patrice as he moved the car out into the street.

"*Toute droite!* - Straight on!"

Lyle's men drove rapidly along Rue des Quatre Fils, arguing about being in the wrong place, whose fault it was that they'd missed the action at the critical moment and where to go next. It was some time before they came across the crashed Bentley. They were still looking at Harutyun's smashed face when the police arrived.

Ralph took the next left, Rue Elzévir, and drove slowly. After a hundred meters they came across Rue Barbette, but it was a no entry. Ahead was the green flashing neon sign of the pharmacy that they had seen when they arrived.

Sabina stirred. "Where are we?" she muttered.

"How're you feeling?" asked Ralph, as they turned into Rue de la Perle.

"Oh, fuzzy. It's as if someone's been shaking my brain loose. What happened? The Noah?"

"It's all right, it's in the boot," Ralph reassured her.

"This is where we parked," shouted Johnny.

"Yes. But how are we going to get back in for Gianni?"

"Is he ok?" asked Sabina.

"I don't know. He was shot in the arm. He's got the remote. I'm going to have to ram the doors. You two had better get out. Will you be all right?"

"I think so."

"Don't worry, I'll hold on to you," said Johnny, quietly. Ralph stopped the car just short of the house. Johnny helped Sabina out and stood with her against the wall of the house. Ralph revved up and drove straight at the wooden doors of the vehicle entrance. He hit them with considerable force, but they hardly moved. He reversed and tried again, this time going as fast as he dared in a lower gear - any more than 25kph and he'd set the airbags off. The doors broke open at the bottom, below the metal arms of the

238

automatic mechanism, and a gap appeared down the middle. Ralph turned off the engine and got out to have a look.

"Dad, you're mad!"

"I know, but we've done it. I reckon we could just squeeze through."

"You'll have to back out: there's no room between the bonnet and the doors."

Ralph climbed back in and reversed a couple of meters. Johnny left Sabina propped up and pushed in through the doors. Gianni was standing in the courtyard nursing his arm.

"Are you ok?" shouted Johnny.

"*Sì*, yes. Not bad. But I cannot find your mother."

"I know - she's not here. We have to go."

Gianni looked at him and reacted like a professional. He came over to Johnny, who led the way out. Ralph had rescued Sabina, who was beginning to lose consciousness again, and put her back in the car. He was just coming through the doors when Johnny appeared.

"Get back, Dad, we're coming out. Without asking any questions, Ralph turned and made for the BMW. He started the engine. Johnny opened the passenger door and ushered Gianni in. He closed the door and opened the rear, settling down beside Sabina. "Let's go!" he yelled, doing up her seatbelt.

"Is she all right?"

"Yes, come on!"

Ralph reversed into the street and put the car into first, his only option to go down the one way system towards where the Bentley had crashed. He looked up. "Let's try something else," he said, finding reverse again. He focused out of the rear window and drove the car backwards the wrong way down Rue de la Perle until he was able to turn right up Rue Thorion, away from where all the action had taken place. "I don't want to bump into those guys or the police," he explained. None of them saw the pool of water and coolant by the wooden gates or the trail of liquid that flowed from the car.

"Hm - good thinking!" commented Johnny from the back. "Gianni, do you want to put your belt on?" he asked. Gianni struggled into his seat belt. Ralph put his on. "Better be careful - she's not really safe like this," he said to Ralph.

"No. There's no rush now. But I've no idea where I'm going." Ralph replied. "We came in from the right, so I'll head that way and see." He veered right into Rue Debellyeme, which led to Rue de Turenne, a wide street that would take them to the Place des Vosges. "This looks good. Keep a look out" He went right and drove slowly. There was nothing behind him - just two cars coming the other way.

"There!" shouted Johnny. "Rue St Gilles - we came that way."

"It's no entry - one way. I'll take the next main road."

Just as Ralph reached Rue des Francs Bourgeois and turned left, a police car went across him, nearly removing the BMW's hood. "I don't think we can hang around. The sooner we're out of the city the better," said Ralph.

At Boulevard Beaumarchais Gianni pointed right: "Place de la Bastille. Down there and take signs to Vincennes. We want the N6 to Melun and Sens."

Ralph saw the tall floodlit column of Place de la Bastille and took the Rue du Faubourg St Antoine, signposted 'Vincennes'. "I think we're ok now, apart from a few banged heads and a bullet wound. But we still haven't found Amanda."

"What is that?" asked Gianni, pointing to the front of the hood. Steam was rising. Ralph checked the water temperature.

"Oh no! We're overheating!" he exclaimed. The needle was in the red. "I'm going to have to stop before it seizes." He pulled over to the left and unfastened the hood.

Gianni got out. He and Ralph looked at the clouds of vapor pouring from the radiator grille, which was broken. The front of the car was badly dented from having been used as a battering ram on the wooden doors of the house. Gianni released the catch with his left hand and raised the hood, which was hotter than he'd expected. The radiator itself was cracked right across the middle. A small pool of water crept towards their feet. "It's finished!" cried Gianni, shaking the heat out of his hands.

It was clear the BMW would be going nowhere that night without substantial repair.

# 45

THINGS WERE PERKING UP for Seymour Lyle. Patrice had called with details of the crashed Bentley. Of course, there was no mention of the fact that he'd been out of position when the action began. He'd given the registration number of the BMW to the police and it would only be a matter of time before the car was found. Eye witnesses had told him about the Louis Vuitton cases, particularly their size and weight, and Lyle guessed that they had found the real Noah. How they had unearthed it and what leads they had been following, he had no idea, but that didn't matter.

On top of that, Niall had discovered that Andreas was booked in to land at Caumont soon after it opened at 6am, presumably to collect the party from Paris. All Lyle had to do now was to wait until they arrived, and make his move. Finally, everything was going his way. And he'd be able to justify the budget overspend.

The main issue was to find a bed for the remainder of the night before returning to intercept Andreas and make sure the Learjet was grounded. He looked at his watch: 3am. He smiled - within an hour, Andreas would be on his way into the trap.

\*

BUT BY 05.00 hrs Andreas was not heading towards Avignon. He had landed at Orly airport, just south of Paris, in response to Sabina's request. There was no possibility of repairing the BMW, so they had pulled the cases out and waited while Ralph walked back a few hundred meters to the Place de la Bastille to pick up a taxi.

Gianni had undone the registration plates, ripped off the road tax and insurance sticker from the windscreen and removed all traces of ownership so that the car could not be easily identified or traced. Finally, he gave the keys to a couple of young Algerians who were hanging around. He knew that by dawn their gang would have stripped the car of its alloy wheels and other saleable parts and then torched it. Not pretty, but highly effective in erasing their tracks.

Sabina had regained consciousness and been alert enough to dress Gianni's wound with antiseptic and gauze she'd found in the BMW's first aid box. It looked as if the bullet had passed straight through as there was a clear exit hole, but he would not be piloting the helicopter for a while.

Ralph had wanted to return to Rochester, but Sabina was adamant that she was not risking taking the Noah into England. Since it was her plane, they set off for Italy. They were completely exhausted and even the excitement of a ride in the co-pilot's seat had not prevented Johnny from dropping off.

Sabina had just been wondering what her anally retentive relative Solange de Brisay would say about leaving the helicopter on her lawn - so untidy - when she, too, fell sound asleep.

# 46

IT WAS LATE IN THE TUSCAN AFTERNOON when Ralph was woken by a call on his mobile phone. It had been automatically redirected from Rochester. For several moments he was unable to work out where he was. The soft pillow, the smooth sheets, the heavily beamed ceiling all seemed alien at first.

"Hello?" said Ralph, sleepily.

"Barton!"

"General Lyle."

"Are you at home? Line sounds odd."

"What do you want?"

"Very simple. We have located your wife."

"Oh, that's brilliant!"

"Yes, but there's a condition."

"What?"

"You and your friends have found the Noah."

Ralph was silent. The man was bluffing. How could he know?

"Well, I'm not going to discuss it," continued Lyle. "You have something I want, I have something you want. Straight swap. You've got 48 hours."

"Forty eight hours for what?"

"Bring me the Noah and we'll get your wife home."

"Or what?"

"Barton, don't be a bloody fool. You know how high the stakes are. Have it delivered to me at the British Museum. Meet me in the café in the Great Court at 4pm on Thursday. Ground floor."

"But I can't..."

"Just do it, Barton." Lyle ended the call.

# 47

ON THURSDAY LONDON WAS WARM FOR MAY but overcast by gray cloud, making the air oppressive. By the time Ralph had maneuvered the two Louis Vuitton cases on the trolley up the twelve stone steps of the main entrance to the British Museum, his clothes were sticking to him unpleasantly.

They had made their preparations. Sabina was convinced that Lyle was not to be trusted and warned Ralph against carrying out the General's request. She was certain that Lyle would try and kill Ralph, and Gianni agreed with her. Ralph knew the man was connected with Billington and must in some way be implicated in his wife's abduction. He understood that his life was in serious jeopardy if he met with the General. But he had no choice - he had to rescue Amanda.

The one thing they had all agreed was that Lyle should not be given the real Noah. As far as they were aware, he had no idea they were in possession of the fake that Sabina's mother had commissioned. They also gambled on the fact that no-one really knew what to expect, as the Noah had only been seen by a handful of people, most of whom were now dead. Gianni and Ralph had carefully removed the real treasure - they were stunned by seeing it finally all laid out, glinting and sparkling on a broad oak table in the vaulted cellars of Castello di Santa Maria Novella. They repacked the Louis Vuitton cases with the fake from the rucksacks. It was a massive risk, but the whole enterprise was so hazardous that they had to do everything in their power to try and outwit Seymour Lyle.

Ralph realized he wouldn't get past security with his luggage and made for the nearest official-looking person - a uniformed guard standing just inside the monumental stone portico of the Museum. He directed Ralph to a stocky woman in a hound's-tooth check suit. She had permed brunette hair, a white blouse and pearls. Ralph took in the plain face, overbright lipstick, dark tights and shoes before noticing the 'British Museum' enameled badge on her lapel. People brushed past - visitors of all shapes and sizes from every corner of the globe. A school party was on its way out, wearing a distinctive uniform of tan shirts and burgundy knickerbockers.

Ralph was told to wait. Three minutes later two men in buff coats arrived and led him and his trolley to a small windowless office, where Lyle was waiting in front of a battered pine table. The walls were painted a dull green, lit by a single fluorescent tube. A set of dark-stained wooden shelves held unbound copies of a periodical. In the corner was a low cupboard with a telephone resting on a pile of directories. A laminated list of internal numbers was blu-tacked above it.

"Barton. Glad to see you could make it," boomed the General, holding out his hand.

"General Lyle." Ralph rested the trolley upright and shook hands, keen not to give the assistants any idea that all was not normal.

Lyle signaled to the men: "Let's have these on the table."

They lifted the cases one by one off the trolley and onto the table in the middle of the room. Lyle indicated that they should leave.

"Thank you, gentlemen." They closed the door behind them. It had a small window at eye height that looked out onto the corridor. "Well, open them," he barked.

Ralph undid the locks and lifted the lids. Lyle immediately noticed that, unlike the fake he'd glimpsed, the wrappings were made of deep green velvet. Sabina had been sorry to lose them, but they needed all the help they could get against such a diabolical mind. The General moved forward and unwound the first roll of jewelry.

"Fantastic! What a thing, eh, Barton, to handle such a prize?"

"Yes, it's remarkable. I never thought I'd see it." Ralph was trying hard to stay the right side of truthful.

"Well, let's get it secure and then we'll go and have a cup of tea." Lyle looked at Ralph, who closed the cases.

Sitting on a bench that ran the length of the table in the Great Court café, Ralph looked up at Norman Foster's brilliant glass ceiling that had transformed the Victorian space into a twenty-first century masterpiece of light and wonder - the largest covered public square in Europe. He hardly noticed Lyle until he plonked the tray down in front of him.

This was the part he was dreading most. Gianni had told him that the most likely thing the General would try was to poison him. He couldn't have him shot or stabbed - far too obvious. Ralph sipped his tea cautiously.

"Have some cake!" invited Lyle, moving a plate with a slice of carrot cake towards him.

"Thank you," responded Ralph, thinking for the thousandth time that he really was not suited to this sort of thing.

"Well, I'm glad you saw sense," Lyle said, looking at his watch. "Your wife will be on her way home as we speak." Ralph took a small bite of cake. It tasted delicious.

At the mention of Amanda, Ralph had even greater difficulty holding himself together. "Oh, good."

"Come on, drink up, eat up! Be happy, man, it's all worked out for the best."

"Yes, I look forward to seeing the Noah on display," Ralph agreed, taking another mouthful of tea.

"Don't be naïve. Really, Barton, you stick to the church - you're not cut out for the real world. You know as well as I that it's never going to see the light of day if I can help it."

"No, you're right. About my lack of experience. That's one thing this whole business has taught me. Would you excuse me a minute - I feel a bit odd. Probably all the excitement."

"Yes. Don't be long. Tea'll be cold."

Ralph extricated himself from the bench and headed for the central British Library Reading Room, looking for signs to the lavatories. He went in through a doorway and down the steps.

Outside the gents on the tiled floor was a yellow plastic sign that read, 'CLOSED Cleaning in Progress - please use nearest alternative'. He stepped past and through the swing door. Dressed in a white coat over green overalls, Gianni greeted him.

"Take your jacket off," he instructed. Ralph slipped out of his linen jacket and rested it on the counter by a basin. He noticed an open black bag full of small vials and other medical equipment. He undid the cuff of his left sleeve and rolled up his shirt. Gianni hovered with a hypodermic syringe. He pressed Ralph's arm and pushed the needle into the blue vein on the inside of his elbow joint, drawing a small amount of blood. Pulling it out he added, "Put your finger there." Ralph pressed down where the needle had gone in. "Here," Gianni passed him a plaster.

Ralph stuck the plaster over the tiny wound and waited. Gianni was testing the extracted blood with a small electronic device.

"Belladonna! *Potrei predire quello.*"

"What?"

"Something I could have predicted. Ok." Gianni took a small bottle and filled another syringe with its colorless contents. He tapped the syringe and squirted a few shots of the liquid to ensure that there were no air bubbles, then injected the antidote into Ralph's arm.

"That should do, but there's a chance we may have missed something." He gave Ralph another plaster to cover the injection: they didn't want Lyle seeing any blood seeping out onto Ralph's clothing. "Try not to eat or drink anything else. Get out as soon as you can."

"I will, don't worry!" responded Ralph.

Gianni held out a cloakroom tag. "Don't forget!"

"No, sure, I'll pick it up on the way out," Ralph agreed, putting the tag in his jacket pocket.

The General smiled as Ralph returned. "Feeling better?"

"Yes, just a bit queasy, but not so bad. All the same, I think I might make a move."

"Fine. I imagine you're keen to get home, see your wife. Well, thanks for everything." Lyle put his hand out again. Ralph was incredulous. This man was too cool. Tea and a handshake!

Ralph handed the tag in to a young Asian cloakroom attendant. She fetched the Arai motorbike crash helmet he was expecting and gave it to him. Stepping out into the warm air, Ralph did feel quite sick and giddy. What if Gianni had missed something? Maybe he hadn't given him enough of the antidote? He'd successfully delivered the fake Noah, but there was more to go. He walked across the broad expanse in front of the Museum towards the road. As he reached the wrought iron gates he pulled on the crash helmet and braced himself. He had to get this bit right. He turned into Great Russell Street and went a few paces, then bent his knees and fell to the ground.

In his desperation to be convincing, Ralph collapsed too quickly. As his head hit the pavement, the helmet cracked like the shell of an egg. For a moment, it looked as if it hadn't broken. It still seemed perfect, whole. But then a thin, sticky liquid seeped out from underneath and began to form a gelatinous pool around his head on the hard stone.

Waiting on the other side of the gateway, Gianni watched Ralph go down and gasped as he realized he'd fallen too heavily. He controlled himself, stayed where he was and called Sabina on his mobile. Once the call was made, he took off the white coat, revealing green overalls and 'PARAMEDIC' badges.

Gianni strode over to Ralph. A few passers-by were staring at him as he lay crumpled on the ground. They couldn't see his face clearly because of the helmet, but it seemed as if his head was bleeding badly. An elderly lady in a heather-colored outfit looked at Gianni as he approached and shouted: "Call an ambulance!"

"Yes, yes I have. Help is on its way. Now please, move out of the way. Give him some air." Gianni knelt by Ralph and took over. The last thing he needed was people interfering. He rolled up his white coat and placed it gently under Ralph's head. Gianni winced as the bullet wound in his arm made itself felt. Ralph looked very pale and was out cold. The coat soon began to turn red.

General Lyle sauntered to the top of the Museum steps and looked out, one hand in his pocket. On the far side of the distant railings, red buses were queuing along Great Russell Street and the pavements were heaving with tourists.

As he waited he thought about Canon Barton. His initial impression had proved accurate - the man was too wet to be relied upon for this kind of caper. Still, Lyle had what he wanted. There was just one more thing. He'd filled the teacup with enough stuff to kill an ox. At one point he thought he'd miscalculated and it was going to kick in too soon, especially when Barton complained of feeling ill. But he'd walked off strongly enough. Seymour Lyle had enjoyed the carrot cake - a shame Barton had wasted his.

Blue flashing lights appeared. Lyle couldn't see clearly, but there was a white vehicle approaching and a crowd. He wondered why there was no siren, and then he heard it wailing. Excellent! Mission accomplished. He wandered off to make a phone call.

Sabina turned the white Fiat Ducato ambulance off Craven Terrace into Lancaster Mews, immediately noticing the change in tire noise as the wheels pattered over the uneven cobbles. To be strictly accurate, it was an ex-ambulance they'd bought off the internet the day before, having traveled all the way to Bristol to collect it. She slowed down as they drew parallel with a DB5 in light Aston Martin Racing Green and drove straight into the open garage. The blue lights were no longer mounted on the roof - she'd switched them off as soon as they'd reached Bloomsbury Square. Gianni had hopped out to detach them in the Southampton Row Multi-Story car park, just out of range of the CCTV cameras.

# 48

JOHNNY JUMPED WHEN THE DOORBELL RANG. He'd been trying to play his guitar but found it impossible to concentrate on the gentle song he'd written. Instead, he had thrashed out some loud cords, venting his jangled emotions at the expense of the innocent instrument. When he opened the door, Amanda was standing on the step in her nightie against the background of the trees in Cathedral Close, looking completely vacant and in danger of fainting. He put his arm round her and helped her inside.

Sabina had responded instantly to Johnny's call and set off for Rochester, leaving Gianni to look after Ralph, who still had a slight headache. A bath and a change of clothes had worked wonders, and he was resting with a large single malt in one hand. The news of Amanda's safe return had flooded him with such joy that he could hardly feel the worn, wide leather sofa he was lounging in. He had his eyes closed, feet resting on the green carpet of the first floor living room. He knew the walls were painted a dirty apricot color, decorated with a gilt-framed painting of thatched cottages and a crude portrait of a young man, its deep white 1960s frame splitting at the miter joints; he thought he'd seen an elaborate chandelier and heavy furniture - a table with barley-twist legs. The house had belonged to Sabina's Armenian grandmother, and it retained a sense of faded Mittel-Europan grandeur.

Gianni was preparing supper and Ralph dozed to the divine aromas of frying garlic, tomatoes, clams and herbs as a pan of fettuccine bubbled on the gas cooker. Gianni himself was dreaming of dinner in Ostuni at the Osteria Piazzetta Cattedrale with Maria and Umberto.

*

JOHNNY SHOWED SABINA to his parents' room, where Amanda was sitting up in bed. It was clear that she had been drugged and had no idea where she'd been. She was bright enough in herself, but Sabina decided it would be best to wait until morning before she launched into an explanation of all that had taken place, and why they would have to stage a funeral and 'cremation' for Ralph to convince Lyle he was dead. It would be a huge concept for Amanda to get her head round.

Sabina had given the matter a great deal of thought, further refined on the way down to Rochester. She would get a death certificate from a doctor she knew in Italy and tell the various authorities in the UK that Ralph had died in an accident abroad - much easier than trying to do it in England. She didn't like the idea of breaking the law or deceiving people, but she was left with no choice after everything Lyle had done. Before then, she'd fly Ralph out to France: she'd decided to give him the Château Roüet-la-Dauphine as a reward for risking his life to recover the Noah. The place only held unhappy memories for her, and she was going to settle in the Castello di Santa Maria Novella and pick up the pieces of her life.

She would suggest that Amanda joined Ralph later in France, once she'd had her treatment and sorted out the house. The Cathedral authorities - Dean and Chapter - were bound to ask her to leave, anyway. From what she knew of Johnny, she thought he'd take to living on a vineyard château. He could perhaps board at King's for a year while he did his 'A' Levels, and then apply for university in France.

"Hi, Mum, this is Sabina," said Johnny, introducing the two women without the faintest idea of the tension that could exist between them.

"Sabina," said Amanda, holding out her hand.

"Amanda - I've heard so much about you," replied Sabina, taking Amanda's hand and holding it tenderly.

"I think I should have said that!" responded Amanda.

"Thank you, Johnny. If your Mum and I could just have a minute," Sabina asked.

"Oh, sure. I'll be in the kitchen," said Johnny, leaving the room.

"I hope you don't mind," Sabina said.

"No. There's a lot to say."

"But not now. In the morning. You've had quite an ordeal."

"It sounds as if you've had some adventures yourself, if half of what Johnny's told me is true," countered Amanda.

Sabina hoped he hadn't said too much while Amanda was still coming out of the morphine trip she'd suffered at the hands of her abductors: "Yes - it's been interesting!"

"You're more English than I expected," Amanda observed.

"Ah, well, that's what boarding school does for you!"

"Is Ralph all right?"

"He's fine. He's got a headache, but he's ok."

"Probably his own fault," joked Amanda.

"Well, perhaps a bit of overacting at the last moment. No, he's doing well. Are you all right?"

"I think I'll be better in the morning."

"That's what I thought. Then we'll have a proper chat."

"Yes, a proper chat. You're not how I imagined at all."

"I'm not sure I should ask!" laughed Sabina, aware that she was beginning to sound more English than usual, mirroring Amanda's speech patterns in an attempt to be liked. Sabina very much wanted Amanda to like her.

"I was afraid Ralph was in love with you," confided Amanda, looking slightly tearful.

'How insecure we are!' thought Sabina. Here was this lovely, devoted woman thinking all the worst things, and she felt partly responsible. She decided to be honest. "I think he is, a bit. And I'm very fond of him. He's a remarkable man. Very correct but full of passion about things he believes in - a rare combination."

"Yes. Dear Ralph. Always charging in - and yet…" Amanda began to cry.

"Don't. You have nothing to fear. He's been amazingly brave and we could never have done any of it without him. But he's in love with you."

Amanda stared at her, searching her eyes to see if she was telling the truth. In theory, Sabina was the last person she should believe - the scarlet woman. But Amanda knew Ralph, and she did not read anything in Sabina that caused her to be concerned. "Thank you."

# 49

RAOUL ARTURO FEDERICO ENESI turned left out of the drive that led to Cezanne's house and walked up the hill on Avenue Pasteur. The August sky was almost cloudless and, because Aix-en-Provence benefited from a micro-climate, it was fresh, unlike most of the South of France at this time of the year. He was looking for the garden at the top where there was a view of Mont Sainte Victoire. The guide in the studio had told him you could see it from the same angle that Cezanne had painted so many times.

He liked Aix. There were broad streets lined with trees, like the main Cours Mirabeau, and narrow alleyways crowded with busy restaurants. Stone fountains and cobbled squares - small and large - and friendly people. The flower market was a heady assault on the senses; the Musée Granet had one of the finest collections of art he'd seen in any town. He couldn't wait to show Amanda - though of course, she'd remember it from her student days. It was she who'd come up with the name Raoul. His mother's father had been called Frederick and his other grandfather Arthur. Enesi? Well, people could work that out for themselves...

His days were full, mainly with French lessons. He wanted to be fluent before moving to Roüet-la-Dauphine. The idea of living in France was not unattractive. It was just that he was more of an orientalist than a Francophile. Still, he could see how that could change.

The hill was steep and he stopped to take a glug of mineral water. Following a sign, he climbed higher and soon found himself on a path laid with flat stones leading to a terrace. Here there were reproductions of some well-known Cezanne paintings printed onto display boards to help less well-informed visitors. Turning round, he saw the mountain for the first time. Its chalky white mass culminated in a high peak, dominating a plain spattered with olive groves. The scene was intersected by cypress trees and Mediterranean pines, while in the foreground the bright flowers of oleanders vied for his attention.

He was surprised that no-one else was around - he had the place to himself. These past three months, he'd had more than enough of his own company. It had been hard at first. He felt like an exile, unable to go anywhere near England. He had been excluded from everything he knew. He'd lived abroad before, of course, but never on his own like this. It was odd to think that he was effectively dead: he could never visit Rochester again, or the place where he was brought up.

Nor had he realized just how much of his identity had been shaped by the national, hierarchical organization of the church. The freedom was alarming at first, and he had lost all sense of belonging. Now, however, he was beginning to think that it would be much harder to return than continue his new life.

He'd never had to forgive such injustice: the way Lyle had treated him and his family had been appalling. But his faith demanded that he let it go. He'd read somewhere that resentment was like drinking poison and expecting the other person to die. How appropriate! He knew the principle was right. He'd not experienced it as a process before - something he had to work at every day, and which was gradually lifting.

And then there was Sabina. What had he been thinking? He had had plenty of time to consider his feelings. He had wondered

258

whether it was possible to be in love with two people at the same time: now he knew that it was not. At least, he was certainly incapable of giving himself wholeheartedly to more than one woman. He might have been convinced at the time that he was falling in love with Sabina, yet he had come to realize that it was something else. Infatuation, obsession, call it what you like. But it was not the same as the way he felt towards Amanda. He must have been deceived somehow, but the strength of his feelings had confused him.

There was a moment when he had nearly told Sabina. He would have destroyed everything. Everything he held dear - his loved ones, his values and his self-respect. And Sabina would have lost all respect for him. Some things are better left unsaid. Certainly, his close call would make him less judgmental in future. Much less judgmental.

Being dead made him wonder what people had been saying about him. He could no longer defend himself against things that weren't true. It had been slightly surreal standing in Cezanne's atelier, which the artist had designed for himself, and seeing the jugs and bowls that featured in his work. Just things he'd borrowed from the kitchen, immortalized in galleries, books and private houses throughout the world. It made him reflect on what he'd left behind. He had another chance - another whole life to live under a new name - but what legacy had Ralph Barton created? How would people remember him? What had he learned - what would he do next time? It was, he supposed, a relatively unusual position to be in.

Ralph is dead: long live RAFE!

# EPILOGUE

SEPTEMBER SUNSHINE GENTLY WARMED the white walls and terracotta roofs of the J Paul Getty Museum in Santa Monica, California. The noise of chatter and laughter rose from the main peristyle garden where a large crowd of the well-dressed - and well-heeled - drank champagne. Glamorous couples stood with linked arms talking to friends; a slim woman with white hair in a chignon introduced an American PhD student to a Professor from Madrid; a large, bearded man who resembled an opera singer had a group in fits over a joke; waiters moved silently among the guests, discreetly refilling glasses.

"So," said Sabina, looking extraordinarily beautiful in a short-sleeved black Armani dress and green lizard high-heeled shoes, "what do you think?" Her hair was up, her cat's eyes matching the brilliance of a large emerald and diamond necklace and earrings.

"I'd never have believed it," replied Amanda, radiant, relaxed and wearing a sapphire blue silk suit. Her treatment had been successful, she was topped up with a preventative chemical cocktail - what she called her 'antifreeze' - and the consultant had given her another five years before the problem was likely to recur. She had brushed her long blonde hair back and held it with a velvet Alice band. "What made you do it?"

"I don't know. I began to realize that my great inheritance owned me, rather than the other way round. I thought I'd never be free while it was locked away. And now look - it's giving so much pleasure to all these people."

"And it's such a great setting - one of RAFE's favorite places."

"I know. He said. That's partly why it's here."

Amanda didn't bat an eyelid. She and Sabina had become the closest of friends. It was either that or they would have seriously fallen out. "And how long is the exhibition on?"

"A month, and then we'll see. I'm looking for a permanent home for it."

"I'm sure you'll have plenty of offers."

"I hope so! It's cost a fortune to put this on! The security alone is outrageous."

Indeed, on the ground floor in well-guarded rooms around the atrium - space normally reserved for the Museum's priceless collection of antiquities - the real Noah was expensively displayed behind bullet-proof glass, its exquisite worked gold and wondrously facetted gems exploding in slivers of reflected light. People stood transfixed, both by its visual magnificence and the thought that they were witnessing a marvel from beyond the Great Flood. Here was skill and design that belonged to human hands but from a culture that had been thought lost. It was hard to say which was more overwhelming - the treasure's unique provenance or its astonishing splendor.

"I must confess I'm surprised you invited General Lyle. I'm sure he was behind my abduction," continued Amanda.

"Oh, I agree, and a great deal more besides. Who else had a motive? No, I can't stand the man, but I invited him because I thought this would be a neat way of showing him that ultimately, he'd lost. And that there's not a damn thing he can do about it."

261

"Yes - elegantly stuffed! He didn't look very happy when I saw him just now."

Seymour Lyle was more than unhappy. He was struggling to comprehend the enormity of his failure. There was no doubt that what he had just seen was the real McCoy: and the thought of the fake Noah now mocked him from the vaults of the British Museum. Following Sabina's invitation, in an effort to gain some understanding of what had happened, he had asked Javier Mendoza to meet him in the East Garden, away from the crowds. Here he sat alone under the shade of sycamore trees on a stone seat whose curve echoed that of the circular fountain in the centre. Beyond the simple basin with its bronze tiger-head spigots spewing streams of water into the pool below was another fountain - in a colorful mosaic and shell grotto flanked by masks of Tragedy and Comedy.

Mendoza approached from the East Vestibule. He moved heavily in his dark shiny suit, unsure whether he wanted the confrontation that would inevitably follow. Lyle heard his steps on the finely raked stones and stood up. They shook hands, eyeing one another with deep suspicion. Billington had commissioned Mendoza to kill Lyle if anything happened to him: Lyle was intent on removing Mendoza for failing to check that the fake Noah had still been in the aluminum cases when he set off to have it destroyed.

Nothing was said. Lyle had hardly been able to control the volcano inside. He lost his cool within seconds and tried to strangle Mendoza. It was a fruitless attempt on a younger and more agile man. For all his ponderous bulk, Mendoza was strong and fast. The two men's feet scuffed the gravel as they fought. Mendoza moved one of Lyle's arms out and back with an ease that sapped the General's confidence. Lyle broke free and stepped back. As soon as Javier saw the knife come out he knew what the outcome had to be.

He grabbed Seymour's wrist, pushing the knife away, and punched him in the temple.

Lyle went down and the knife flew out of his hands. He tried to get up: as he did so, Mendoza used the General's movement to ram him into the pool of the fountain. He held his head down until Lyle's legs stopped thrashing the clipped hedge surrounding the fountain's stone ledge.

Amanda decided she'd had enough champagne for one afternoon and Sabina asked her if she'd seen the Herb Garden.

"Oh, you must. It's fabulous. I'd love something like it at home. Do come and look. It's all in raised beds. There are over fifty types of herbs -- can you imagine? And there are fruit trees - apples, peaches, pears, figs, oranges, lemons..."

"I've always wanted a lemon tree in my garden."

"Well, you can in France. It's far enough south."

"I wish RAFE could be here."

"Give it time. We have to be careful while Lyle's still around."

"Yes, sorry. And are you feeling more settled?"

"Not sure. Sometimes I miss the ship. Especially the swimming."

"Viaggiatore. What does that mean in English?"

"Traveler. That's me. Restless. At least, it has been up till now. Who knows? That reminds me, I'm giving you the Bridget Riley as a wedding present."

"Wedding present?"

"Well, presumably you'd like to be married to Raoul?"

"Of course, but…"

"With his changed name and new identity, it would be much better if you went up the aisle again."

Amanda thought for a moment. Such a thing hadn't occurred to her. "Wow! Yes, I see. That'll be a day."

"It will!"

"But the Bridget Riley - that's too much!"

"No, it's exactly right."

Lyle knew he'd been outwitted over the Noah and now he feared for his life. Mendoza was much stronger and faster than he'd reckoned: his only option was to feign death and hope Mendoza wouldn't hang around. He lay as still as he could. The air was trying to force its way out of him, but he couldn't risk any bubbles. The General's reactions may have slowed down, but he was still army-fit.

He submitted himself to the kind of hectoring lecture he normally reserved for subordinates. Bloody fool! Fool to have underestimated Barford, the Contessa - all of them. And Mendoza. Of course he was Billington's weapon of choice. Of course Mendoza would be on his guard. Idiot!

There was only so long he could resist the reflex to seize a new breath. Giddiness announced the limits of consciousness and he had to blow out, pushing himself off the bottom of the fountain and sucking new oxygen into his lungs.

As the crash of his ascent from the water and braying inhalation subsided, Lyle slumped down on the gravel, held up awkwardly by the hard stems of topiary, arm out, head slapped sideways on the marble surround, gasping like a carp. No one saw him, but even if anyone had been there, he was beyond caring, intent solely on survival, on recovery.

Javier had decided to leave as fast as he could, taking the lift down to the garage and driving out along the lava-stone driveway. He would have been infinitely less relieved about his meeting with the General if he could have seen him at that moment: Lyle's waterlogged linen suit clung to him in carved stone folds: he lay there, still, staring, gaping, cast like a victim of Pompeii - but alive.

Seymour Lyle watched Sabina's guests, blurred tribespeople in a heat haze as they crossed the inner peristyle garden. Its sunlit

264

narrow pool was guarded by the bronze statues of women, who seemed to breathe deeply in the diamond-bright day.

He would not rest for long.

# ABOUT THE AUTHOR

## Robert Barnes

Educated at the universities of Grenoble, Oxford and Reading, Robert taught English & Drama in Sussex, London, Oxford and Cambridge for fifteen years. During this time he also wrote and directed a number of children's plays and musicals, one of which was reviewed in The Times Educational Supplement.

Having held posts including Housemaster, Director of Studies, Academic Director and Deputy Head, Robert left the classroom for Los Angeles, where he wrote two screenplays. Returning to London, he managed a Mayfair art gallery before being selected for a writing course at The Guardian, which led to a job in advertising, working for an Omnicom agency.

After a spell in marketing, running a portfolio of European accounts, he went freelance and worked as a communications consultant for many blue-chip clients. He won the D&AD Yellow Pencil in the category 'Writing for Design'.

In 2002 he took on responsibility as Principal and Senior Partner of the independent school his father founded in 1955. He was appointed Headmaster in 2004. In 2006 he successfully negotiated the sale of the school to a large educational charity, The Girls' Day School Trust.

In 2009 Robert left the school to pursue his writing career full time.

CPSIA information can be obtained at www.ICGtesting.com
Printed in the USA
LVOW101606111112

306825LV00002B/53/P

9 781456 588250